The DEAD WOMAN *of* DEPTFORD

ANN GRANGER

headline

First published in 2016 by
HEADLINE PUBLISHING GROUP

First published in paperback in 2017 by
HEADLINE PUBLISHING GROUP

1

Cataloguing in Publication Data is available from the British Library

ISBN 978 1 4722 0454 7

Typeset in Plantin by Avon DataSet Ltd, Bidford-on-Avon, Warwickshire

Printed and bound in Great Britain by CPI Group (UK) Ltd,
Croydon, CR0 4YY

HEADLINE PUBLISHING GROUP
An Hachette UK Company
Carmelite House
50 Victoria Embankment
London EC4Y 0DZ

www.headline.co.uk
www.hachette.co.uk

. . . the very existence of London depends on the navigation of the Thames, insomuch that if this river were rendered unnavigable, London would soon become a heap of ruins, like Nineveh and Babylon . . .

The Picture of London for 1818

This book is dedicated to my family, my friends, and my neighbours, in gratitude for their invaluable support at a difficult time. Thanks in particular to Tim and to Chris, my sons, who have had to manage their loss as well as mine; and to my agent, Carole Blake, and editor, Clare Foss.

Chapter One

Inspector Ben Ross

HIS NAME was Harry Parker. He was a small, scrawny figure and scruffily dressed. In the yellow light cast by the police lantern, he peered up at us with the trapped look of a stray dog, cornered and at bay. He gripped a cloth cap in his hands, pressing it against his chest, and his little eyes flickered from one to the other of us, always returning to my face. I could not have said what kind of an impression he would make, as a witness, on a judge or jury. I only knew that he made a very poor impression on me.

A little under an hour earlier, I had thought myself finished for the day. I had even uttered the words: 'Well, Morris, I think we might at last go home!'

The sergeant and I had been out of London, clearing up a matter in Cambridge where assistance had been requested. Police duties apart, it had been a pleasant break. Cambridge had seemed quiet after London and we'd appreciated the cleaner air, the atmosphere of the university town, its fine Gothic buildings and the open meadows on which cattle grazed. It had truly appeared a different world.

Returning home, we had been able to see from the train the grey pall of smoke that hung above our great capital. It could have been worse. This month, November, normally saw more fog rolling up the Thames estuary. Mixed with the coal smoke, it often formed a dense, bad-smelling, yellowish mass that invaded every nook and cranny, right down to pavement level, and cloaked the buildings with a dirty veil. You could not brush by without your clothes being marked with black smears. But, though cold and damp, we had so far been spared 'a London Peculiar'.

Morris and I left the train to be swallowed up at once in the scurrying crowds and made our way through packed thoroughfares. Our ears were assaulted by the rattle of wheels and clip-clop of hooves; the cries of street vendors and jangling of barrel organs. All life was here. With respectable citizens mixed beggars – who made their trade obvious – and pickpockets – who did not. Cambridge's lively but scholarly atmosphere might have been another country. When we passed through the doors of Scotland Yard, it seemed we had reached sanctuary. I registered our return, promised our report first thing in the morning and all that was left now was the pleasant expectation of supper with our families.

That was when Fate conjured up a herald of Doom, in the person of a red-faced, breathless young constable. The clatter of boots on the stairs heralded his appearance in the doorway, clutching a letter. He was perspiring profusely.

'Who are you?' snapped Morris, not recognising the

newcomer but identifying an obstacle between himself and his own fireside.

'Evans, sir, from Deptford!' squeaked the newcomer. He peered doubtfully from one to the other of us. 'They told me downstairs to ask for Inspector Ross.'

'Did they, indeed? I am Ross.' I stepped forward and took the letter he held out. 'Well, lad, what's brought you so urgently?'

'We have a murder, sir!' declared the youngster excitedly. 'They only just found the body. It's in Skinner's Yard. Oh, and sir, Inspector Phipps sends his compliments and his apologies,' he added belatedly.

'Good of him!' muttered Morris behind me.

We both now knew that there was no telling when we would get home that night. The building had emptied of most officers and those remaining were busy – or busy enough to send Constable Evans to me. I read the letter slowly. 'Murdered woman, eh?'

'The body's still lying where it was found,' urged Evans. 'I'm to take you there, sir.' The lad was actually hopping from foot to foot.

It was necessary to do something before this eager young Mercury was so overcome by excitement I had to pour water over him. There was nothing for it. I sent him out to find a four-wheeler cab that could transport all three of us to the scene.

'Sorry, Morris,' I said to him, as we made our way out of the building.

Morris mumbled some reply but I did not catch it. I didn't need to.

3

I reread Phipps's letter on our way south of the river. I was seated next to young Evans, as he was of slighter build than Morris, whose generous bulk nearly filled the opposite seat. To read, I had to twist myself into an awkward position and hold up the paper to the eerie glow of the gaslight from the street. It made the document look like some mediaeval parchment. The jolting of the cab sent the words leaping up and down but I could just manage to make them out.

The murder had some unusual features, wrote Phipps. But he did not divulge what those might be. He was, however, strongly of the opinion the investigation would be better handled by the Yard. At Deptford they had not the resources. A recent increase in drunken brawls and fights among seamen, many of them off foreign ships and speaking no English, kept them fully occupied.

I did not know Inspector Phipps; though I'd heard of him and his reputation was of a capable officer. But I found it difficult to believe that such anarchy raged in Deptford that a murder investigation could not be given priority, at least initially. If there proved to be complications, it might later come the way of the Yard. That we were called in immediately brought to mind the expression 'hot potato'.

I peered from the window. Deptford had long had a claim to being the most insalubrious area in London; and that against some stiff competition. Yet the scenes we passed revealed a lively place. Along the river lay ships at anchor on one hand, their tall masts a forest against the night sky. Occasionally the darkness of the winter sky was illuminated by a shower of red and gold sparks, as if someone had set up a spectacular firework. The impromptu display marked where men worked on the hull of an iron-clad vessel in one of the shipyards.

We rumbled by the dark bulk of the great warehouses of the wholesale traders. Cargo ships came into the port of London from all over the world. With other smells that found their way into the cab, my nose caught the scent of spices and tobacco. Many small businesses also depended on the docks: chandlers, smithies and wheelwrights. We clattered along the high street, which boasted the usual grocers, fruiterers and wine merchants, many of them busy even at this late hour. From the brief glimpses afforded me, many shop premises appeared small and cramped within, with low ceilings and exposed wooden rafters. Already every drinking den we passed was full. We caught snatches of raucous singing and the scrape of a fiddle. Above us the upper storeys of the buildings blotted out the sky, human anthills in which families were crammed, often in a single room.

I had not seen any evidence of the rioting mobs, yelling abuse in a variety of languages, suggest by Phipps's request for assistance from the Yard.

I could say nothing aloud before the Deptford constable, but I had deep misgivings about this whole business. I passed Phipps's letter to Morris, who scanned it as best he could before we turned off into less well-lit streets. Aloud, as poor consolation, I said to him, 'Perhaps it will turn out something that Deptford can cope with perfectly well, after all.'

'Then why don't they?' muttered Morris. Perhaps he did not intend me to hear him. Perhaps he was hungry and tired and didn't care.

But Evans heard him and I felt him flinch. When, shortly afterwards, the cab rocked to a halt, his voice came nervously in the gloom. 'It's here, sir!'

We scrambled down. I paid the cabbie, and got him to scrawl a receipt on a scrap of paper I hunted out of my pocket. I trusted I would be reimbursed. The Yard had already funded our return train fares to Cambridge that day, so an additional claim might well be declared above the set allowance.

The cab rattled away, leaving us in an area somewhere between the river and the commercial heart of the place. Eyes watched us from all the buildings around, but the actual watchers had retreated out of sight. We followed young Evans, who led us through a gap and into a dark, evil-smelling space, inadequately lit by the light from windows overlooking the spot and the bobbing rays from police bull's-eye lanterns. The bearer of one such lantern raised it on high so that the beam targeted my face, and revealed the carrier to be a sturdy figure in heavy caped uniform coat and helmet.

'Barrett, sir!' said the uniformed man, as I shielded my eyes from the sudden glare. 'I've got him here, the fellow who found the body.'

My eyes were adjusting to the poor visibility. The area in which we found ourselves was not so much a proper yard as a gap between tall brick buildings, extending twenty feet to the rear and measuring some fifteen to twenty feet in width. Rubble scattered about suggested a building here had been demolished, perhaps an old warehouse, and no one had seen any purpose in replacing it. Taken together with the surviving houses flanking the gap, the effect was of a row of aged teeth, slowly crumbling and falling out.

The street behind us was lit by gas lamps, but they cast little light into this desolate nook. Only the oil-fuelled beams of the lanterns barely reached to the far end, where dilapidated wooden lean-to buildings suggested privies. Once everyone living here probably used these: and they were still used by some, if the stench was anything to go by. Bazalgette's sewer system for London had not yet tunnelled its way here. Those privies must drain into some rarely emptied cesspit, or, even worse, still channelled their refuse into the river. Elsewhere the new sewers had done much to banish the spectre of cholera. But if it were to return, this yard was an ideal breeding ground for its horrors. Litter and rubbish of all kinds was heaped about, festering and odorous. Rats scuttled here and there boldly, lured out by easy pickings and tonight by the scent of blood.

Like his colleague, Evans, Constable Barrett was young but keen. He hauled his prize out of the shadows and into the light with a flourish; rather like a conjurer producing a rabbit out of a hat.

'Here he is, sir!' he declared triumphantly.

I clapped my chilled hands together, partly to dispel the numbness but also to underline I was in charge here; and scowled my displeasure at the miserable specimen of dockside riff-raff before me.

He, in response to my glare and the echo of my hands round the brick walls, cowered back. He looked even more terrified. Good. It might be unfair at this point to blame him for my delayed return home and hot dinner. But I was only human and, in the absence of Inspector Phipps, had to focus my resentment on some target.

'What's your name?' I demanded of the unprepossessing specimen of humanity pushed under my nose. I had seen a 'rat circus' once, performing in a large cage, prodded and bribed by a human ringmaster. It was as if one of those performers had escaped and stood before me, dressed in jacket and trousers, and standing on its hind paws.

My nose, in fact, conveyed the first information about him. The witness had spent his recent hours in a pub. He reeked of beer, sweat, sawdust and tobacco smoke.

'Parker,' our witness mumbled, 'Harry Parker.' In a spurt of courage, fuelled by resentment, he pointed at Barrett. 'I already told that rozzer, didn't I?'

'What's your occupation, Mr Parker?'

'I work in the docks,' he muttered. 'I wait at the gates early in the morning when they hire men for the day. If I'm hired, I do anything I'm set to – loading or unloading, fetching and carrying . . .'

And a bit of thieving, if you can manage it, I thought to myself. The casual labourers hired at the dock gates in the morning were searched on leaving the docks at the end of the day. But with a crowd of weary, ill-tempered, fellows pushing by; and only a couple of men at the gates to check each one, it was not possible to stop pilfering.

'How did you come to find her?' I asked him next.

'I fell over her!' His voice rose indignantly to a squawk. 'I told the rozzer that, an' all! It's not my fault, is it? I never went looking for her, did I? I come in here – ' he waved a hand to indicate the yard – 'I came in here on account of *a call of nature.*' He spoke the euphemism with a ludicrous dignity and pointed towards the wooden sheds at the back of the yard. I doubted he'd been making for them. No one in his right mind would willingly enter one of them after nightfall and risk tumbling head first into a stinking pit.

'I never saw her in the dark!' Parker went on. 'There's no light here except what comes in from the street or shines down from up there, if someone pulls back a curtain.' He jabbed a finger upward. 'It give me an 'orrible shock. I ran out back into the street and there was a—' He checked himself, perhaps realising, from Barrett's scowl, that he would not like being described as a 'rozzer' for a third time. Parker amended his closing words. 'I told this here constable. Ask *'im!*'

'That's correct, sir!' said Barrett. 'I was on my regular beat. The witness came rushing out into the street and nearly knocked me over. He was gibbering with fright and making no sense at all. "In there!" he kept saying. So I pushed him back in front of me, into this yard, making sure to keep my hand on his collar. Sure enough, there we found the poor woman.'

I wondered, if the constable had not happened to be on the spot, whether Parker would have gone in search of him. More likely, he'd have run home and left the grim discovery to someone else.

Parker snuffled into his cap. 'I'm a decent working man . . .' he concluded in tones of self-pity as if even he believed the fiction.

I glanced upwards. There was no knowing how much light had fallen into the yard from above earlier. Now that word had got round, and that word was 'murder', every window overlooking the yard was open and had one or more figures leaning out, eager to watch the show below. A theatre in the round, I thought, and we are the players. A babble of excited voices floated down.

'Can yer see the body?' demanded a shrill female voice.

'Nah . . . they got it covered over. Over there by the wall, see, there's something there.'

'I can't see nuffin',' grumbled the first voice.

'We shall have to send officers into those buildings, asking if anyone saw or heard anything,' I said to Sergeant Morris. 'They're showing enough interest now! I wish Phipps had sent men in there already.'

Barrett, anxious to defend his own colleagues and his senior officer, said, 'There's no one to send, sir. There is a Russian cargo ship docked, and it's been very lively around here this evening.'

'So I understood from Inspector Phipps's message,' I said. 'Though things seem quiet enough at the moment – apart from this unfortunate dead woman, of course.'

'We've had every man we can spare out on the streets, sir,' said Barrett. 'To make sure things don't get out of hand. You should've been here yesterday, sir. It was like the bloomin' battle of Waterloo.'

'I'll drum up a number of constables to go round knocking on doors first thing tomorrow, sir,' said Morris. 'It's too late to get hold of anyone extra now. The delay won't make a difference, because I reckon no one will have heard a thing. It's too dark here to have seen much, either. If anyone did, they won't admit to it. But, let's face it, who would take any notice of a few shouts or a scuffle? There's generally some kind of a hullabaloo somewhere around here, as that lad Evans says.'

Well, after all, that was true enough; even though I still suspected Phipps had exaggerated the latest outbreak of fisticuffs. We were attracting a lot of interest now, but my guess was that Morris was right. No one would admit to having seen anything earlier; or to having heard a call for help or a woman's scream.

As for suspects, we would have more than we could wish. Around us were countless drinking dens and bawdy houses; and squalid rooming establishments providing cheap shelter for seamen of all nations. So yes, there was often violence, and tonight there was murder.

The body lay a short distance off, decently covered with a tarpaulin. I signalled to Evans to pull back the covering so that I could view it as well as was possible by the lantern light. He obeyed and scuttled back, gulping. I hoped he was not going to be sick.

Even in the gloom, and with the horror of her injuries, it was clear to me this was not one of London's countless street women. Perhaps it was that which had alarmed

Phipps. She was sturdily built and respectably dressed, though I could see no hat or bonnet, nor any shawl or coat. She appeared simply to have walked out of some nearby house into the cold night air, just for a moment, on some trivial errand. Even at this late hour, as I'd remarked earlier, many of the little shops were open to catch the very last of the day's trade. Together with all the rogues and ruffians lurking in the neighbourhood of any port, there were still citizens of the more decent sort to be seen: home-going working men, or housewives scurrying to buy something needed to make the evening meal, or a child sent out with twopence to buy a pinch of tea. If you are poor, you don't buy tea by the packet. You buy as needed to make a brew, a tiny amount in a twist of paper. The dead woman, had she been on such an errand? Was her family, even now, waiting for her at home?

I stooped and fingered the hem of her skirt. In the inadequate light, it appeared dark in colour. It was of quality cloth, the hem trimmed with braid but otherwise unadorned. She had not been a very poor woman and my first idea, that she might have been paying a last-minute visit to a grocer, seemed less likely. She was the sort to keep her larder well stocked. A respectable woman, at first view, and that could be enough to worry Phipps.

It was hard to judge her age, as one side of her head had been viciously battered. I thought her probably in her fifties. She wore no earrings and no wedding ring. Her killer may have made off with those. Or the wretched Parker might even have robbed the body before he raised the alarm. I wouldn't have put it past him.

I drew Barrett aside. Parker, though clearly relieved to be free of the constable's surveillance, watched with apprehension.

'Has that fellow blood on him?' I asked Barrett.

'Some,' replied the constable in a low voice. 'On his right sleeve, sir, and on his hands. He says he stooped down and shook her shoulder, when he first stumbled over her. He thought she might be drunk. But then he struck a match, saw her injuries and the blood, and knew she must be dead.'

'Well, we mustn't lose him,' I warned. 'Take him back to the station and make him turn out his pockets. Then get a statement and his details. Make sure he gives an address that's genuine. Either go yourself, or if need be send a colleague with him to his house. If any of his clothing is bloodstained, get him to change into something else and bring the stained clothes away for further examination. I am not prepared to take anything said by Mr Harry Parker as gospel.'

A rumble of wheels came from the street; a closed van had arrived to take the victim to the morgue. The chattering voices about our heads fell silent in a moment of respect.

'I leave you in charge here, Morris,' I said to him. 'Secure the area so that we can come back and search by daylight. Report to me in the morning.'

'Yes, Inspector Ross,' said Morris resignedly.

I was sorry to abandon him there, but there was nothing more I could do for the moment. I set off home to my wife.

Chapter Two

MY LITTLE house is near the great rail terminus of Waterloo, so I was on the necessary south bank of the Thames but still a tidy distance away and unlikely to find any cab plying for hire here. I directed my steps towards the Thames, hoping to find a ferry able to take me upriver to a spot near Waterloo Bridge.

To find the river was straightforward enough. I had only to follow my nose. The docks and wharves were just a few streets away. They began building ships for the Royal Navy at Deptford in good old (or bad old, depending on your point of view) King Henry VIII's time. With such patronage, what area could fail to thrive? And so Deptford did, for a time. Open countryside had lain between it and London's plague-ridden hovels; so fashionable people raised fine houses here. Good Queen Bess had visited in person to greet Francis Drake on his return from his adventures. In Deptford she had created him a knight, right there on board his own ship at anchor. It was over a Deptford puddle, they claimed locally, that Sir Walter Raleigh had spread his cloak to save his monarch from soiling her shoes. Even such an exotic visitor as the Russian Tsar Peter had come here to watch the shipwrights at their work, amid the hammering and sawing and overpowering fug of boiling tar.

London's sprawl has since eaten up the fields and smallholdings, sucking everything into its capacious brick maw. Now almost permanently enveloped in the pall of London smoke, Deptford has lost favour with the well-to-do. Worse, its great dockyard has recently also fallen from favour with the Royal Navy. Modern ships are iron-clad. The work will go to private yards.

Another piece of government trade has disappeared now that the notorious convict transports to Australia have finally ceased. 'Pity about that,' lament the ship owners and sea captains of Deptford. 'It was regular cargo.'

I turned into a narrow and deserted lane. There were gas lamps positioned at either end, but their glow only cast an eerie sheen on the nearer walls and did not reach the middle where a pit of black uncertainty awaited me. I wondered if I had been wise to leave behind bustle and crowds and whether I was indeed really alone. The loudest sound was that of my own footsteps; yet there was something more. My ear caught the creak of unoiled wheels behind me, and a rumble and rattle as they bounced unevenly over the cobbles. I stopped and spun round.

I was not surprised to see a handcart had turned into the lane and was being propelled laboriously towards me. It was piled high with some load partly covered with a tarpaulin. An extraordinary creature was in charge of it.

I say 'creature' – for at first sight it hardly appeared human. With the corner gas lamp behind it, I could at first only distinguish a broad shapeless form, entirely black and with flapping wings to either side, like a gigantic bat. It crouched forward with the effort of pushing the load. Then the cart trundled into the dim circle of light cast by an oil lamp fixed above a storehouse door. I saw better who propelled it: a rag-picker.

It was a common enough trade and nothing to be surprised at. Under the tarpaulin I could glimpse a jumbled heap of old clothing and other junk. A wave of relief swept over me. I chided myself for giving way moments earlier to my imagination. What on earth could I have expected? The moon then chose to come to my aid and cast its pale light upon my companion.

The ragman appeared to be wearing a selection of the tattered garments he'd gathered over the years: baggy trousers, some sort of coat of Prince of Wales check, and a grubby neckerchief. Over all this, he wore a big black opera cloak that must once have been worn by some theatre-goer in a more wealthy area of the city. I could see it had what looked like a velvet collar. It was this cloak that had given the wing-like effect. His hair, long, grey and uncombed, fell to his shoulders from beneath a battered high hat, such as might also have been worn by a dandy, some forty or so years earlier. His face was gaunt and marked with deep creases. He looked incredibly old and I wondered he had the strength to push the cart over the cobbles. Seeing my eyes on him, his withered lips parted in a grotesque grimace revealing a row of rotten teeth that reminded me of the buildings I had just left behind me. There were even a few gaps, such as the one leading into the yard where the murdered woman had been discovered.

'Good evening, sir,' he croaked and tilted his head sideways at the same time. The wrinkled skin on his cheeks folded into deeper crevasses. His gaze seemed to be looking at me, around me, and even through me, all at once. It was like being surveyed by some sort of wild animal. He was certainly elderly but not, perhaps, quite as old as I'd first judged him.

'Good evening,' I replied.

He made to push his load on down the street, but I put out a hand to stop him and he did as I wished, setting down the wooden feet at one end of the barrow and releasing his grip on the handles. He did not, however, straighten up, but remained in the semi-crouched stance. Perhaps he had some deformity of the spine or perhaps he had spent so many years pushing this barrow that he'd just forgotten how to stand up straight. His elusive gaze still played over me. I felt uncomfortable under it.

'You work this area regularly?' I asked him. To encourage a reply, I took a shilling from my pocket and held it out.

A hand, more a talon than human, shot out and grabbed the coin. Cold scaly fingertips brushed mine and I recoiled from the touch.

'P'lice officer . . .' he said hoarsely. 'Plain-clothes sort, ain'tcha?'

I wasn't surprised he identified me so easily. The poor,

whether gainfully employed or not, easily recognise the law.

'That's right,' I said.

'I collect rags everywhere,' he told me, 'not just round here. Where there's people, there's what they throws out. I even go over the river, up west. I get good pickings there.'

That must be where he'd obtained the opera cloak and tall hat. But I wondered he had the strength to push the barrow so far.

'Were you in this area a little earlier this evening?'

He squinted at me. 'I was, after I come back from Greenwich. I was at the Seamen's Hospital.'

I recalled the Seaman's Hospital was anchored there. It was housed not in a building but a ship, and one with a fine history as a ship of the line. No longer needed by the navy, she had been purchased by a philanthropic society and set up as a hospital for merchant seamen, the river providing a cordon sanitaire between their diseases and the shore.

'What took you there?' I asked. It wasn't a place many volunteered to visit.

I caught a cunning glance from the corner of his bleary eyes. His upper body tilted towards me as if he would make some confidence; I wasn't sure I wanted to hear it.

'They usually have scraps of stuff for me. The fever patients and such, the 'ospital burns the rags what they're wearing when they come in. What they don't burn, the dead don't need no more, and no one else claims, they let me have.'

Despite myself, I took a step back. He noticed it and grinned hideously at me.

I could not but look again with horror at the stack of rags on his barrow, and tried not to imagine what diseases might infest them along with the fleas and lice. I hoped he was right and the hospital did burn the discarded clothing of the fever victims. Foreign sailors had been known to arrive carrying smallpox.

'You have not . . .' My voice sounded, to my own ears, strained. 'You have not noticed a well-dressed woman, middle-aged, sturdily built, in the area earlier? Perhaps three hours ago? Perhaps alone or perhaps with a man?'

'Drab?' he croaked.

I shook my head. 'No, a respectable woman in appearance.'

He shook his head. 'Nah, not that I noticed. I only notice them if I think they might have something for me.' Then he said suddenly, 'There was a murder done earlier, wasn't there? Just back there?' And he pointed down the way I'd come.

'Yes. How did you learn of it?' I asked sharply.

He snorted and rubbed his grimy claw across his face. 'Murder? Everyone hears about it and they don't talk about nothing else for days. I stopped to wet my whistle at the Clipper public house, and I heard it there.'

'What's your name?' I asked him.

'Raggy Jeb, they call me,' he replied. 'You can ask anyone round here for me. They all know me.'

'You have a surname?'

'Fisher,' he said. 'They give me that name at the

workhouse; on account I was fished out of the river when I was a baby. Someone threw me in, like I was a bag o' rubbish. My swaddling clothes got caught up on a spar and kept me afloat long enough for a lighterman to fish me out. Workhouse was all my family.'

A childhood in such a grim institution was no childhood at all. But he had survived it.

'Well, Jeb Fisher, if you hear anything regarding this murder you might think would interest me, if you hear anyone say he thought he might have seen the woman earlier, you come and tell me, Inspector Ross, at Scotland Yard.'

'Worth my while?' he bargained.

'Yes, if what you tell us proves true. Don't come with fancy inventions.'

He nodded and, without another word, seized the handles of his barrow to push it, and its load of festering rags, onward. Then, hardened by my experiences though I was, I received such a shock that I let out a cry of alarm.

The tarpaulin covering the rags moved. The first thought to flash through my mind was that a rat had hitched a ride. But it was far worse. A small, very small, human hand emerged from the tarpaulin. Tiny fingers gripped the edge to pull it back into place. I reached out and snatched it back. There, before me, crouched amid the rags, was a child.

It was a little girl, perhaps no more than four or five years of age, with long, tangled, fair hair and the bright eyes of something feral. She appeared to be wearing a crumpled and grimy velvet dress, much too big for her frail body, a crocheted shawl pinned over it. She stared up at me with something calculating and totally unchildlike in her expression.

Appalled, I demanded of Fisher, 'Who is this?'

He responded with a hoarse chuckle. 'She's my grand-daughter. She often comes with me when I do my rounds. Say "good evening" to the officer, Sukey.'

The child, who appeared to have no fear of me, obediently said, 'Good evening, gen'leman.'

'What do you mean by putting a child on this barrow amongst all that filth?' I almost shouted at him.

'She's learning the trade,' he said complacently.

'At her age? She is an infant!'

'Never too young,' he retorted. 'She's very good for business, is Sukey. If we go around respectable places, streets where people have a bit of money and good stuff, I send her to the door and wait by the barrow. They might refuse me, see, straight off. They say they got nothing, just to be rid of me. But they don't like to refuse her. They tell her to wait. Then they dig out something or other for her, generally something a pretty colour. I've got some nice bits and pieces that way.'

'But what is she doing under there, that dirty tarpaulin and those unspeakable rags?'

'Keeping warm, ain't cha, Sukey? Cold night. She's nice and snug in there.'

'But the risk of disease!' I protested.

'She was born among the rags and she lives among the rags, same as her mother and all my family. We don't catch no diseases. We've got what you'd call natural

22

protection. There's no healthier man than a rag-picker. Say goodnight to the officer, Sukey.'

''Night, sir!' piped the child and scrabbled back under the tarpaulin.

'We'll be home afore long, sir,' said her grandfather (if, indeed, that's what he was). 'She'll be out of there soon.'

With that, he shoved hard against the weight of the barrow and trundled it away.

I watched him leave. A door was suddenly opened as he passed by; and he and his load were briefly illuminated by a shaft of brilliant light. Then he was gone, around the corner and off to whatever den he and his wretched family inhabited. Whoever had been curious enough to open the door had spotted me. The door was slammed shut again, sending me back into the gloom.

I had not physically touched the fellow or his unsavoury load of rags, but my skin itched.

Chapter Three

Elizabeth Martin Ross

IF YOU are married to an officer of the law, there is no telling what time he will arrive home of an evening. As a result, our little house near Waterloo Station saw a procession of overcooked suppers varied, on extreme occasions, with plates of cold cuts left out to await Ben's return. Today Ben would be later than usual because he had travelled out of town to Cambridge. This had given me some unexpected free time which I had used to pay a duty visit to my Aunt Parry, across the river. She is a woman of some property, who lives in the smart district of Marylebone, in Dorset Square.

Because of this, I had also been late arriving home. I'd more than half expected to find Ben already there, even allowing him the travel time from Cambridge. But the parlour and upper floor were dark and empty. I had taken Bessie, our maid, with me so the house was cold. I set Bessie to the task of building up the sitting-room fire before she went into the kitchen to peel potatoes. Then I went upstairs to take off my best hat and tie on an apron before joining her there. I had stopped at a meat pie shop on the way home and bought a large dish of steak and kidney with a well-browned crust. If all this sounds a scraped-together hurried meal, it was.

I should explain that Aunt Parry is not really my aunt, but the widow of my godfather, Josiah Parry. She had been good enough to offer me a home and a situation as her companion when I had first arrived in London. That I had left her to get married and, to her further dismay, to marry a policeman was something she found difficult to forgive me. Not that I had been a great success as a companion, with a tendency to become involved in matters no lady should trouble with (like murder). But Aunt Parry easily felt neglected and liked to remind me I had abandoned her. Bessie had worked in Dorset Square as kitchen maid and, when I left to set up my own home, I had taken her with me. Aunt Parry occasionally chose to complain about that, too, although a kitchen maid was easily replaced. It wouldn't have surprised me if Aunt Parry had never set eyes on poor Bessie, toiling in the basement; nevertheless it added to her list of grievances.

Today my visit had been even more difficult because, to my astonishment, I had discovered Aunt Parry in greater distress than usual. Her medical man had imposed on her a strict regime: in short, a diet.

'A regime?' I asked.

'A *regime*!' Aunt Parry's voice quivered with emotion. The quiver rippled outward like the circles caused by a stone thrown into a pond, until the whole of her substantial form was a-quake.

When I'd been her companion I had often been present when Aunt Parry had made her morning levee. While Nugent, her maid, carefully tonged her hair into elaborate curls before pinning the whole lot up into a wedding cake of an arrangement, I had listened to my aunt list the tedious calls I was to make with her that day. My eyes had often sought escape by studying a portrait in oils hanging on the wall. I knew that the sitter was a young Aunt Parry and the likeness had been done just before her marriage to my godfather Josiah. She had been his second wife and there had been some age difference. The painting showed a young woman in a pink silk ball gown in the style of around 1830, with the low-set ballooning upper sleeves of the period, attached to a 'bateau' bodice cut straight across the bosom. The girl is sitting with a freshly picked assortment of wild flowers in her lap; as if going out to pick flowers in the countryside, while wearing pink silk, was the most natural thing in the world. Her hair is dressed in fat ringlets, framing a round but attractive face, with small mouth and large blue eyes. An enigmatic smile touches the rosy lips. Atop her head, her hair (real or false) is twisted, with the help of hidden frame, into an 'Apollo Knot'. The image reminded me of a large cherub forced into a corset, but I could see what had attracted Uncle Josiah.

Sadly the cherub had since become a vastly overweight middle-aged woman with a peevish expression. The blue eyes now held a look of disappointment with the world, except when contemplating a groaning dinner table. So I was not surprised to hear a doctor had finally summoned

27

the courage to suggest a diet. Still, it had taken a brave man . . .

'Is this the advice of your usual medical man?' I asked.

Aunt Parry's turquoise drop earrings danced furiously as she shook her head. 'Dr Bretton is a dear man. I don't think he would ever have been so harsh. But he was at a loss to explain my breathlessness, my fatigue, the terrible heartburn I suffer. He referred me to a specialist, Dr Bruch.'

She heaved a deep sigh. 'He is a German and, apparently, very distinguished.' She brightened. 'He is consulted by all the very best people.'

'I'm sure Dr Bretton would not have sent you to anyone less well recommended,' I said. So Dr Bretton had balked at the idea of making the suggestion himself and 'passed the parcel', as in the party game, to the nearest person as fast as possible.

'Certainly not. Dr Bretton has always been dedicated to my health. Well, anyway, Elizabeth', went on Aunt Parry briskly, 'I called at Dr Bruch's consulting rooms in Harley Street with the utmost confidence. I described my symptoms in detail, including . . .' She lowered her voice again. 'Including the repeated gastric disorders.'

She threw her pudgy hands in the air. 'And this is his advice! That I should exercise! A woman in my delicate state of health? How can I? That I should lose weight! Even if such a thing were desirable and possible, his horrible diet means that I am deprived of the innocent pleasure of a decent afternoon tea. You no doubt wondered why Simms brought in such a paltry tray this afternoon.'

Aunt Parry gazed sadly at the crumbs that were all that remained of a seedcake, and the now-bare plate that had held thinly sliced bread lightly smeared with strawberry jam. It was true, I had wondered about the unaccustomed frugality.

'No scones.' Aunt Parry spoke with quite sepulchral regret. 'No muffins, teacakes, Welsh cakes or any sort of biscuit, even the plainest. As for any more dainty treat, and an éclair or two, a meringue . . .' She heaved a sigh. 'I have almost forgotten what they look like.'

'And the exercise?' I inquired, wondering if mention of it would cause further upheaval in the layers of silk and lace opposite.

The reaction was quite violent. Aunt Parry gripped the arms of her chair. Her complexion, always florid, darkened to an alarming shade of magenta matching that of her gown. Her eyes flashed outrage.

'As you know, Elizabeth, normally I would attend to my correspondence from my bed and only rise when it is all answered. Then Nugent helps me dress and arranges my hair. In happier days, it would then be time for a light luncheon.'

I had eaten at Aunt Parry's luncheon table when I'd lived here and the quantity provided by the indefatigable Mrs Simms, toiling at the stove in her basement kitchen, had always been more than enough to last the rest of the day. Needless to say, in Aunt Parry's case, it only lasted until afternoon tea and cake, followed by dinner in the evening.

'However, thanks to Dr Bruch, I must now rise and

dress at ten in the morning, *ten o'clock*, Elizabeth!'

'Our household is astir at half past six,' I said unwisely.

'By your household, I suppose you to mean that one maid you employ. She should indeed be at her work at half past six. But what time do you rise?'

'Not long after,' I confessed. 'You see my husband has to be at Scotland Yard by eight.'

Aunt Parry gazed at me more in sorrow than in censure. 'You would marry that policeman. You could have stayed here with me, in a comfortable home.'

'I shall always be grateful for your kindness to me, Aunt Parry.' I didn't ask where her latest companion was that afternoon. Had she, like her predecessors, fled?

Aunt Parry had already returned to her first concern: herself. 'So now, I must dress, and eat a ridiculous breakfast of a single boiled egg and two slices of toast. Dr Bruch told me I could also have a bowl of porridge, if I wished. Porridge, Elizabeth! It is made from oats! Am I a horse? After that, I am to ignore my correspondence and have James drive me to Regent's Park. There I walk for half an hour, attended by Nugent. At this horrible, cold time of year, mark you! I have told Dr Bruch that if I succumb to a chest infection of the very worst sort, it will only be because I have followed his advice.' Aunt Parry's well-corseted upper body tilted towards me. 'He laughed, Elizabeth!' she told me in a strangled whisper.

'*Laughed*, Aunt Parry? Surely not . . . A professional man?'

'Well, chuckled, then,' Aunt Parry conceded. 'He

received my words with undue levity. He told me I had only to wrap up well, and I should be perfectly all right. Anyhow, after that, James drives me home here, to a frugal luncheon of cold meat and rice pudding. And no decent afternoon tea to compensate for it! However,' she concluded, 'when Patience arrives, I'll ring for some more tea and I am sure Mrs Simms can find something suitable to accompany it.'

'We are to be joined by Miss Wellings, Frank's fiancée?' I asked in surprise.

Frank Carterton was Aunt Parry's nephew. He had recently been elected to Parliament – and become engaged to be married – in quick succession. Aunt Parry worried about both things. I had met Patience Wellings briefly, when she had travelled down to London just after the engagement had been announced, together with her parents. Mr and Mrs Wellings had clearly been in awe of Aunt Parry. Patience had been much more at ease. She had struck me as a cheerful, practical sort of girl, with pretty dark curls. I had liked her very much. This was just as well, because Frank had drawn me aside to ask me seriously, 'What do you think, Lizzie?' I had been able to assure him I thought he had made an excellent choice. He'd seemed relieved to hear it.

'I shall be pleased to see Miss Wellings again,' I said. 'Are her parents also in London?'

Aunt Parry shook her head. 'No, her father's business requires him at home and her mother has other obligations. Patience is staying with some relatives who live in Goodge Place. Their name is Pickford.' She hesitated before tilting her upper body forward again, signalling another confidence was to be made.

'Elizabeth, I fear dear Frank is rushing into wedlock! The engagement was so sudden. I am sure it was brought about at Mr Gladstone's insistence. I am not finding fault with Patience. She is a nicely brought-up, polite, cheerful sort of girl. One can easily be fond of her. In a year or two, with encouragement and the right influences, she could shine. But her family is provincial, lacking experience of fashionable society. Patience is very young and could easily be led into some awful faux-pas. She is scarcely more than a child, only nineteen. Oh, Elizabeth! She is a veritable little savage in her lack of knowledge of the world. Every time she opens her lips, I fear to hear what she will say. Dear Frank, of course, finds this enchanting.'

'She will learn,' I comforted her.

'From whom?' demanded Aunt Parry sharply. 'Have I not just said that her close circle is not sophisticated?' Perhaps she felt she was sounding over-critical. More graciously she went on, 'I gather they are a leading family in Frank's constituency, well respected, and have played their part in local affairs. There is a statue of her grandfather in the park there. But I think that is because he was instrumental in bringing the railway to the town, adding greatly to its prosperity. Frank tells me her father has built a fine house in the Gothic style. However, the town remains a workaday place. Frank told me it is permanently under a dense black cloud of smoke from the kilns.' She sighed. 'I am afraid that dear Frank himself remains – despite an excellent education and the advantage of spending much time here in Dorset Square – an innocent!'

It was a good thing I had set down my teacup or I should have dropped it. Frank? An innocent? Hardly that. Kind-hearted, yes, and well meaning. But when I had first met him he had been busily sowing his wild oats. He'd been very clever at hiding this from his doting aunt. What's more, after a brief diplomatic career, he now sat at Westminster representing a constituency in the Potteries, with all the problems of industry. I doubted Frank lacked knowledge of the world.

'Um . . .' was all I could find to say.

Fortunately, at that moment, we heard the distant front doorbell.

Aunt Parry sat up straight. 'Oh, good,' she said brightly, 'here is dear Patience. We shall have more cake. Mrs Simms must have more cake downstairs.' Quietly, she added, 'We'll continue this conversation another time, dear Elizabeth.'

Whatever was worrying Aunt Parry, I was not to learn it, not just yet, anyway.

Shortly after that, Patience herself fairly bounced into the room. Her glowing cheeks were framed by bunches of black curls that seemed to quiver with a life of their own. She wore a dark blue gown, trimmed with braid and looking brand new. The gown was pinned up around the hem to protect it from wet pavements. The colour had perhaps been chosen to enhance the blue sapphires set in her engagement ring. Apart from the ring, she wore no jewellery except small coral earrings. She brought a breath of fresh air with her into Aunt Parry's overheated drawing room.

'My dear child,' said Aunt Parry to her when first greetings had been exchanged. 'You looked very flushed.'

'It is because I walked here, Mrs Parry,' said Patience cheerfully.

'Walked – from Goodge Place to Dorset Square!' cried Aunt Parry in disbelief.

'Oh, yes,' said Patience. 'It is cold, but the rain has stopped, the sun is beautiful and I am used to walking, you know. At home, I walk all the time. I have good boots,' she concluded. Indeed, we could see, beneath the pinned hem, her neat little walking boots of the type called 'balmorals' and made popular by the ladies of the royal family, with their liking for walking during their Scottish holidays. Patience's boots had begun the day highly polished; now they were heavily smeared with mud.

'Alone?' asked Aunt Parry, raising hands in horror, both at the idea and at the mud. 'They did send a maid with you from Goodge Place, I trust?'

'Oh, no. Well, my Aunt Pickford offered to send one with me, but I told her I was sure of the way. I have a street map,' she added.

'Map?' Aunt Parry's voice was barely audible.

'Yes, Mrs Parry, a street map. Frank gave it to me. It's very useful. And, of course, I allowed myself plenty of time.'

Aunt Parry cast me a look said that clearly, *You see what I mean?*

To Patience she said firmly, 'A map, dear child, is not a substitute for a companion of some sort. An unmarried young woman, Patience, does not wander around London with no protection other than a map! I shall speak to Frank.'

'Oh, Frank doesn't mind,' said Patience, not at all dismayed at the criticism.

I remembered that when I'd arrived in London all alone, to be companion to Aunt Parry, not even a maid had been sent to meet me at the station. I had taken a cab and arrived in Dorset Square without mishap. Subsequently, I had walked everywhere on my own. But then, I had not been engaged to Frank.

It was clear that Aunt Parry found conversation with Miss Wellings a strain. With the arrival of fresh cake and tea, few words were exchanged. Once the last few crumbs had disappeared, she retired to her room to rest; and left entertaining Frank's fiancée to me. As she passed by me on her way to the door, Aunt Parry gave me a meaningful look. Something was expected of me.

What was I supposed to do? Turn Patience into a society belle with the help of a few instructions? I was never any kind of society belle myself and couldn't have done so, even had I wanted. Anyway, I liked Patience as she was. So, more importantly, did Frank.

I need not have worried how to begin the conversation now Patience and I were alone. As soon as Aunt Parry had left us, Patience leaned forward and began, 'Dear Mrs Ross, I am so glad you are here. You are the very person I wanted to see.'

'Please call me Lizzie,' I said, wondering what was coming next.

'Thank you!' Patience beamed at me. 'I have wanted to do so, because Frank always calls you that, but I did not want to seem forward. Aunt Pickford tells me every day I must observe all the niceties, and not put my foot in it. You will call me Patience, I hope?'

Mention of her feet drew my eye back to the muddy boots and I wondered if I should . . . No! I decided. This was none of my business. But clearly, there was something that Patience was anxious to make my business. My heart sank. Surely Frank had not got into a scrape? I really had thought him older and wiser. At least, one hoped so, for his constituents' sakes.

Some of the animation left Patience's manner and she fidgeted with her cuffs. 'It is very difficult,' she burst out suddenly, 'and I do not know where to turn. Oh, Mrs Ross, Lizzie, you are the only person I can talk to about this!'

'Your Aunt Pickford—' I began in alarm.

'Oh, no, Lizzie, not Aunt Pickford! She would write directly to Mamma, or worse, to Papa!'

Keep calm, Lizzie, I told myself. I knew I was about to be the recipient of information that, in some way, was going to be either embarrassing or downright alarming. Whatever it was, I didn't want to hear it. But poor Patience was clearly in a terrible state about it and she was, after all, only nineteen and living in a strange city.

'Patience,' I said, 'you had best begin at the beginning and go slowly, I beg. I hope you have thought about this and won't tell me something you may later wish you hadn't.'

'But I can't tell anyone else!' burst out Patience, clenching both fists, so that the knuckles showed white and the sapphire engagement ring stood out. 'It concerns my brother, Edgar.'

'I don't believe I've met Edgar,' I said cautiously. 'Does he know you are talking to me about this, this problem? Because, whatever it is, if it's Edgar's business—'

'Only hear me out!' begged Patience. 'You'll understand when I've told you. Edgar is older than me, he's twenty-five. He came to London to study medicine at St Bartholomew's College of Medicine. He is now a junior doctor and continuing his training at the hospital itself. They call it "Bart's", Lizzie.'

'Yes, I know,' I said. Medical students were apt to get into scrapes. I knew this from stories my late father, himself a physician, had told me.

'The trouble is that Edgar has a very good heart but not much commonsense,' said Patience. 'Perhaps I should not say that, but really, it is the truth, so I have to.'

Edgar was beginning to sound much like the younger Frank Carterton.

'I do understand,' Patience said earnestly. 'Edgar came to London from our provincial town, as I have now done. Our town is thriving and over the last years many people have built fine houses. We have a new concert hall. People receive and entertain in style and are anxious to do things properly. But, well, London is quite different. One does feel, well, one does feel *awkward*. I make mistakes. I know

I do. I should have let Aunt Pickford send a maid with me today, shouldn't I? Not walked here all the way from Goodge Place alone? I saw Mrs Parry's face when she heard I'd done that. Mrs Parry fears I will be an embarrassment to Frank, doesn't she?'

'No, Patience, of course not.' I hoped I sounded convincing, but that was exactly what Aunt Parry thought. I am clearly a poor liar.

'Yes, she does,' said Patience, 'and I don't blame her. But I shall try very hard not to let Frank down. They all like him at home, you know, and are so pleased he is to represent our interests at Westminster. But, how can I put this? Because Aunt Parry already thinks I am a bit of a problem, I can't let her find out about Edgar.'

'What on earth has Edgar done?' I demanded.

'He's been gambling and he owes a lot of money. He can't pay it,' said Patience. 'I can't tell my parents. I can't tell my Uncle and Aunt Pickford, because the news will go straight home.'

'Have you told Frank? Because, really, Patience, you ought not to tell me things you keep from Frank. It puts me in a very difficult position.'

'I have told Frank that Edgar has been foolish, got in with a rakish set of other young medical men, and has been gambling. I have not informed him, because I really am unable to do so, that Edgar came to me and asked me for money.'

'Asked *you*?' I cried.

'Yes, because I have a little money of my own, left to me by my grandmother. She stipulated that, if I remained unmarried, it would be mine to dispose of at twenty-one. But if I became engaged to be married before then, and was over the age of eighteen, I should be allowed to put some of it towards the cost of my trousseau and setting up home. Her intention was that, even if my father's business should fail and he become poor, my prospects would be protected. I should be able to be married in style. Well, Papa's business didn't fail. It has done very well. He is paying for my trousseau and all the costs of the wedding. Mrs Parry has also settled a handsome sum of money on Frank, in recognition of the fact that he is about to be married. My Uncle and Aunt Pickford have been generous in allowing me to live with them in Goodge Place and paying nearly all my expenses. So my sum of money has remained untouched. Edgar knows it.'

'Really!' I said angrily. 'Edgar has no business to ask you. He should go to your father and make a clean breast of it! I am sure your father, though disappointed, would pay.'

'Oh, yes, he would. And I told Edgar, when he came to ask me for money, to do exactly as you say. He should go to Papa and confess. I refused to give him any money because Frank and I may need it. It costs a lot to live in a suitable style for a Member of Parliament. We shall have to maintain two homes, one in the constituency and one here in London. Edgar said he would pay back any loan. But how ever could he? So, although I felt cruel and Edgar was disappointed, I refused.'

'You did quite right, Patience', I said. 'I am relieved to hear it.'

'After all, I know Papa would pay the money, if he must, and Frank wouldn't be cast into some awful prison.' Patience was anxious I should understand.

'People are not so much imprisoned for debt now, Patience. It is not as it used to be twenty years ago,' I consoled her.

'It would still be a scandal and Bart's might tell Edgar he must leave. "You have no choice, you must go to Papa!" That's what I told Edgar. After all, any scandal in my family would reflect on Frank's career.'

'So, did Edgar take your advice and go to your father?' I asked, without much hope.

'No,' said Patience. 'He went to a moneylender. That paid his gaming debts, but now he is being pursued by the moneylender. Honestly, Lizzie, when I heard that, I could have— have thrown something at Edgar. We had a terrible quarrel. He said it was my fault, for not helping him out. I said it was his, because he gambled in the first place, and because he was too much the coward to go and confess to Papa. So we parted on very bad terms.'

There was a silence while I turned all this over and Patience sat watching me hopefully.

'What do you think I can do?' I asked bluntly at last.

Hope faded in Patience's face. 'You might have some ideas. You know about things. You live here in London. You are married to an inspector of police. I don't know about anything!'

'All right, Patience, here is my advice,' I told her. 'Although I dare say you will not like it. In the first place, you were right not to lend or give any money to Edgar yourself. It is certainly not what your grandmother intended in her will, and it would encourage Edgar to continue in a downward spiral. He cannot always be "robbing Peter to pay Paul", as the saying goes. He will never be clear of debt, if that is what he tries. Things will get worse, because the moneylender will be charging interest.'

'Yes, Edgar told me the interest on the original sum is mounting alarmingly,' agreed Patience.

'There is only one avenue he can take. He must go to your father. It will not be pleasant for him or for your parents. They are rightly proud of him for doing so well in his medical exams, and becoming a junior doctor at Bart's, and it will be a shock to them. But your father will understand. Edgar is not the first young man to be led astray by wild companions. Your brother is ashamed and trying to hide it all from your parents. But he cannot. Either he must go to them and confess – or you must tell them.'

'Oh, but I can't!' wailed Patience. 'Edgar will say I've betrayed him!'

'At the moment, Edgar is betraying everyone else. You have to do it, Patience. But, before you do, you must tell Frank all about it. You and he are to be married quite soon. It is no way to start a marriage with a secret like this on your mind. What's more, Frank's career does leave him vulnerable to scandal. So it is vital this all be cleared up before you marry.'

'You couldn't tell Frank, I suppose, Lizzie?' Patience asked in a very small voice. 'Frank does think so highly of you.'

'I am not the one about to marry Frank,' I said firmly. (I fought back the memory of the occasion when Frank did ask me to marry him.) 'You are. There must be trust between husband and wife, Patience. Frank is very understanding.'

'Yes, Lizzie,' said Patience dolefully.

'And now,' I said, getting to my feet and making toward the bell rope, 'it is already getting dark. I shall summon Simms and have him go out and find a cab to take you back to Goodge Place. Have you sufficient money with you?'

'Yes, Lizzie.' Patience made an effort to regain some poise. 'And in future I will take a cab when I come here from Goodge Place, I promise.'

'I'm pleased to hear it because it will set Aunt Parry's mind at rest. Oh, do make sure you always take a closed cab, a four-wheeler. Only fast women ride around unchaperoned in open-fronted hackney cabs.'

'Do they?' Diverted by this information, Patience brightened. 'I shall look out for them! I don't think I've ever met a fast woman.'

'When you are going about in fashionable society, I am sure you will,' I told her.

Chapter Four

Inspector Ben Ross

I ARRIVED at Scotland Yard the following morning with a guilty conscience. I had arrived home so late the previous evening, after my visit first to Cambridge and then to Deptford, that Lizzie had quite given up waiting for me and had gone to bed. It had, after all, been just on midnight. My dinner sat between two plates on the hob, keeping warm, but I had little energy to eat it. If I'd been hungry earlier, my hunger had worn off with tiredness. I crept into bed, trying not to disturb my wife. She muttered, 'Ben?' and I replied back, 'Yes.' And that was the sum of our conversation.

I had completely forgotten that Lizzie had spoken yesterday morning of going to visit her Aunt Parry in Dorset Square. It was not until Lizzie began to tell me, at breakfast this new day, about some diet or other Mrs Parry was on; and something about Miss Wellings, the girl Frank Carterton was to marry, that I remembered. But I was unable to disguise the blank look on my face and the conversation went no further.

It occurred to me, before I rushed out again, that Lizzie looked preoccupied. Then on my way to work I began to think that it was not so much preoccupied as offended. Perhaps she thought I neglected her? She never complains at the irregular hours I am obliged to keep. That evening, I decided, whatever happened during the day, whatever progress or lack of it, we might make into the Deptford murder, I would arrive home at an earlier hour and have some civilised conversation with my wife.

The road to Hell, the saying goes, is paved with Good Intentions.

My first task of the day was to send a message to Deptford, asking that they bring in Parker again for questioning. Following this, I had to make a necessary but unpleasant visit to the mortuary at St Thomas's Hospital, where Dr Carmichael was to carry out a postmortem.

Carmichael is a surgeon of the old-fashioned school and had only recently been persuaded to accept new ideas about infection. The result was that the mortuary reeked of carbolic, and moisture from the spray that had dispensed it trickled down the tiled walls; so the atmosphere was not only pungent, but damp. It practically took my breath away and had me spluttering. At least it masked other noxious odours about the place. When I had mopped my watering eyes, and greeted the surgeon, I saw that scientific progress had not succeeded in parting Carmichael from his dissecting coat: an old and dirty frock coat. He was proud of that garment. Its stains were honourable, he had told me, a record of his career as good as any written account.

Nor had he been parted, I saw on arrival, from his assistant, Scully. Scully is a pale-faced creature with lank, long dark hair and pale protruding eyes. He stood nearby now wearing a long rubber apron. He had put out Carmichael's instruments on a table and waited patiently to hand them to his master. His pallid features wore an oddly satisfied expression. Scully enjoyed his work.

'I have examined the victim,' said Carmichael briskly. 'But only externally, you understand. However, I do not expect, when we begin the investigation proper of the body, to find anything to add to the conclusions I have already formed. She was severely beaten about the head with some heavy object. It could have been almost anything. You will need to find the murder weapon, so that some comparison can be made to the injury. There is no indication that she struggled. No other injuries, I mean, such as might have been inflicted if she had raised her arm to ward off the blows. No torn fingernails from scratching at her assailant.'

'More than one blow, then?' I asked.

'Decidedly. A quite frenzied attack, and I would suggest she was taken by surprise.'

'How old do you think her?' I asked him.

'Oh, not more than five and fifty. Perhaps not even that. She is a sturdy female, well nourished. She was not accustomed to manual work.'

Carmichael lifted one of the corpse's stiff hands as much as he was able. 'See here, the nails, as I have already mentioned, are undamaged. They are neatly shaped, the palms of the hands are smooth. But if you will look closer, Inspector Ross . . .'

Reluctantly I edged nearer to the table. I thought I saw Scully hide a grin and glared at him, but he had already turned aside and was fidgeting with the array of tools. I looked down on the victim. It is always a distasteful moment and any officer dislikes it. It evokes both horror and pity, for even the most fearsome bullyboy seems a poor, vulnerable creature laid out flat on a mortuary slab. The carbolic spray canister set up nearby still dispensed its droplets over the corpse so that the glistening skin looked like marble.

I saw her first last night, in the mud of Skinner's Yard, I thought. *But now I am meeting her for the first time.* Last night she was only 'a body'. Today she is the enigma of a human experience.

I had not been able to make her out clearly the previous evening. Now I saw that she was a stout person, with a round face, snub nose and skin marked by faint scars, probably from some childhood illness, such as chickenpox or measles. Her hair was reddish-brown, streaked with grey. It had been worn in a bun at the base of her skull, but events had loosened it and I could see that it was strong and coarse in texture. Well fed, I thought. Not a poor woman.

I turned my attention to her hand, held up by the surgeon.

'There!' declared Carmichael. 'See there? These dark stains on the fingertips, and dark traces beneath the nail of the index finger on the right hand? Also, although there are no other calluses on the hand, there is a slight one here, just above the knuckle of the same finger, on the side, facing the thumb.' Carmichael put down the hand. 'Now then, Ross! What does that say to you?'

'She was right-handed,' I said.

Carmichael showed signs of impatience. He wanted more from me than that. The stains? They were bluish-black. But not bruises, I decided, so what else?

'Ink?' I suggested.

Thank goodness I was right. Carmichael was nodding. 'Yes, ink. The hands always tell a lot about a person. So, she did not wash dishes or scrub floors. But she did a powerful amount of writing; enough to stain the finger almost indelibly and form this small callus. She worked with her pen, sir!'

'Copying documents?' I mused. 'She would have to write quantities of private letters to stain a hand like that. But if she copied legal documents, for example, that might do it.'

'Book-keeping!' Carmichael voiced his own opinion in a decided manner. 'Mark my words, Ross! You may depend upon it. You will find out that she kept a regular ledger, or more than one, probably to do with monies. You know, columns of figures.'

'A counting house usually employs male clerks,' I said. 'Perhaps she helped to run a small business? A shop?'

'Well, you will find out, no doubt,' said Carmichael, showing a cheering confidence in my abilities. 'Now, the left hand . . .'

He moved round the table and lifted the left hand in

order to demonstrate. 'See here? The ring finger? The pressure mark? She normally wore a ring on this finger. I would guess a wedding band.'

'We did not find it,' I said. 'I noticed that she wore no jewellery of any sort.'

'The ears.' Carmichael was moving towards the woman's head and gently moved aside her hair. 'Pierced to take earrings and the large nature of the holes suggest she habitually wore them.

'But see here . . .' Carmichael reached towards Sully, who promptly handed him a magnifying glass. 'Look, both earlobes have some damage to the holes for jewellery, small tears. The earrings, I would suggest, were pulled out in haste.'

'The body was robbed,' I said. 'I had expected as much.' We would have to quiz Harry Parker closely.

'I took a look at her clothing. It is over here, on this bench.' Carmichael led me to a high bench against the far wall. He put a hand on the neatly folded pile.

It consisted of a dark-blue skirt and a matching fitted bodice, separately made. The light woollen cloth was of good quality, and of plain design. There were three narrow braid trims stitched around the hem of the skirt. The bodice had a simple lace collar and plain, cloth-covered buttons down the front. Chemise, corset, petticoat and drawers were of equally plain but fine cambric. She had not worn a crinoline. (My wife informs me this fashion is on its way out, not before time, in my opinion. But if you cannot afford to be changing your clothes with every season's whim, you cling to the old.) I wondered if the absence of any crinoline meant this woman had been of a practical rather than a fashionable turn of mind. A folded pair of black lisle stockings and light but sensible shoes stood to one side. Two crumpled lengths of ribbon lay neatly stretched straight, side by side: her garters. I found the sight unexpectedly pathetic.

'She was no lady of fashion,' I observed, more flippantly than I would normally have done. I was concealing my moment of weakness. 'But, neat, and certainly not a poor woman,' I added with more appropriate neutrality.

Carmichael, ever professional, pointed at the bodice. 'Here, on the bosom, you can distinguish pin-holes in the cloth. Do you require a magnifying glass?'

'Thank you, no, I can see them. She was wearing a brooch,' I guessed.

'Possibly, but it would have been a heavy one, and she wore it every day. The material is well punctured and the damage to the cloth permanent. This is only a guess, mind . . .' He turned his head and fixed me with his sharp gaze.

'Your guesses, Dr Carmichael,' I said, 'have often been of great help to the police.'

He looked pleased. 'Well, in my line of work, the powers of observation must be kept well honed, eh? My view is that she may have worn a watch. You know, a small fob watch, on a ribbon or short chain, pinned to her bodice, so that she could consult it regularly. Her daily timetable was important to her. You will make of that what you will.'

'She liked to be prompt or she expected others to be

prompt.' I had learned several important things from Carmichael. 'She was a businesswoman,' I said.

'A businesswoman, eh?' said Dunn, when I reported all this back to my senior officer.

The superintendent drummed his fingertips on his desk and squinted at me. His appearance always suggested more the farmer than a police officer. He was stocky in build, florid in complexion and had a liking for tweed. Today, with his thick bushy hair and cheeks reddened by a brisk walk to work, he appeared more than ever the country squire.

'It's a possibility, sir. I have already sent over to Deptford and asked them to bring in the fellow, Parker, who found the body. We can be reasonably sure she was robbed.'

'Robbed after death?' asked Dunn. 'Or was it a robbery that ended in a battering and death?'

'My suspicions are that it was robbery after death – and that brings us back to Harry Parker. If he did not kill her, but stumbled on the body as he claims, it would not surprise me if he took everything of value before he rushed out to find a constable. There was, for example, no purse or reticule. If she had stepped out to go to a shop, for example, she would have had money. The thing that really struck me as strange, sir, is that she had no hat. Sergeant Morris and a constable looked all around for one.'

'Ah,' said Dunn. He pushed himself away from his desk, stood up and went to the window. There he stood, staring out, with his hands clasped behind his back, and addressed me over his shoulder. 'She would not have left her house without some sort of head covering, eh? Quite so, every beggar woman, every street-corner prostitute, has some kind of headwear pinned atop her hair. Are you suggesting, Ross, that she was killed indoors and the body brought out to be left where it was found?'

'It has puzzled me from the start how she came to be in such a foul, abandoned corner. What could possibly have taken her there of her own free will and on her own two feet?' I told him. 'No, no, my guess is that she met her death elsewhere.'

'So, we must concentrate our search on the buildings around!'

'Morris is there now, sir, with two constables, going door to door.' Not that it will gain us much, I thought.

Dunn swung round on his heel. 'What do you intend to do next?'

'Go over to Deptford, sir. I hope they will have brought Parker back in for me to interview again. I have also sent Constables Biddle and Murphy around the local pawn-shops there. If anyone took her earrings, wedding band and fob watch or brooch, then the thief will try to sell or pawn the items. At any rate, the constables will tell the pawnbrokers to look out for such items and let us know immediately if any are brought in.'

'They are the kind of items brought in for pawn all the time,' said Dunn. 'And we have no detailed description of them. If they were all three brought in together, that would indicate . . . But yes, yes, the pawnbrokers must be alerted. There are other means of disposing of stolen jewellery, of course.'

'Now the police are visiting the pawnbrokers, sir, the receivers of stolen goods will soon hear of it. The thief may find the items too sensitive and be unable to dispose of them immediately.'

'The longer they remain in his possession, not only is he unable to profit by his theft, they are evidence of it. If he still has 'em,' said Dunn with a rare smile, 'he will be a worried man.'

Elizabeth Martin Ross

I was sleeping so soundly the previous night when Ben had eventually arrived home that I'd hardly been aware he had joined me in bed. Conversation at breakfast this morning had been hasty and disjointed. I told him I had visited Aunt Parry the previous afternoon: and he looked as though I'd said I'd been to the moon. He then told me there was a new case of murder, that it had taken place in Deptford and there were no suspects. I knew from experience that until this case were solved it would occupy his mind completely, and it was pointless trying to talk to him about anything else.

Thinking it over, after he had left for Scotland Yard, I was glad I had not had time or opportunity to explain Patience's worries about her brother. It was neither a matter for the police, nor would Ben have any personal interest in Edgar. Neither of us had ever met that young man. On the other hand, Ben had met Patience; and the only family of any sort I had in London was that of Aunt Parry and Frank. Not that Ben approves of Frank. In short, Ben already thinks the entire Parry family a nuisance. No need to make things worse with the tale of Edgar's debts. But I did wish Ben liked Frank Carterton more. I cannot help being fond of Frank; that, of course, is the reason Ben doesn't like him!

But Patience was still on my mind. She had to persuade Edgar to go to his father, no question about that. I could support her decision though otherwise I could do little. I was, however, aware that this whole affair would become an embarrassment to Frank and that did worry me.

My worries were about to increase. In the early afternoon, our maid-of-all-work, Bessie, appeared to tell me, with an air of conspiracy, that someone had brought me a message from Miss Wellings.

'Where is it?' I asked, not unreasonably.

'In the kitchen,' said Bessie.

'Can't you bring it in here?' ('Here' being our minuscule parlour.)

'I can bring *her* in, if I make her take her boots off,' returned Bessie. 'She's already messed up my clean floor.'

'You mean Miss Wellings is in our kitchen?' I got up hurriedly to go and investigate.

'No, missus, it's a maid from a house in Goodge Place. It's not written down, the message. I asked. If it'd been written down, I'd have brought it in proper, on a tray!' said Bessie reproachfully.

I debated whether to wait while the messenger took off her boots, or whether to save time and return with Bessie to the kitchen. I went to the kitchen.

Awaiting me, gazing about her critically, was a no-nonsense young woman. She wore a black bombazine dress with a lace collar, a small felt hat, and large Paisley shawl. She had pinned up her black skirts and her boots were, indeed, very muddy. There was a trail of footprints from the back door to where she stood by the table.

'You have come from Miss Wellings?' I asked her. 'Did she not give you a note?'

'No, ma'am,' said the girl briskly. Her accent was certainly not a London one and I identified her tones as probably Staffordshire. She might be Aunt Pickford's personal maid, who had accompanied her mistress to London. 'She didn't want to write anything down, ma'am', continued the girl, 'in case Mrs Pickford got hold of it. She asks if you would be kind enough to call this afternoon in Goodge Place.'

I glanced at the kitchen clock. I would have to leave at once.

The maid saw me look at the clock and added, 'If you can, ma'am, you could come back with me. Then I'll slip through the basement and you go up to the front door, like a regular afternoon visit.'

Aha! The plot thickened. All this could only be about Edgar. Patience was determined that the Pickfords should not learn of Edgar's difficulties. I was to arrive that afternoon under the pretence of a social call. It was all highly irregular and I suspected that Ben, had he known about it, would have recommended me strongly to make an excuse. But I was here, Ben wasn't, the maid had spoken to me, and I had no excuse.

'Bessie,' I said, 'would you run up to the cab stand at the railway station and fetch me a closed cab?'

The brusque young woman brightened visibly at the thought of making the return trip to Goodge Place in comfort.

Whether his cab had really, by fortunate chance, been the next in line for hire – or whether Bessie had ignored the other cabs and sought out Wally Slater, she didn't say. But it was my old friend who arrived. His four-wheeled 'growler', drawn by his horse, Victor, rumbled to a halt before our door; and Wally climbed down from his perch.

'Nice to see you, Mrs Ross,' he said, as he opened the door for me with a gallant bow. 'You off investigating again, are you?'

'No, Mr Slater, only paying a social call.'

He clearly didn't believe me. His battered ex-prize-fighter's features contorted into a conspiratorial wink and grin as he handed me up into the cab.

The maid, with a look at Wally that mingled curiosity with alarm, scrambled in after me.

Wally whistled to Victor and off we jolted. It was only when we were well underway and passing over Waterloo Bridge that I thought to ask the maid her name, and whether she knew of any particular reason for her mistress wishing to see me so urgently.

'It'll be to do with Mr Edgar,' said the girl, confirming my suspicions. 'And my name is Lucy, ma'am.'

'Mr Edgar isn't going to be there too, is he?' I asked, far too late.

'Yes, ma'am. Leastways, Miss Patience hopes so. She sent out earlier to ask him to come. He sent back that he would. But,' concluded Lucy with the familiarity of the trusted family servant, 'you can never tell with Mr Edgar.'

'I'll wait for you, Mrs Ross,' said Wally, after he'd handed us down in Goodge Place. 'Don't worry that I'll charge you a lot extra for it. I brought you here and I'll take you back. The inspector would wish it.'

I thanked him, secretly relieved.

It was fortunate I'd spoken to Lucy before my arrival. When I was shown into a small back parlour, two people rose to greet me. One was Patience, who looked so relieved and happy to see me that I feared the worst. The other was a tall, well-built young man who, like Patience, had a head of dark curls and would have been handsome if he hadn't looked so mulish and discontented.

'My brother, Edgar!' declared Patience, with a sweep of the hand towards the gentleman.

Edgar Wellings made me a stiff bow and said bluntly, 'I am obliged – my sister and I are both obliged . . .' He cast his sister a brief glance. 'We are both obliged,' he repeated, 'to you, for your kindness in coming.'

He then fell silent; having obviously said what he'd been instructed to say. I had to repress a smile because he resembled nothing so much as a rebellious small boy who had been drilled on how to greet a visiting adult.

'And we're aware that it was very impolite of us to ask you at such short notice, as we did,' Patience took up, 'but Edgar has to be at Bart's for much of the week; so we had to take advantage of the one afternoon when he's free.'

'I quite understand,' I said.

We all sat down.

'I have asked them to bring some tea,' said Patience, 'as soon as visitors come. The reason we are in this small morning room is because Aunt Pickford receives her visitors in the main drawing room.'

'And I am hiding from Aunt Pickford,' said Edgar drily.

'No!' protested Patience.

'Yes!' retorted Edgar. 'It's no use pretending this is to be a genteel tea party. I stand in the dock, Mrs Ross! I am here to defend myself, if that were possible, which it is not. And I am to be told what to do. It is something I don't want to do; and I have sound reasons for it. Only my sister won't listen to them!'

'Dr Wellings,' I said, now quite unable to hide my smile, 'I'm not going to lecture you. That would be quite out of order. In fact, if you prefer we won't talk of your predicament at all. I can leave, if you wish.'

'Oh, no, Lizzie!' cried Patience, as I made to stand up. She threw out her hands imploringly. 'Oh, Edgar, don't be so awkward! Lizzie has come to help. She's very wise. Frank says so.'

Edgar pulled a wry face. 'Well, I am not wise, Mrs Ross.'

I decided I liked Edgar. That didn't mean he was not a problem and likely to remain one for quite a while.

'Please call me Lizzie,' I said. 'When your sister and Frank are married, we shall be almost family; although I am only the late Mr Parry's goddaughter, you know.'

'This meeting is really more about Frank than about me, isn't it?' said Edgar, throwing himself back in his chair with a sigh. 'You have no idea, Lizzie, how proud my parents are that Patience is to marry a Member of Parliament, and one representing our town as well. I, on the other hand, am the fly in the ointment.'

'But they are rightly proud of you, too, are they not?' I countered. 'They don't know about your being in debt and having to pay back the moneylender, who is charging you interest.'

'No, they don't, and I don't want to tell them. As you say, they are proud of me. It will come as a terrible shock. I am not just embarrassed for myself,' he added urgently. 'Believe me! But it is all very well, you know, for Patience and you too, Lizzie, to tell me I must go home and throw myself on my father's mercy, like the prodigal son. But you don't know what they are like in a provincial town.'

'Oh, but I do!' I contradicted him. 'I came to London from Derbyshire only four years ago, when my father died. He was a medical man. I know provincial society very well, believe me.'

'Then you know how – how *moral* they are!' burst out Edgar. 'How damn – oh, sorry – didn't mean to swear – how *censorious*. They criticise the smallest lapse. Respectability is their guiding star! My parents will be horrified to hear what I've done. They won't dare to speak of it. Every time an acquaintance asks how I am doing in

London, they will have to hide the truth. It will be difficult for them, because they are so very honest themselves. People will soon guess.

'And, oh, Lizzie . . .' Edgar shook his dark curls. 'People there are so very quick to sniff out any scandal! My mother's friends will know at once, from her embarrassment, that something is wrong. As for my poor father, as soon as a rumour starts concerning my lack of prudence with money, it will reflect on him and his business.'

Edgar suddenly adopted an accent similar to that of Lucy, the maid, and declaimed: '"Young Wellings has gone to the dogs! It'll cost his father a pretty penny to bail him out. They've got that daughter to marry in style, as well. It will be the ruin of them!"'

'Stop it, Edgar,' stormed Patience, reddening. 'You're embarrassing Lizzie and you're embarrassing me!'

'Calm down, both of you,' I ordered. They fell silent obediently and sat, looking at me, like a pair of school children caught out misbehaving and faced with a stern teacher.

'All you say may well be true, Edgar,' I told him. 'Nevertheless, you will have to go to your father, and the sooner the better. You know that as well as I do. But perhaps, before you go, we should try and persuade this moneylender firstly to give you more time to pay; and secondly to fix the sum at its present level – not add yet more interest. If he is assured he is to be paid soon, he may agree.'

'*She*,' corrected Edgar unexpectedly. 'The moneylender is a woman, and a sour, fierce old dragon she is. I have studied medicine and know the human body needs a heart to function; otherwise I'd swear Mrs Clifford has no heart at all. She's all business, like some sort of machine. She lives in Deptford.'

He gave a sigh of exasperation. 'Mrs Ross, I must tell you that you are hopelessly optimistic in your suggestion. Mrs Clifford will listen to no kind of reasoned argument. It would be a complete waste of time going to see her. Worse, it would humiliating.'

'Edgar,' I told him more sharply than I'd intended, 'you can't allow yourself the luxury of hurt feelings! That is another price you will have to pay. Think of it as a part of the interest on the loan. It cannot be avoided.'

He flushed a dull red. 'You are right, of course. But consider that it would also be humiliating for a respectable woman such yourself to have to argue with the old witch. You have no idea how unpleasant she is. I hate to think what language she might use. And all to no avail! As for my sister going to see her, that's quite out of the question,'

'Why is it out of the question?' demanded Patience, the light of battle in her eyes. 'I am not afraid of Mrs Clifford or of anything she might say. You came to me, I would remind you, Edgar, with your problem. You cannot just say now that I am not to be embarrassed. Do you think I am not embarrassed enough? Do you think it was not humiliating to have to ask Lizzie's advice? Oh, Lizzie . . .' She turned to me. 'That didn't sound quite polite. I meant that Edgar has already embarrassed himself and me; and I, clearly, have embarrassed you. I should not have troubled you with it all.'

Her voice quavered on the last couple of words and I realised that Patience, for all her fighting stance, was not far off tears.

'I am very glad you came to me, Patience,' I told her. 'Now then, we'll talk no more about it. It will just end up in recriminations and time-wasting. We'll do without tea, and we'll go to Deptford to see Mrs Clifford now. It will grow dark soon, so we shouldn't delay.'

'Me, too!' she insisted. 'I won't be left behind! Stop scowling, Edgar. I am coming too.'

'Then let's be off,' I told them before Edgar could speak again. There was a sheen of perspiration on his face. He was now incapable of sitting still, twitching and crossing and uncrossing his legs. During his last speech he'd begun marching about the room. Any moment now and he'd say things he'd later regret, fling himself out of the house and we'd be able to do nothing.

'My cab is waiting outside and we can go at once.' I stood up.

At that moment the tea tray arrived, carried by a parlourmaid. She looked astonished at seeing us preparing to depart. Patience sent her and the tray back the kitchen where, no doubt, the girl would have a good story to tell of raised voices and arguments above stairs. If Edgar thought that, having let the genie out of the bottle, he could persuade it back in again, he was mistaken. What was more, it was only a matter of time – perhaps very little time – before the Pickfords got wind of dissension in their household, and demanded to know what was going on.

As for me, I knew I was already more tangled up in this than I wanted to be; but I had no idea how much worse it was about to become.

Chapter Five

Inspector Ben Ross

DEPTFORD, WHEN I reached it about two, had a
subdued air about it. The little shops were all open and
busy enough and the customers appeared respectable:
housewives, for the most part, shopping for foodstuffs.
The carousing seamen, who had given Phipps such
trouble recently, were nowhere to be seen. They were
either back aboard their vessels; or Phipps had them
locked up in a police cell. Public houses had cleared the
debris of the night before, and looked swept and clean.
Last night's roisterers were now sleeping off their excesses.
New customers were beginning to arrive, but were, as
yet, still sober and well behaved.

I passed the Clipper public house, where Raggy Jeb
Fisher had heard the news of the murder. A brewer's dray
was drawn up outside, and the two magnificent shire
horses waited patiently while the delivery was completed.
Their coats shone with diligent brushing and the brass
medallions fixed to the harness gleamed like gold. There
was something of a competition between breweries to

have the best turned-out teams.

The kegs of beer that had been unloaded were directed by a potman from the public house towards an open trapdoor in the pavement. Through this, the brawny draymen rolled the kegs down a ramp into the cellars. They crashed down into the depths with a tremendous rumble, as if a sudden thunderstorm had burst on a perfectly dry day. The drayhorses did not twitch so much as an ear.

An elderly man in a ragged coat, sporting a battered tarred hat such as sailors used commonly to wear, was searching patiently all around the frontage of the Clipper and in the gutters for cigar butts. Whatever he found, however small, he stowed away carefully in a cotton bag. When his bag was full, I knew, he would sell the contents to the makers of cheap cheroots. They would unpick the scavengings, dry out the tobacco, and reuse it. The old fellow even foraged among the hooves of the great horses, reaching under their bellies. They might occasionally turn their great heads towards him in mild curiosity, but otherwise were less troubled by his presence than by the flies that settled on their gleaming coats.

A few urchins ran about, and one or two old men stood talking together. In short, the area was looking its best, and its rough reputation unwarranted.

'Wait until this evening!' warned Morris, who had accompanied me, when I remarked on this.

I was curious to meet Inspector Phipps. He proved to be a middle-aged man of military appearance, standing very straight, with a fine sandy-coloured moustache.

Otherwise his hair had receded to leave a polished dome of a head. What remained around the back and sides was also sandy in hue, with streaks of grey.

When we had shaken hands, he set forth a succinct account of the latest circumstances with the same military precision suggested by his bearing.

'The witness, Harry Parker, is unfortunately not to be found this morning,' he said. 'I had already sent a constable to bring him in before I received your request. But he has flown the coop. Others in the house say he left his lodgings last night.'

'To be expected, I suppose,' I said with a sigh.

'He'll turn up again,' said Phipps confidently, 'unless he really does have something to hide. This is his natural haunt. He will be lost anywhere else. In the meantime, I have left word at the docks that, should he show his face there, I am to be informed. Sooner or later, he will need to earn some money.'

'If he robbed the body and is successful in disposing of any valuables, he won't be back until he's spent his ill-gotten gains,' I said.

'I understand you have men visiting the pawnbrokers,' said Phipps. 'I have sent a man to seek out known handlers of stolen property. They have been told that if items are returned promptly, with information as to the person who brought them in, they will have done their duty, and need not fear arrest. Unfortunately we cannot be sure exactly what items are missing. However, they know there's been a murder; and that is an incentive to them to be more helpful that they usually are.' Phipps paused.

'Though, frankly, I am not optimistic. The thief may decide to keep the items hidden until the hue and cry has died down.'

'Or throw them in the river, if he thinks they'll hang him,' I said.

Phipps slapped hands together. 'On the other hand,' he said cheerfully, 'I do have someone for you to interview and her information might prove important. It is a young woman, a maidservant. She came in about half an hour ago to report her employer missing. The informant's name is Britannia Scroggs. The employer is a Mrs Clifford; and Scroggs last saw her yesterday, early evening around half past six. In view of the victim being female, I thought you'd want to talk to the girl. We have her in our interview room. We have taken a basic report.' Phipps produced a sheet of paper and handed it to me.

I read the report through quickly. It was very basic indeed. Phipps had no intention of doing Scotland Yard's job for them.

Britannia Scroggs, aged twenty-three, stated a Mrs Stefanie Clifford employed her as cook-housemaid. Mrs Clifford was a widow and Britannia 'lived in', her room being in the attic. She rose early and Mrs Clifford some time later. However, her employer was generally downstairs by half past eight. But this morning Mrs Clifford still had not shown herself at ten o'clock. By then, the maid was beginning to fear her employer was sick. Britannia had gone to Mrs Clifford's bedroom and knocked on the door. Receiving no answer, she'd looked into the room and found that the bed had not been slept in. She had eventually come to the police station to voice her concerns.

'I should certainly like to talk to her,' I told Phipps.

Britannia Scroggs was a pasty-faced young woman in a brown dress and a dark green crocheted woollen shawl. What could be seen of her hair beneath an old-fashioned bonnet appeared to be fair. She looked older than her twenty-three years and her eyes held the wary expression of the London poor, mixed with defensive belligerence. Yet she did not seem displeased to see me. I suspected she was enjoying a moment of being the centre of attention in her downtrodden life. Mindful of Carmichael's observation that hands could tell the observer a good deal, I glanced at the maid's. They were already work-worn, and the distorted knuckles suggested rheumatism might be setting in. If that happened, Britannia would not be able to work. I felt a spasm of pity for her. She had probably toiled since childhood.

'Well, now, Miss Scroggs,' I said encouragingly, 'tell me about your employer, Mrs Clifford.'

'She's gone,' said Britannia bluntly.

When she moved her lips to speak, I caught a glimpse of a chipped front tooth.

'I understand from the statement you made earlier at the police station that you realised she was missing at ten o'clock this morning.'

'Didn't come down to breakfast,' said Britannia, nodding. 'Generally half past eight, she's there at the table and

I serve up two lightly boiled eggs and four slices of toast.'

The chipped tooth, flashing in and out of sight as she spoke, was distracting to the eye. I concentrated harder to make up for it.

'Lightly boiled eggs . . .' I mused. 'So, you cannot prepare the breakfast until she actually comes downstairs.'

'Of course not', said Britannia impatiently. 'Or the eggs would be as hard as rocks, wouldn't they? Gone cold, too.'

I sensed there was a strict routine to Mrs Clifford's household and it would be useful to know it. 'What time did she lunch?'

'Lunch?' Britannia snorted. 'She doesn't eat fancy like gentry. She eats her proper dinner at half past twelve, in the old-fashioned way. Generally boiled beef and carrots, or beefsteak pudding or, on Friday, a bit of fish. She's also partial to tripe and onions. What's this got to do with it?'

I ignored her indignation and prompted, 'And in the evening?'

'Evening? Six o'clock sharp I take in the tea tray to the parlour, toast again or muffins, if the man comes round selling them. Half past six, I go back in to fetch out the tray and take it to the kitchen to wash up the crockery. Then I'm finished for the day.'

'Do you go out of an evening?'

'I don't go round the pubs, if that's what you mean!' snapped Britannia. 'I can't afford it, I'm too tired, and anyway, Ma sent us all to the Methodist Sunday school when we was kids. No drink, no gambling, no bad language – that's what they taught us, or you to straight down to hell.'

'I see,' I said, impressed by the warlike glint in her eye, and hoping she was not going to demand that I sign the Pledge. 'So, what do you do, after work?'

'I mends me clothes or washes me hair,' said Britannia, after some thought. 'Once a week I goes to visit Ma. Generally I get into bed early and fall asleep. I get up at half past five of the morning, you know. Mrs Clifford likes the house all straight, dusted and polished before she comes down to breakfast. That's so I don't disturb her later. Anyway, last night I never went out.'

'Right,' I said, coming back to recent events. 'When Mrs Clifford didn't appear at the normal time, at ten you went to see what was wrong.'

'Well,' said Britannia, 'I thought she might be ill. Until I knew, one way or another, whether she was coming downstairs, I couldn't get on with my work. I needed to know what she wanted for dinner. I'd have to go out to the butcher, if it was meat. I knocked and she didn't answer, so I opened the door a crack and just peeped in, you know. I could see straight away the bed was all made up, never slept in, if you ask me. But I thought she might have gone out for something. You know, made up the bed herself although she didn't do that usually. That's what she pays me for, ain't it?'

'But you hadn't heard her.'

'No, so I went to look in the cupboard, to see if she'd taken her cape and boots. But they were still there. The cape is a wool one, dark blue, and she always wears it in winter. It's got velvet ribbon stitched round it, really nice. She's got a bonnet goes with it, small, sits on top of her

69

head, tied with ribbons. That was on the shelf and the boots was on the floor of the cupboard, so she hadn't gone out!' concluded the maid triumphantly.

'What time was it by then?' I asked. The maid said she thought probably about a quarter to eleven. 'But,' I said, 'you did not come to report her missing until half an hour ago, so Inspector Phipps tells me.'

'She might've come back, right? I had to wait a bit.' Britannia clenched her fists and burst out fiercely, 'You've got to *understand*! Mrs Clifford is a very private person. She don't like anyone knowing her business. I daren't even go and ask the neighbours if they'd seen her, because it would have started some gossip. If she'd come back, and found I'd done that, she'd have skinned me alive!'

'So, what changed your mind, Miss Scroggs?' I asked her.

'The hearthrug,' said Britannia. 'When I went into the parlour to straighten up, same as usual, I noticed the hearthrug was in the wrong place. I thought she must have moved it but I still thought it was a funny place because it was in the middle of the floor, on top of the big Turkey carpet in there.'

'Where should it have been?' I asked foolishly.

Britannia gave me a withering look. 'In front of the fire, where d'you think? Anyway, I thought I'd ask Mrs Clifford, when I saw her, why she'd moved it. But when I hadn't seen her, I began thinking again. First I wondered if she'd left me a note, in the parlour, and I hadn't noticed it. So I went back in. No note, but there was that rug in the wrong place and it really annoyed me, you know? It's a rag rug and it looked odd, stuck in the middle of the floor. Because the Turkey carpet is a really nice one, so why would she want to go covering up the middle of it with a rag rug?' She paused and glared at me.

I realised I was supposed to indicate I followed her reasoning. 'Yes, of course,' I said.

Britannia nodded acknowledgment that I was keeping up. 'So, I decided I'd move it back where it should be. I was thinking that today everything was out of sorts. I didn't know where *she* was, her breakfast eggs were still sitting in a bowl out in the kitchen and now it was nearly dinner time and I didn't know what I was supposed to cook for her dinner. So I thought to meself, right, my girl! At least you can put that rug back where it should be.

'So, I rolled it up, to be easier to carry over to the fireplace. Then I saw that, underneath it, there was a big damp stain on the Turkey carpet. I thought, she must have spilled tea, the evening before, only I hadn't noticed it when I'd gone to fetch the tray and she hadn't said nothing. Well, the Turkey carpet is patterned all over, mixed-up colours, so I couldn't have said for sure it was tea, but I thought it. I went out to the kitchen and got a bowl of water and a clean rag, come back to the parlour and got down on me knees to try and clean it up. Only it wasn't tea, because the rag was stained a rusty-red colour straight off and had a smell to it. It was blood.'

'What?' I shouted, jumping up. 'Are you sure? For goodness' sake, girl, why didn't you tell us this straight away?'

71

'I'm telling you things the way they happened,' said Miss Scroggs primly, 'like I tried to tell them here when I came first. Only I didn't get a chance, did I? As soon as I started telling 'em about her being missing, that other inspector with the moustache, he said perhaps I should be telling my story to a plain-clothes inspector, who was on his way over here from Scotland Yard. "You must give all the details to him," he says. "He will be here directly."' Britannia managed a fair imitation of Phipps's manner and speech. 'That would be you, wouldn't it?' she demanded unexpectedly.

I nodded, silenced for a moment by her complete confidence.

'So I didn't have to wait long, did I? Because here you are. Anyway, once I saw it was blood – and I do recognise blood when I see and smell it, thank you! – once I saw that, I took another good look round. One of the brass fire-irons is missing too, from the companion set. The poker,' concluded Britannia. She sat back, her work-worn hands folded in her lap, and looked at me in triumph.

After that, we all returned to the Clifford house *en masse*. With Sergeant Morris and myself came Inspector Phipps. He was clearly seething. I guessed he felt he had 'lost face' as the Chinese say, in not finding out about the bloodstains on the carpet. He had previously passed the case to the Yard and had been resolutely refusing to know about it. But now, in the light of Britannia's revelations, he'd decided he wanted to be part of the investigation. He had brought along Constable Barrett. We marched down the road, led by a grumbling Britannia Scroggs.

'Look at us all!' she accused us. 'Like a blooming parade! What'll the neighbours make of it? Bring along a brass band, why didn't you?'

The house, like its brethren in the terrace, was in the plain but pleasing style of the Regency, brick built then stuccoed and whitewashed. The terrace would have been built early in the century as homes for respectable artisans and aspiring clerks. Many would have been employed in the naval dockyard. The black-painted front door was reached via a well-scrubbed and whitened pair of stone steps, doubtless Britannia's work. The gleaming brass knocker also bore witness to her energetic polishing skills. Above the door a projecting ledge, supported by fat stone cherubs, shielded callers from the rain. The house was narrow but tall. The main parlour window was to the left of the entrance. On the floor above a pair of sash windows indicated the rooms behind and, above them, a dormer window projected from the steep, tiled roof, indicating Britannia's bedroom in the attic.

'Hm,' observed Phipps, studying the exterior, 'does Mrs Clifford rent this?'

'No, she owns it,' said Britannia. As she spoke, a curtain twitched at the parlour window of the house next door. Britannia produced a key. 'Come on,' she said impatiently, 'everyone's gawping at us. Come inside.'

We all squeezed into the narrow hallway with the exception of Constable Barrett, who was left outside to deflect inquiries.

This did not please Miss Scroggs. 'What do you want

to leave that bluebottle out there for everyone to see?'

She led us into the parlour and we could see for ourselves the ominous stain on the carpet. Britannia produced the rag and bowl of water she had used when trying to clean the damage away. The water in the bowl was an unpleasant brownish-orange shade and the blood had dried on the rag. Phipps and I exchanged glances.

'Miss Scroggs,' I said to her, 'do you know of any relatives of Mrs Clifford? What about her husband?'

'Never heard her mention him,' said Britannia. 'He might've died, or he might've run off, like some of them do. Leastways, she's never said a word about him.'

I looked around the parlour. Mrs Clifford did not follow the current fashion for cluttering up the place with knick-knacks, potted plants and antimacassars. There were no pictures on the walls other than a small framed sampler reading 'Be Wise Today' and with a border of cornflowers. There was a mirror above the hearth and a pair of china dogs on the mantelshelf, together with a hideous black marble clock with brass pillars. There wasn't a cushion anywhere. I had seen convent parlours more comfortably furnished. Struck by the absence of photographic portraits, I asked Britannia if there were any of Mr Clifford elsewhere about the house.

'No, she doesn't go in for them photographs,' said Britannia.

'How about children? Had she any?'

'Not that she's ever mentioned. She could've had some and they died,' offered Britannia as a practical explanation. 'Ma had seven of us and now there's only me left to look after her. My eldest brother, Billy, went to sea when he was fifteen. We haven't seen him since, nor heard from him in twenty years, so he's probably drowned. My sister, Maria, she died with her first baby, childbed fever. My younger brother, Eddie, he died in an accident, under the wheels of the coalman's cart. The other ones all died when they were really little, of the diphtheria. They all three died in one week. So there's only me left.'

'I'm very sorry to hear it,' I said, touched by this tragic tale and the no-nonsense way Britannia told it.

'Ma was really upset about Eddie,' she said. 'But it was his own fault. He was hanging on the side of the cart, hitching a ride, you know, like boys do. Only the horse set off suddenly, and Eddie lost his grip.'

I should have been concentrating on the case, but I heard myself ask, 'What about your father?'

'Accident in the dockyard,' she said briefly.

I didn't want to hear any more of the disasters afflicting the Scroggs family, and wished I hadn't asked. 'Now then,' I said, 'was your mistress wearing any jewellery when you last saw her, yesterday evening? Does she own some favourite pieces that she always wears?'

'Wedding ring,' said Britannia promptly, 'and her watch, pinned to her bodice.' She paused in thought. 'Earrings,' she added, 'nice ones, gold with rubies in them. I reckon they're real stones, not paste.'

Full marks to Dr Carmichael. 'She wore these items yesterday?' I asked.

Britannia said Mrs Clifford wore them every day. I suggested she go into the kitchen, accompanied by

Morris, and write down a list, describing the pieces as well as she could, even, in the case of the earrings, sketching them, if she could.

'And then,' I said to Morris, 'take her over to the mortuary and ask her if she can identify the body. It appears there are no family members.'

Morris went with Britannia to the kitchen. Before the kitchen door closed on them, I heard Britannia protest, 'What? Now I got to go and look at a dead body?' She sounded more annoyed at the inconvenience than distressed.

Phipps looked at me and said: 'The Clifford woman never married. She styled herself "Mrs" for respectability, mark my words. They're very particular about things like that, around here.'

I saw through the window that a sizeable crowd had now gathered in front of the house. When I went to the front door and opened it, the beleaguered Barrett appeared relieved to see me.

'They won't disperse, sir.'

'Go to your homes!' I shouted at them. 'You are hindering a police investigation!'

'Ah!' went up a collective murmur of satisfaction. So there *was* a crime.

'Go on, now!' I ordered.

Some of them began to move away.

Back in the parlour, Morris had returned. He handed me a sheet of paper on which Britannia had listed the items of jewellery her mistress had been wearing when last seen. She had sketched both the fob watch and the earrings, and done it with a confident hand. She hovered nearby with an air of someone expecting praise.

'I was always good at drawing,' she said complacently when duly complimented. 'They give us paper and wax crayons at the Sunday school so we could draw Bible scenes. I was good at drawing donkeys 'cos my uncle kept one to pull his cart. He was a costermonger, my uncle. The teacher said I had an eye.' Britannia frowned. 'She meant I drew good pictures, not that I didn't have two good eyes.'

'Perhaps you'd now go with the sergeant, Miss Scroggs. He will take you to view the body.'

Britannia sulked and now decided to object. 'Who's going to be here, watching you lot?' she muttered. 'I'm responsible for the house, when she's not here.'

'Come on,' ordered Morris, taking her arm.

'You let me go!' she ordered him. 'I ain't your prisoner and we ain't sweethearts, neither.'

But she left.

'Well, at least now we have something more specific to show the pawnbrokers!' I said to Phipps. I waved Britannia's drawing.

'That girl,' said Phipps, 'has altogether too much to say. But none of it is what we'd want to know, if you take my meaning! There's a lot she could tell us, but she doesn't.' He paused. 'Not until she has to.'

'I'd noticed that,' I agreed. 'I fancy she enjoys the public attention. She says her employer is a very private person. Miss Scroggs must have little opportunity to shine.'

We looked again around the gloomy parlour and by common instinct made for a writing desk in one corner. It had appeared to be locked but when we got closer we saw marks of the lock being forced.

'Neatly done,' said Phipps, peering at the scratches. 'Whoever did this, he's done it before.'

'Did Mrs Clifford interrupt a burglar?' I wondered aloud. 'Does this property have a rear entrance?'

We went to investigate and found that behind the house was a small, narrow garden, some of it paved over. Another area was taken up with an outside privy, a washhouse and a large bin for coal. A wooden door in the rear wall opened out on to a narrow alley running behind the entire terrace of homes and exiting into a side street.

It was an arrangement similar to that at my own house. I made a mental note to fix a new and stronger bolt on our alley door, as soon as I had half an hour free for domestic odd jobs – whenever that might be.

Back in the kitchen I examined the lock on the back door carefully. 'This has not been forced. No intruder came in this way.'

'Unless he was admitted by an accomplice. That girl Scroggs must be questioned again,' growled Phipps.

We had so far ignored the small dining room, situated between the front parlour and the kitchen. Now, we went to investigate. Nothing here had been touched, as far could be seen. The dining table was covered with a red chenille cloth to protect the surface. The sideboard contained dishes of various kinds, comprising a good quality china service. Something about the way they were stacked suggested they had not been taken out and used in a long while. The baize-lined drawers held cutlery and damask napkins yellowed with age and lack of boiling. I did not imagine Mrs Clifford held many dinner parties and I guessed this room, together with its contents, was largely unused. The air was fusty. We checked the window, giving a view of a side passage running along the kitchen wall before debouching into the backyard. No one had forced the sash.

We returned once more to the parlour, stepping carefully around the grisly stain on the carpet. I opened up the damaged lid of the desk, pulling down the flat writing surface.

Inside we saw the usual arrangement of pigeonholes and a larger space beneath containing several ledgers. But someone had been here before us. All the documents and scraps of paper had been pulled from the pigeonholes, apparently searched through in haste, and then stuffed back into the larger space, crammed in with the ledgers.

'He was in a hurry,' I said to Phipps. 'I wonder what he was looking for?'

'Money . . .' muttered Phipps.

We took the ledgers to the table and opened them up to find rows of neatly entered dates. Against each was a symbol we could not understand. A code, I thought. In a third column were entered varying sums of money, some of them considerable.

Phipps turned a few pages and then straightened up. 'Ross,' he said to me in his clipped military way, 'the woman was a moneylender, mark my words. No doubt about it!'

I pointed to the code of symbols. 'The names of her clients?'

'Probably, but if there is a key to them, she may well have kept it in her head.'

'Come now,' I said to him. 'She would have demanded some acknowledgment of the money borrowed, a signature on an IOU, from any client. But she didn't keep the proof in that desk. Perhaps she feared just such a break-in by a desperate debtor unable to pay. So, where?'

We returned to the desk and began to look carefully through the papers pulled from the pigeonholes. The first thing to take our notice was a letter with the heading of a well-known banking establishment, which I folded and put in my pocket.

'We'll look into this,' I said. 'If she was a moneylender there could be large sums banked.'

Phipps was subjecting the room to careful scrutiny. 'Cashbox,' he said elliptically.

'Where?' I looked round the room.

'Can't see one,' said Phipps. 'But if she was a money-lender I'd expect to find a cashbox with some money in it, here in the house. She might bank her profits, but she'd keep some cash here, either for emergency loans or monies paid back by a client; but not yet banked.'

We searched the house high and low, including the maid's attic room, but we found no cashbox. In the house owner's bedroom, however, we pulled a chest of drawers from its position against the wall in order to look at the back of it. This may seem a strange thing to do, but it is common enough for people to 'hide' something by taping it to the rear of a piece of furniture that would not normally be moved. There was no key or letter, the usual items concealed in that way. But when we went to push the chest back into place, Phipps noticed a loose floorboard by the skirting. It lifted easily, with the aid of a penknife, and beneath it was a small box. It was not the missing cashbox, but the sort of fruitwood container made for cigarettes. Inside, we found a heavy silver crucifix and chain and a man's gold half-hunter watch.

'Worth a bit, that,' said Phipps, of the watch. 'She hid it away behind this chest of drawers, so that maid wouldn't find it.'

I examined the watchcase for an inscription, but there was none. 'Is this,' I mused, 'a relic of the late Mr Clifford, and means he did once exist? Or was it taken as repayment of a loan in lieu of cash?'

Phipps had no trouble making up his mind on the subject. 'I told you, I don't believe the woman was ever married. Or never in a way the law would recognise. She took it in lieu of cash.'

I was curious enough to ask just what made him so certain. 'I agree, women sometimes claim to be widows, when they are not – for the sake of social standing. But why are you so certain in this case?'

Phipps gave me an unexpected mirthless grin. With his sandy moustache and narrow features, it gave him an unsettling foxy appearance. 'Money, Ross. The woman liked money. She knew how to make money. She did not need a husband to support her; and she would not have wanted any husband to control the money she made.'

He had a shrewd point. The law, generally speaking, gave the husband full control over any money a wife might have on marriage, or earn during it. There was much discussion about changing it; but so far that had come to nothing. A single woman, on the other hand, or a widow, controlled her own money. 'Mrs' Clifford might well have seen the benefit to herself in remaining single. The assumption of widowhood would then be purely for status.

'Well, when Morris gets back with the maid, and if the girl has identified the body as that of her mistress, I'll remove all those ledgers downstairs, and this watch and the silver cross, as evidence,' I told him. 'I will leave a receipt with the girl – and one with you, if you wish.'

'I'd be obliged,' said Phipps. 'Someone might turn up and start asking about it.'

'As to that, we'll place an advertisement in the press, asking for relatives of the woman to come forward.'

'We shall get a throng of people claiming to be close relatives, unaccountably out of touch with her, and all demanding to know if there is a will!' warned Phipps.

'Those we shall tell to go and find themselves a solicitor. We need someone who can give us detailed information about her. A murder victim about whom one knows nothing gives us no leads.'

We returned to the parlour where Phipps began speculating again about the theoretical cashbox. It was worrying me, too.

'If there was an intruder, he could have taken it with him, if it was a small box,' I pointed out to him. 'Our failure to find one is not surprising, perhaps, and does indicate an intruder. We've examined the locks and they are untouched, but a window could have been left open?'

Phipps, however, was anxious to make life difficult for Britannia Scroggs. His own failure to get her whole story from her, before I arrived, still rankled with him.

'How do we know that girl hasn't taken it? She had plenty of time between establishing her mistress was missing, and coming to the police to report the disappearance. She could have used the time to spirit away a cashbox. If Mrs Clifford had one, Scroggs must have seen it at some time.'

'I will keep her in mind,' I said firmly. I wanted it clear I was in charge. Phipps had not wanted to be involved at first. He'd sent for the Yard immediately. Now that he appeared keen to recover the reins of the investigation, I wasn't about to let him.

We had spent some time examining the papers in the desk until a commotion at the front door signalled the return of Morris with Britannia.

'It's 'er!' shouted Britannia, erupting into the parlour with Morris vainly trying to restrain her. 'Some villain has bashed in her head!'

'Miss Scroggs identified the body as that of Mrs Stefanie Clifford,' said Morris woodenly.

'Miss Scroggs,' I said to her. 'Sit down there.' I indicated a chair.

Britannia sat down, took out a handkerchief and blew

her nose noisily. 'She treated me all right,' she mumbled. 'She was a bit of a tartar but as long as I did things the way she wanted, and kept my mouth shut about her business, she was good to me.'

'Was your employer a moneylender?' I asked her bluntly. 'We have reason to believe so.'

Britannia raised reddened eyes. 'Yes,' she said sullenly.

'Did she keep a cashbox of any sort on the premises?'

'Brown box with a brass handle atop,' said Britannia. 'It's in that desk.' She pointed to the forced writing desk and seemed to see its disturbed contents for the first time. 'Here!' she exclaimed. 'Who did that? Did you? She never kept it like that. She was regular neat and tidy, was Mrs Clifford. I knew I should've stayed here with you lot. Police or not, you've got no right to go round damaging people's property!'

'So,' I said, ignoring her protest, 'you knew she was a moneylender. You knew she kept money in that desk.'

Britannia was quick to catch the drift of these questions. She bridled. 'Oy!' she snapped. '*I* never took it. I never messed up that desk, either! I worked for her for five years. She trusted me.'

'Someone took it,' I pointed out.

'Then *he* did!' shouted Britannia.

'Who is *he*?' I was shouting myself now.

Britannia grew quiet and sullen. 'She had a visitor yesterday evening. He come about eight o'clock or a bit before. They had an argument. I didn't see him leave.'

'*What*?' yelled Phipps and I in unison.

I forced myself to be calm. 'Britannia, why must you

dole out information in little scraps? Why don't you tell us the whole story at once?'

'Because it was *her business*!' Britannia defended herself stoutly. 'I didn't *know* she was dead until I saw her laid out on that slab. I couldn't go telling you everything, could I? She might've come back. I couldn't go telling her business, not to you nor to no one!'

'Britannia Scroggs,' began Phipps in a manner suggesting he was about to seize the reins again and arrest her, 'I put it to you there was no visitor and you've just invented him.'

I signalled him urgently to silence. 'Listen to me, Britannia. If there is anything else, anything at all, do you hear me? You must tell us now.'

'Nothing else,' muttered Britannia, again disposed to sulk. 'And there *was* a fellow came to see her. I'm not lying.'

'Did she often receive late visits?'

'Yes.' Britannia gave me a shrewd look. 'She was a *moneylender*. People don't want anyone knowing they've gone to a moneylender, do they? Otherwise everyone would know their credit is no good. So they often came quite late at night. She let them in herself. Perhaps she didn't want me to see them. Anyway, I was usually upstairs in my room, up the top in the attic, when she had late visitors.'

'But you could hear them?'

'Depends how much noise they made and how late they came!' snapped Miss Scroggs. 'Otherwise, it wasn't my business. It was her business and, like I told you already, she didn't like anyone knowing it. That went for me, as well. She didn't tell me anything and I didn't snoop. She wouldn't have put up with it.'

I pictured the façade of the house, and the attic window overlooking the street. 'Very well. But did you ever chance to see a visitor, from your window in the attic? Did you see the person who came last night? Is that what makes you so sure someone was here? Did you look out?'

'Yes,' agreed Britannia, 'as it happens, I did. I just happened to look outside, and I saw a bloke standing under the gas lamp. He was looking at the house, and he was just taking off his hat. He tucked it under his arm.' She mimed the action. 'I didn't know who he was. I mean, I don't know his name or anything But it was a top hat and he was dressed quite the gent.'

I seized eagerly on her equivocation. 'Had you seen him here before?'

'I might've done,' admitted Britannia cautiously. 'Handsome fellow, he was, young, bit of a dandy. That's all I know.'

At that moment there came a rumble of wheels outside and a vehicle drew up before the door. Shortly after, we heard Constable Barrett arguing which someone who wanted admittance.

I left the room, strode down the narrow hall, and pulled open the front door. A small group of people in the forecourt exchanged lively conversation with the doughty Barrett. It appeared they were demanding entry. Behind them, in the street, the audience of neighbours had reconvened and, also, grown. Word had reached the streets around that 'something was happening'. Young and old, they were there, from young children to an old fellow in a bath chair pushed by an eager girl in a maid's uniform, complete with frilled cap. All watched, agog with curiosity. In the distance, new figures hurried to catch the activity before it was too late.

Waiting there, too, was a familiar cab. Beside it stood the burly form of the driver, Wally Slater, holding the horse's head, and beaming his terrifying grin. It was like some fantastical bad dream.

I closed my eyes and opened them again. No, I was not hallucinating. At the house door, demanding to know why Constable Barrett was barring the way, stood a tall and agitated young man I did not recognise. But I did identify the young woman with him. It was Miss Wellings, Frank Carter's fiancée. Behind them stood – oh heaven, was it possible? My wife?

'Lizzie!' I gasped.

'Ben?' cried Lizzie, spotting me at the same moment. 'What's happened here?'

Before I could answer, Britannia, who had followed me into the hall, pushed by me and flung out her forefinger, with its swollen joints, to indicate the young man. 'Him!' she shouted. 'That's him! He was here last night. That's the one I was telling you of. I saw him clear in the lamplight, clear enough, anyway. That was him, I'll take my oath.'

She advanced on the young man like an avenging Fury; and was intercepted by Barrett, who struggled to hold her back. The crowd, scenting fisticuffs, set up a roar of approval.

Over Barrett's restraining arm Britannia shouted, 'You done it! You bashed poor Mrs Clifford's head in. You're a murderer, that's what you are, and you'll swing for it!'

Chapter Six

Inspector Ben Ross

THERE WAS nothing for it but to bring Lizzie, Patience Wellings, and the young man into the house and close the door on the crowd. Deprived of more entertainment, they jeered or whistled. Phipps went back outside to help Barrett disperse what was becoming a mob.

'What terrible people! Where have they all come from?' gasped Patience.

I could have told her that the London mob gathers round a disturbance as flies swarm around meat.

'Why at this house?' demanded my wife, ever practical, and fixing me with a stern eye, as if I were somehow responsible. I suppose, in a way, I was.

I suggested they follow me and led them into the kitchen, after I had prudently closed the parlour door, so that the newcomers should not see into the room as they passed down the hallway. I sent Britannia to wait upstairs in her attic bedroom. This enraged her.

'I've got questions of me own I want to ask him!' she stormed. She rounded on the young man. 'What d'ya want to murder her for? Standing there looking at us so innocent! You hope we'll all think you too fine a swell to do anything so horrible, eh? Well, I saw you, right? I saw you outside here, last night, on the pavement. Right under that lamppost, you were, taking off your hat and tucking it under your arm, like the young fancy you think yourself!'

Morris gripped her elbow and bundled her, still protesting, out of the hall. We listened as she stamped upstairs, abuse flying back to us partly directed at Morris, who followed her to make sure she did as ordered, and partly at Wellings. The tirade was stemmed when a distant door slammed. Morris returned down the stairs.

'She fair makes your head ring,' he muttered.

'You had better stay here, in the hall, in case she attempts to creep back down again and listen at the door,' I told him.

I returned to the party in the kitchen. Lizzie and Patience Wellings were obviously brimful of questions but managing, for the moment, not to speak. The young man, however, did address me.

'I didn't . . .' he said, sounding and looking bewildered. 'I didn't do anything, to anyone. What's happened?'

'Who are you?' I asked him sharply.

He pulled himself together. 'My name is Wellings, Edgar Wellings.'

'He's my brother!' declared Patience, bursting into speech and darting forward to take the gentleman's arm. 'He hasn't done anything wrong, whatever it is has happened.' She glared at me, red in the face, small but determined.

'What has happened, Ben?' asked Lizzie in more moderate tones.

A four-way conversation would be disastrous. 'Ladies,' I requested them, 'I see Slater is waiting outside with his cab. Allow him to take you both to your homes. Perhaps you would remain, Mr Wellings. It seems you may be able to help.'

'I want to stay with my brother!' stormed Patience, who clearly did not have the quality her parents had hoped to bestow on her when she was christened in that name.

Lizzie, thank goodness, took charge. 'Come along, my dear,' she urged and guided Patience out of the kitchen.

'Let us sit down, Mr Wellings,' I invited him. 'I am Inspector Ross of Scotland Yard's plain-clothes division, by the way.'

He looked surprised. 'Then you are Lizzie's husband?'

'I am, but that has no bearing on my presence here.' I again indicated a chair.

This time he did as bid, taking off his gloves, stuffing them inside his top hat and then putting the hat, after some hesitation, on a nearby stool. I recalled the description Britannia Scroggs had given, of a young man – she claimed it to be this one – standing outside beneath the lamppost, and tucking his silk hat beneath his arm. Britannia had also described the visitor as handsome and 'a swell'. It was a pretty fair description of Wellings. But it would also describe many other young fellows.

I had allowed him enough time to compose himself. But I did not mean to give him so much time he could invent some plausible tale.

'Now, then, Mr Wellings,' I said. 'Why are *you* here? And why, I am curious to know, do you arrive accompanied by two ladies, one of them my wife?"

He stared at me, his dark brows puckered. 'But I came to see Mrs Clifford. My sister and Mrs Ross came with me because we had all three been discussing the – er – situation in which I find myself.' He grew less certain. 'Where *is* Mrs Clifford? The maid was shouting out that she was dead. Surely, that cannot be?'

'She *is* dead,' I told him. 'Moreover, evidence to date suggests she was murdered in her own parlour.'

He turned so white I thought he might faint. But then he rallied. 'When?' he asked bluntly.

'Yesterday evening,' I told him.

Now Wellings shook his head decidedly. 'No, no, she was alive and well yesterday evening.'

'You sound very sure of that. Were you here, then, as the maid told us? '

Wellings drew in a deep breath. 'You might as well know the whole story, but I know nothing of her death! I paid a short call yesterday evening. She was alive then, very much so, and alive when I left here.'

'Begin at the beginning,' I invited him. 'How do you know the lady?'

'No lady!' said Wellings with a scowl. 'A heartless, grasping, unscrupulous old harridan.'

Phipps had returned, slipping into the kitchen and

stationing himself against the far wall behind Wellings, unseen and unsuspected. The Deptford man raised sandy eyebrows but, thankfully, remained silent. I understood his surprise. Wellings had not begun to defend his innocence very well. In his first sentence, he had told us he was on bad terms with the deceased.

Perhaps Wellings had also realised that he had spoken out too frankly. 'Normally,' he said stiffly, 'one does not speak ill of the dead – or not immediately, anyway. But the woman was a moneylender and had all the worst traits of that miserable trade.'

'And that is how you knew her? You are a client?'

'Yes,' said Wellings briefly. When I remained silent, he continued. 'I came to London to pursue my studies at St Bartholomew's Hospital College of Medicine. I am now a junior doctor, continuing my training on the wards at the hospital itself.'

He fell silent as if he expected I would make some comment. When I merely nodded, he continued, becoming visibly nervous. 'As a student, I fell in with some rather wild company.' He leaned forward, 'You have to understand, Ross, as a student of medicine – and even more so as a doctor – a fellow sees some dreadful sights and tragic, distressing events.'

'So does a police officer,' I told him unsympathetically. 'If he cannot stomach them, then he is in the wrong line of work.'

That set him back briefly and he flushed. 'Yes, of course. I did not mean to suggest . . . Well then, you will understand, perhaps?'

'Try me,' I invited. 'I am listening.'

'One needs to be able to put these things out of one's mind,' Wellings said. 'A fellow needs to get out and about and cut loose, you understand? Among other things, I got in with a crowd who played cards – for stakes. The stakes were quite modest and at first it didn't matter if I lost from time to time; because on other occasions I was a winner. But— but it moved on from that to more serious gaming. I was introduced to clubs where the stakes played for are very high and— and I was not among friends. When I lost, I had to pay up. I soon found myself short of cash. Then, someone I'd played cards with and knew well from my student days mentioned this woman – the woman who lives here. The chap was willing to introduce me to her. He said he'd dealt with her himself and everything was very businesslike. As she lives across the river here in Deptford, my visits to her would be unremarked by anyone who might recognise me. So, that is how it began.' Now Wellings did fall silent and waited for me to speak.

'So last night, did you come to borrow money?'

He shook his head and looked miserable. 'No, to ask for more time to repay what I had borrowed. I had a losing streak. I kept playing because I thought, sooner or later, my luck must change. But it didn't.'

How familiar a story this was and how many youngsters like this one had tried to beat the odds. And how many desperate actions had originated in this way!

Wellings looked even more despondent. 'I swear to you, Ross, I began to feel I must be cursed! She – Mrs

Clifford – she charges interest, of course. That is how she makes her profit. When I couldn't pay, even something on account, she became unpleasant. She threatened to inform Bart's. That would finish me. My medical career would be over before it had hardly begun!

'Of course, I could go to my father, cap in hand, and explain. I could ask him to pay what I owed. But I didn't want to do that. The very thought appalled me. I dreaded not only his anger, but also his disappointment. I thought— I hoped there was another way.'

'Which would be?'

Now he turned brick-red and fixed his downcast eyes on his clasped hands. 'You will think me a cad,' he said dully. 'And you will be right, because that is what I am. There is no pretending otherwise. You see, my sister, Patience . . .' He paused and raised his eyes to my face, a question in them.

I nodded. 'I have met Miss Wellings.'

'She is engaged to be married to a chap called Carterton. He's the Member of Parliament for our town. Patience has some money in her own right. It was left to her by our grandmother. The legacy stipulated that if Patience became engaged to be married before she reached the age of one and twenty, the money would become available to her to spend on wedding preparations, her trousseau, that sort of thing. My grandmother wanted to be sure Patience's prospects would not be harmed if my father lost his business. Such a thing can always happen in trade or industry. My father is not a landowner, able to sell off a few acres when he is short of cash. Well, happily our father did not lose his business; he prospered, and is well able to marry off Patience in style. So she does not need our grandmother's money right away, and I thought . . .' His voice tailed away.

Behind his back I could see Phipps scowling. But mercifully he kept silent.

'You thought to borrow money from your sister, money intended for what they call her "bottom drawer" or "hope chest",' I said.

He looked up and met my eye. 'Yes,' he said simply. 'I can see you think me a scoundrel and I don't blame you. I would pay her back. Once I am established as a doctor, I will have the funds to do that. It might not be for a few years, but as a family arrangement, that would be all right, and my sister would get her money eventually. The situation would be quite unlike that I find myself in with Clifford.'

'And did Miss Wellings agree to make the money available to you?'

'No,' said Wellings disconsolately. 'She didn't. She told me to go to our father. I should go and own up and throw myself on his mercy.'

Sensible girl, I thought to myself. If she lends this young wastrel money, she will never see it back, no matter how brilliant a medical career he may make for himself. This sort will owe money somewhere, to someone, all his life.

'So, let us come to last night,' I said. 'Why did you come to see Mrs Clifford? To tell her you could not pay?'

'Yes, and no,' young Wellings told me. 'You see, I

thought that Patience would relent – eventually. If I kept at her, you know, I thought she'd agree.'

Behind him, over by the wall, Phipps's scowl was now so ferocious that, with his foxy colouring and features, he really did look as though he might attack the speaker.

I began to think that Frank Carterton was going to acquire just the sort of brother-in-law a man making a political career doesn't want. That would worry Lizzie. What worries her also worries me.

'Mrs Clifford presumably holds – or held – some kind of note from you, acknowledging the debt? An IOU?'

'Yes, yes,' he muttered resentfully. 'She had proper forms printed out, very much the businesswoman. They show the amount borrowed, interest it will attract, date it is due to be repaid. If you look around the place, you'll find them – mine and those of other clients.'

Phipps and I had looked around the place very thoroughly, but we'd not found the all-important IOUs. We'd found the ledger but that, in itself, was not enough. What had happened to the all-important signed documents described by Wellings?

'How did you get here, last night?' I asked. 'By what means did you travel, when did you arrive and how did you gain admittance?'

'I took the train from Charing Cross, across the river,' said Wellings. 'I descended at the station at New Cross.'

'Did you keep the return ticket?'

'No, I had to give it up. There was a guard collecting the stubs at the exit at Charing Cross. Anyway, from New Cross station I walked to Deptford High Street, and turned off it to reach here. It is not so very far at a brisk pace. I arrived here at twenty minutes to eight. I am certain because I looked at my watch. I tapped on the window, to the left of the front door.'

'Why did you do that? Why not use the knocker?'

Unexpectedly, Wellings grinned. 'Because the old woman was secretive about her business. Well, to be fair, her clients didn't want to advertise their arrival. Rapping at the door on a quiet evening would bring all the neighbours to their windows. So the drill is – was, I should say now – to tap on the window. If she was in the parlour, she would come and look through the glass to see who was there.'

That, I thought, is why, when Britannia looked out, she saw you removing your hat. It was so that Mrs Clifford would be able to identify her visitor.

'There is a lamp standard just outside the house, so she had a good view of a caller,' said Wellings, confirming my theory. 'Then, if she wanted to let you in, she did. If she didn't, she'd signal the caller to go away. If she didn't come to the window, she wasn't there, so there was no point in waiting. I tapped on the window and she let me in. We went into the parlour. She conducted all her business in there. Until this moment when we find ourselves here –' he gestured at the kitchen around us – 'I had never seen any other room in the house. Just the hallway and the parlour.' He paused. 'You say that— that is where . . .'

'There is evidence of a murderous attack,' I said.

'She was alive and well when I left here,' he repeated

obstinately. 'How can I persuade you? I can only repeat the truth.'

'We had reached the point in your account where she had let you into the house and the parlour,' I prompted him.

'Oh, yes, well, we talked – argued. I told her I thought I could get the money from a relative. I didn't name my sister or say that the relative was female. So, I said, there was no need for her to threaten me with informing Bart's. She gave a most unpleasant laugh. It sounded like a rusty hinge grinding. "Bright young spark, like you," she said. "Families will always pay up eventually. I reckon you'll be the shining hope at home. You tell your relative, whosoever that might be, that you've got ten days. That's to give your relative time to get the money together."

'I tried to explain that it might take a little longer. After all, I hadn't talked Patience round yet. But Clifford wouldn't listen. Just threw me out, more or less. So, I left.'

'But you admit you and she quarrelled. Harsh words were exchanged, threats made. It went no further than that?'

'It wasn't a pleasant social call!' snapped Wellings, colouring. Then he made a gesture of appeasement. 'I am sorry, but yes, we quarrelled. She was so obdurate and unreasonable. I told her to her face that she was. I was very angry, I don't deny it.'

'You might even,' I suggested, 'have felt justified in striking her.'

'Yes,' said young Wellings with a scowl. 'Anyone

would. But I didn't. I wasn't here above twenty minutes. I looked at my watch again after I left because I needed to catch a train back again. So, if someone came here and killed the— killed her, it was someone who arrived after I did.'

I signalled to Phipps. Wellings spun round and saw the inspector for the first time. He looked first alarmed and then furious.

'Who is that?' he demanded.

'Inspector Phipps from Deptford,' I told him. 'Wait here, Dr Wellings.'

Phipps and I went into the hall and joined Morris there. I closed the door on Wellings in the kitchen, and spoke quietly.

'I'll take him with me to the Yard, by train and cab, to write out his statement and sign it. You, Sergeant,' I turned to Morris, 'go upstairs and tell that girl to put her things together. The house is the scene of a dreadful murder and she cannot stay here. We cannot risk her "tidying up" or moving things around. There is also her safety to consider, if the killer should return. He may not have found all he was looking for.'

I looked at Phipps. 'He was obviously searching for something in the parlour, but we cannot assume it was the cashbox. We know from Wellings that clients signed a properly drawn-up document detailing the money borrowed, the interest payable, and time allowed before, presumably, penalties ensued. My guess is that whoever cracked open the desk was looking for the document with his signature. He could have taken the cashbox to disguise his true purpose. If he did not find it, he may come back and try again. In any event, Scroggs's employer, the house owner, is dead; so there is no justification for her remaining.'

I turned back to Morris. 'If the girl cannot take everything she owns, tell her she can come back under police escort another time to fetch the rest. She should take what is necessary for a day or two now. Then take her to her mother's house. We need to be able to find the maid again easily, so try and impress on the old woman, if she objects, that she should offer her daughter shelter for a time.'

'Yes, sir,' said Morris woodenly. He set off back up the staircase to where Britannia Scroggs sat fuming in her attic eyrie.

I addressed my colleague, Phipps, again. 'I would be much obliged to you if, during my absence, you could oversee this house being sealed. I would like a seal on the parlour door here, one on the front door, another on the kitchen door – and one on that wooden door into the alley, at the back of the yard. I would also like the parlour window sealed up.'

'I'll see to it,' said Phipps. 'We can nail a couple of planks of wood over that alley door, and the kitchen door. The windows in the front and the front door can have wax seals and I'll leave a man on watch.' He cleared his throat and added quietly, 'You didn't tell that young gent the body was found in Skinner's Yard.'

'No. If he is innocent, let him go on thinking it was found here where she was attacked. If he is not, then he will be wondering why we haven't mentioned it; and it will worry him and make him unsure what tale to tell.'

As I prepared to leave the house with Wellings, we heard an eldritch screech above our heads.

'What do you mean, go and stay with Ma?' yelled Britannia's voice. 'How can I do that? She's only got one little room and one narrow bed! Where am I going to sleep, on the floor? And suppose she don't want me there, what then?'

Outside the house, a remnant of the earlier crowd lingered hopefully. Sighting Wellings, they sent up cries of: 'Is that the murderer? Have you arrested him? Where's the Black Maria?'

The old fellow in the bath chair became quite danger-ously excited, waving a stick and shrieking, 'Murderer, murderer! Hang the damn fellow!'

Wellings had turned a deathly white and appeared terrified, as well he might. To be the object of concentrated abuse from a crowd is a frightening thing.

'Ignore them,' I advised him. I gripped his arm, not to stop him running off, but to ensure he didn't faint away on the pavement. He stumbled along beside me.

I had feared the throng might accompany us and wondered if I would have done better to bring Constable Barrett with me. But some remained before the house in case anything new happened there. Most of the rest gave up at the corner of the street. One or two people tagged along further but were soon bored. After that, although we got a few curious looks, only one ragged boy of about nine or ten years of age followed us all the way from the house to the station. Eventually, as Wellings had put up no resistance and there was no more entertainment, even this spectator got bored and deserted us.

Outside the railway station, I spotted the old man with the tarred hat again, still hunched in his search for tobacco among the cobbles. This was probably a good spot for it. Perhaps as a youngster he sailed with Nelson, I thought; ship's boy, perhaps? The old fellow took no notice at all of us. All that mattered to him was to fill his little cotton bag with the precious tobacco.

Chapter Seven

Elizabeth Martin Ross

PATIENCE WAS in no state to go home to Goodge Place so I had Wally drive us back to my house near Waterloo. There, Bessie and I plied Frank's fiancée with strong tea, and waved a bottle of sal volatile under her nose until she protested. I also sent Bessie down to the public house to buy a small flask of brandy.

'Never – drink – alcohol,' gasped Patience between sobs.

'Medicinal!' I said firmly. I wondered quite how she would manage as hostess to dinner parties with Frank's political friends, once they were married. She could hardly refuse to provide wine, port and other liquors.

So Patience drank the brandy. It made her cough and splutter, but it did the trick.

'I feel a little better,' she told me. 'Well, not better about what has happened. That's— terrible! I can't believe it! Of course, Edgar didn't do— didn't do what that girl accused him of. Edgar wouldn't attack anyone! Anyway, he's a doctor now. He couldn't kill anyone deliberately.'

There had been convicted murderers who had been

doctors, I knew that. Generally, as I understood it, they tended to poison, rather than bludgeon. But had Edgar been desperate enough to panic and just strike out?

'In the absence of his denial, we must accept,' I said cautiously, 'that your brother was there, at that house, last night. The maid seemed very sure of it. That was where he went to borrow the money from Mrs Clifford and it does appear that Mrs Clifford is dead. Of course, the girl could be mistaken; and Edgar may already have denied being there. Ben bundled us away before we had time to find out.' Ben could have done nothing else, but all the same, I was a little annoyed about that.

'Even if he was there,' burst out Patience fiercely, 'he didn't – wouldn't – couldn't kill anyone!'

Bessie's head appeared around the parlour door. 'More tea, missus?'

'Not for me, thank you,' said Patience dismally. 'And I won't drink any more of that brandy, either, thank you, Lizzie. Aunt Pickford will smell it on my breath when I get back to Goodge Place.' Alarm filled her eyes. 'Oh, my goodness, oh heavens, what are we to tell Uncle and Aunt Pickford? They will find out. I mean, if Edgar is arrested . . . Will your husband arrest him, Lizzie?'

'I don't know,' I told her frankly. 'He might, I suppose, if he believes that girl. But he might not. It will depend, I dare say, on what Edgar has to say for himself, what explanation he gives.'

'Oh, how I wish I was there in that house, listening to what he has to say, and supporting him!' wailed Patience.

So did I, but I didn't say so.

Patience had fallen silent and I sensed a change in her mood. 'Lizzie,' she said, suddenly calm. 'We must go and tell Frank, right now, straight away.'

'He might be in the House,' I said. 'If Parliament is sitting, that is.'

'We'll try his rooms. Can your maid go and find that cabman again?'

So Bessie was sent out again to find a cab, preferably Wally's if possible. I heated water to enable Patience to wash her face. Then I helped her comb and pin up her hair afresh; and by the time we'd done, Patience looked and sounded her usual sensible self.

Bessie reappeared, flushed with success. 'He was in the pub,' she said. 'But I got him out of there sharp. The cab is outside.'

In the street we found Wally. It was not yet late in the day, but the light was already fading.

'Neither of us,' said Wally to me, 'neither me nor the horse, that is, has dined, as you might say.'

'I am sorry, Mr Slater. It's an emergency,' I told him.

'When duty calls,' he said, 'the Slaters always hear it. I'd an uncle, fought all the way through the Peninsular Campaign with the Iron Duke. You can rely on a Slater. Blow the trumpet and we're ready to advance.'

'He is a funny man,' whispered Patience to me, when we were inside the cab. 'But he looks so frightening, I wonder anyone hires his cab! Still, he's very – very obliging, isn't he?'

I agreed that Wally was, indeed, both kind and reliable. I did not say that, in view of his speech about duty, I also suspected he'd downed a pint or two before Bessie hauled him from the public house. I hoped it didn't affect his driving.

Frank Carterton had found himself comfortable furnished rooms on the second floor of an elegant house in Bedford Square; and he was at home. He was in fact lounging on a chaise longue with his feet up, in his waistcoat and shirtsleeves, and reading some correspondence.

'Good grief!' he exclaimed when the landlady ushered us in. He jumped to his feet. 'I mean, what a pleasant surprise!' He kissed both of us on the cheek – Patience with more warmth than me.

'We did not mean to trouble you, Frank,' I said, indicating the correspondence that now lay scattered on the carpet.

'Oh, don't worry about that. Letter from a constituent, you know . . .' He scooped up the papers and put them on a table. 'Let me ask for some tea.'

Looking around his sitting room, while Frank went to organise refreshment for his visitors, I wondered what the rent of these rooms might be. He needed a respectable address, and one with some style. I was reminded of what Patience had said to me: after the pair married, they would have to maintain two homes, one in London and another in his constituency. Patience's legacy from her grandmother would be needed. Could Edgar not see that? Or was he so wrapped up in his own affairs?

I decided that Edgar Wellings, although likeable, had been thoroughly spoiled by a doting family. He'd arrived in London lacking the awareness that other people would not treat him with affectionate indulgence. He was now finding out the hard way that it is a cruel and unfeeling world, particularly if you are a silly young man easily parted from his money.

I didn't doubt he might make a very good doctor one day. His intelligence was not in question. But he had no commonsense; and I did wonder if he would ever acquire any. He had begun his adult career with falling into debt through gaming, and was now entangled in some sordid business in Deptford. In our brief conversation over breakfast that morning, Ben had spoken of a new case of murder. The nearly hysterical maid at the house in Deptford had flung wild, incredible accusations at Edgar. What were we now to tell Frank?

'Well, ladies,' said Frank, reappearing. He was pulling on his coat as he spoke. 'Tea will be brought up shortly. I am, of course, very pleased to see you, both of you. But I confess I am a little puzzled. There is not some emergency with my Aunt Julia?' He looked at me.

'Oh, no, Mrs Parry is quite well,' I assured him. 'Only a little downcast because of the diet the doctor has insisted she follow.'

'Oh, the diet!' said Frank with a wide gesture of dismissal. 'She's been complaining about that almost without drawing breath. I've told her, she's got to stay with it. It's for her own good.'

A knock at the door heralded the tea tray. We all waited while it was deposited. Once the landlady had departed, Patience took it upon herself to pour out. I guessed it was because she was not anxious to begin the tricky business of telling Frank the purpose of our visit. Perhaps she hoped I might start first.

I looked at Frank, who was gazing proudly at his betrothed as she demonstrated her skill with the teapot, without spilling too much in the saucers. I knew he had just turned thirty. It was young to begin a parliamentary career. But his diplomatic travels, first in Russia and then in China, had matured him. He wasn't the scapegrace he had been when we'd first met, only four years earlier. He'd also given up the dandyish fashions and no longer curled his hair with tongs. (I fancied he had taken the opportunity to brush it when he'd gone to fetch his coat.)

Perhaps I had been too harsh in my earlier judgement on Edgar Wellings. Perhaps he, too, would learn from his experiences? But I could not rid myself of my doubts, although I hoped I would be proved wrong.

Patience set down the teapot with a trembling hand and raised imploring eyes to me. Well, this was what she had come to me for: help.

'Frank,' I said. 'We all know how much you have on your mind, and how busy your day is. But there is a matter we'd like to discuss with you. Patience did not want to trouble you unnecessarily, but there has been a development.'

'In what?' asked Frank. He looked at Patience and asked with a smile, 'You have not got into a scrape in the big city, Patience?'

'No,' said Patience dolefully. 'My brother, Edgar, has.'

Then it all came out; all, that is, except for the fact

that Edgar had asked his sister for money. We had decided, Patience and I, during the drive there, that as she had refused her brother the money, the matter was closed. Frank need not be troubled with it. There was certainly enough to tell him without that.

Frank listened in silence, then stood up and went to the window to gaze down into the square outside, his hands clasped behind his back.

Patience stood the silence for as long as she could, then burst out tearfully, 'Oh, Frank, I am so sorry!'

'Not your fault,' said Frank from the window, but without turning round.

'I should have told you before, straight away,' Patience cast me an imploring glance.

'Frank,' I said gently. 'Patience is very upset.'

Frank swung round, walked quickly to where Patience sat, dropped down to balance on his heels, and took her hand. 'Come on,' he said. 'No tears, now. The sight of them gives me indigestion.'

'Oh, *Frank!*' cried Patience, laughing in spite of her distress.

Frank patted her hand, stood up and stooped to kiss her again, this time on the forehead. Then he turned to me.

'I shall have to talk to Ross,' he said. 'But that won't be easy, will it? I cannot interfere in a criminal investigation.'

'Let me speak to him first, this evening,' I suggested. 'Not that he would tell me anything he should not, you understand. But I will tell him that Patience and I called here to tell you what has been happening. Of course, we only heard the maid shouting at Edgar. She could be mistaken in what she was saying. I really don't see how it could be otherwise.'

Patience sat up straight. 'Edgar would not kill anyone! That maid was half out of her mind. I don't know if it was from shock that she made such horrible accusations, or whether she is simple. But she was talking a lot of nonsense!'

'I would be grateful, Lizzie,' said Frank to me, 'if you would take Patience back to Goodge Place now. In fact, I will come too. Someone has to explain it all to the Pickfords.'

'Oh no, I had forgotten Uncle and Aunt Pickford!' wailed Patience.

'I'll take care of them,' said Frank firmly. 'Now, let us be on our way. I have to be in the House later this evening.'

In Goodge Place, Frank helped Patience down from the growler. 'Slater can take you home now, Lizzie,' he said. 'And thank you, my dear, for being such a good friend to Patience. I am sorry if this makes difficulties for you with Ross.'

He went to give instructions to Wally and also, I saw, to pay him. When he came back he said, 'Slater has been paid until the end of the day.'

'I did not mean for you to do that, Frank,' I protested.

'Nonsense, this whole affair is not of your making. Patience and I are extremely grateful to you. Now, then, let us beard the Pickfords in their den!'

So he and Patience set about the fraught business of breaking the bad news in Goodge Place and Wally, and the weary Victor, took me home.

Chapter Eight

Inspector Ben Ross

I HAD arrived with Wellings at the Yard. He collapsed on to a chair and stared at me wild-eyed. 'That old man,' he gasped. 'He wants to hang me!'

'I dare say he wants to hang a good many other people, too,' I told him 'That sort of old gentleman is very keen on Law and Order and punishing the guilty with the utmost severity. Such people resist any mention of prison reform or making penalties less severe. Put him out of your mind.'

He rubbed his forehead and muttered, 'How? Oh, dear Lord! But she was alive when I saw her last, I swear.'

I explained he must tell his story again, leaving out no detail, while Constable Biddle wrote it down.

Biddle is conscientious in taking dictation, but slow. A couple of times Wellings showed signs of impatience. But, in the end, we got it all down and Wellings signed it.

'What now?' he asked me with some trepidation. 'Am I under arrest?'

'No,' I told him. 'You are free to go. If I were to charge you, you would be detained. The hospital would know about it. Likewise, if you decide to leave London in a hurry, Bart's will know and that will be the end of your medical career. So, I am not afraid you are going to run away. You must, of course, stay in London. You understand that? No inventing sick relatives or any other emergency at home.'

'I'm not going anywhere!' snapped Wellings. He drew a deep breath. 'It looks bad for me, doesn't it? I was there last night and that maid saw me. I won't deny I was there; and Clifford and I exchanged some hard words. But you have only my word for it that I didn't leave her, dying or dead, on the carpet when I left.'

'Oh, I know you didn't do that,' I told him. I held up my hand to forestall the words about to burst from him, and the look of hope in his eyes. 'I know you didn't leave her on the carpet, I mean. I still don't know whether you struck her, perhaps fatally.'

Wellings had now realised that some vital information had not been given him. 'How so?' he asked bluntly.

'Because, although we have good reason to believe she was attacked viciously in her home, her dead body was not discovered in her parlour. It was found elsewhere.'

'Elsewhere?' Wellings shouted, jumping to his feet.

Biddle's alarmed face appeared at the door. I signalled him to go away.

'Sit down, Dr Wellings, and calm yourself. Mrs Clifford's body was discovered late last night in a neglected spot called Skinner's Yard. It is some distance from her house, about half a mile away.'

Wellings sat quietly for a short time. Then he said in a wounded tone, 'You have not been open with me, Inspector Ross.'

'I am investigating a murder, Dr Wellings. We are not chatting as friends.'

He flushed. 'But you let me think I am suspected of her murder! Am I now to believe that after I left her, the woman quitted her house for some reason and – perhaps in a random act of violent robbery – met with her death in this yard? No, no,' he corrected himself immediately. 'Because you say you have good reason to believe she was attacked at home. Am I allowed to ask what makes you so sure of that?'

'Bloodstains on the carpet, for one thing, among other indications,' I told him. There was no reason to tell him about the ransacked desk.

'Then I am in the clear!' exclaimed Wellings with relief. 'Why on earth did you make me dictate a long statement to that young constable?'

'Because your account is evidence, Dr Wellings. You were at the house, you admit it. The maid saw you, as you know. You exchanged heated words with Mrs Clifford. I should stress that you are still a suspect. Don't go away from here thinking otherwise. You are far from being "in the clear", as you put it.'

But Wellings had regained confidence and, in a swing of mood, become angry. 'Look here, I could hardly have thrown Clifford over my shoulder and carried her through the streets! I don't know where this Skinner's Yard is. Anyway, every person I met along the way would have seen me. Deptford is not a quiet spot, Ross.'

Wellings paused and frowned. 'Let's see, she may have been attacked at home. Symptoms – I mean clues – point to that, you say. But she couldn't have been fatally wounded or she would not have been able to get to her feet, go out of the house – as she must have done – and make her way to the place where she died.'

I said nothing. Wellings studied me and, when he spoke, showed that he had put aside his earlier panic and had a cool head. Now he was the doctor faced with a difficult diagnosis.

'Badly injured subjects are capable of considerable exertion. The hospital regularly sees accident cases arrive, having suffered serious injury to internal organs or other parts of the body. Yet the sufferers are able to walk into the casualty department on their own two feet. We had a man walk in, only last week, with a knife in his head.'

I was almost tempted to smile because Edgar Wellings appeared to have no sense of self-preservation. He had earlier insisted that he'd left the woman alive and there-fore could not be her murderer. Now he was saying she could have walked out of the house, even if severely injured.

'So, your medical opinion is that Mrs Clifford could have walked, bleeding from an extensive head wound, to the spot where she was found?' I asked.

But Wellings was not such a fool – or was beginning to gather his wits. 'One can understand an injured person seeking medical help. But if Clifford were so seriously injured and bleeding, she could not have travelled far unaided. Look here, Ross. You say her body was found in some yard. Was she – the corpse – was she dressed in outdoor clothing? Hat? Cloak? That sort of thing? It was a cold night.'

'No, only what she would have worn in the house, her gown and so on,' I told him. It was interesting to see how Wellings was torn between defending his own innocence and a desire to speculate.

'She would not have walked out of the house bare-headed and without a shawl, at the very least,' he muttered.

'She might have done so if seeking help was her prime consideration,' I pointed out.

'True,' he was kind enough to agree with me. 'But would she not have simply gone to a neighbour . . .'

It was time to remind him that it was for me to ask the questions. 'Can you remember, when you were talking to her earlier, whether she wore any jewellery?'

He looked surprised. 'I wasn't looking to see if she wore any. I was there to talk business. Oh, she had a little fob watch; I remember that, because she consulted it while I was trying to explain. I couldn't swear to anything else.'

That caught my attention. 'She looked at her watch? Was this near the beginning of your conversation with her? Or towards the end? Did you gain the impression she might have been waiting for another visitor that evening?'

'Not long before I left. I have to say,' Welling told me openly, 'that I thought she was indicating to me that I was wasting her time, and she had nothing more to say to me.'

'That's possible, too,' I mused. 'Was she wearing earrings?'

He looked even more astonished at what he clearly thought a trivial line of questioning.

'I told you, I can't swear to anything other than the fob watch. I wasn't in the mood to study her jewellery! Why on earth should that be of any interest to you?'

I wasn't about to satisfy his curiosity.

'Cast your mind back, go through it all slowly, playing it in your head,' I invited. 'See it as frozen images, if you can, like a magic lantern show.'

This suggestion of mine had a most unexpected reception. Wellings, who had clearly been thinking I was wasting his time and taking an unworthy pleasure in tormenting him, now smiled and grew enthusiastic.

'Yes, yes, a magic lantern show! That is an excellent suggestion. I am very interested in the working of the human mind, you know,' he continued earnestly. 'Interested from a medical point of view, that is. What do we remember, really remember? And what do we only *think* we remember? It's easy to muddle up random memories, isn't it? But to put the disparate snatches of memory in some order, as a story told with the aid of magic lantern slides, yes, yes, excellent!' He beamed at me. 'I shall write a paper on it, mark my words. A first-class suggestion, Ross! Well, why did I never think of that?'

Now I was disconcerted. 'I don't want to muddle you, or for you to invent, or give flight to your imagination,' I told him. 'I have enough witnesses who do that in any case under investigation. Often they will swear to a thing, quite false, because they have persuaded themselves it is true.'

'Yes, yes!' Wellings leaned forward eagerly. 'There is true memory and false. I believe, as you clearly do, that there is also buried memory. That is the sort you were trying for when you told me to imagine the scene as a set of magic lantern slides. The subject may know – or have seen – something that he's forgotten. I also believe there is learned memory. The subject believes something, but it may never have happened.'

Welling appeared so happy to discuss his theories that he would now prattle on until I stopped him. Perhaps I had been unwise to send him, with his medical background, down this path. So I did stop him and draw him back.

'Quite so. Let me ask a question. When you arrived outside the front door of the house, you took off your hat, so that she could see your face when she came to the window, after you'd tapped on the pane, is that right?'

He nodded. 'Yes, that's right.'

'Did she seem surprised to see you? Angry? Disappointed?'

'Annoyed,' said Wellings. 'But she only appeared for a moment. She pulled aside the lace curtain, stared out, recognised me, grimaced and then let fall the curtain. I wasn't sure, to be honest, that she meant to let me in.

But I waited. After a very short time she opened the front door. She whisked me inside and slammed the door behind me.'

'Whisked you inside? Why would she hurry to get you indoors?'

'So that the neighbours shouldn't see me, I suppose,' said Wellings.

That confirmed Britannia Scroggs's statement that her mistress was a 'very private person'.

He had nothing to add to his previous account. I let our young medical genius go home. I stressed that he must not discuss anything of this with anyone, particularly not with any of his fellow doctors. He must particularly not be tempted to discuss his theories on the working of the human brain. 'And try,' I asked, 'not to discuss it with your uncle and aunt, the Pickfords, or with your fiancée. Or with my wife,' I added.

'I'll have to say something,' he told me, 'above all, to my Uncle Pickford. And the ladies already know, well, know some of it.'

'You must, of course, tell your uncle the basic facts. Beyond that, tell him you are under police instructions to keep silent.' I added, 'This may be a good time to confess that you have run into debt. I don't see how you can avoid doing so.'

He sighed, got to his feet and put on his hat. 'This is a damn awful business, and knowing I have got myself into the middle of it does not help. Yes, yes, I shall own up to Uncle Pickford and write to my father.'

I wondered whether he would; or whether it would be

left to Patience to carry the message. Wellings was quite capable of asking his sister to be the bringer of his bad news.

When he had left, I went to see Superintendent Dunn and explain what had happened, taking with me Wellings's statement.

'Between you and me, Ross,' said Dunn, 'I am ready to believe that fellow Phipps at Deptford, when he says he was so quick to call us in because he was short-handed. But when that girl Britannia Scroggs arrived today to report her employer missing, you can be sure Phipps recognised the name Clifford. A moneylender operating her business in his division? Yes, he will know about that! It would have made him doubly anxious not to be the investigating officer; and to await your arrival, let you hear the girl's story. He does not know to whom she lent money and he would be afraid to disturb the drawing rooms of some outwardly very respectable people.'

'Indeed, that is just what has happened. She lent money to Wellings. That young man was there the night the woman was attacked. He doesn't deny it. As the maid has identified him, he has little choice but admit it. Worryingly, Wellings's sister is engaged to a Member of Parliament.'

Dunn leaned back in his chair and made a steeple of his stubby fingertips. 'See here, Ross, that same MP is known to your wife. The young lady, Patience you say her name is, also knows Mrs Ross. This is not going to be an obstacle in your investigation of the case, eh?'

'No, sir,' I said firmly. 'And if I thought it would become one, I would tell you.'

'I would then have to take you off the case and replace you with someone else. Perhaps I should do so, anyway. On the other hand, with your family connections, Mr Frank Carterton MP cannot say he is too busy to see you; and neither Dr Wellings nor any of his family can object to your asking personal questions, either. There is just one other thing . . .'

Dunn peered at me over his fingertips. 'You will forgive my asking, but past experience has made me wary. Mrs Ross isn't going to be playing detective in this, is she? She has done so before in other cases. I admire Mrs Ross's intuition and her tenacity, but it won't do to have her meddling. You must make it clear to her, Ross.'

'Yes, sir, I'll tell her that.' I'd tell her, certainly, but whether Lizzie would listen was another matter. 'As regards Inspector Phipps, sir,' I went on. 'I do believe he is torn between not wanting to be responsible and a natural urge to be in charge in his own division. He is furious with Britannia Scroggs because she didn't tell him of the blood-stained rug – or more accurately, he gave her no chance to tell him.'

Dunn un-steepled his hands and slapped his palms on the desk. 'Then he shouldn't have shillyshallied about! Either he calls in the Yard and lets us do the job. Or he keeps quiet and takes our instructions.'

He shook his head of wiry hair. 'At worst, we should have to let Phipps get on with it and investigate the case himself, whether he wants to or not.' He chuckled but immediately grew serious again. 'But we cannot. We must oversee it here, at the Yard. We are indeed going to trample over the drawing-room carpets of some influential people!'

Some time later Morris returned, red-faced and weary, from his task of escorting Britannia to her mother's home and making sure that Mrs Scroggs understood her daughter must stay there.

'Sit down, Sergeant,' I suggested. 'Let me know how you got on. Britannia safely delivered into her mamma's keeping?'

'You could say that,' returned Morris, subsiding gratefully on to a wooden chair, rather small for his solid frame. 'Well, Mr Ross, it went like this.'

The report of Sergeant Frederick Morris

'I don't think that maid stopped talking all the way there. When I say *talking*, perhaps I should say *shouting*. Everyone around us could hear what she had to say. Of course, that's what she wanted! Besides, they could see by just looking at me that I was an officer of the law. So they reckoned she'd been arrested. Word spread. Every loiterer passed it on. People kept demanding to know what she'd done. They came running out of the shops and public houses. We had a pack of street urchins at our heels all the way. It all served to slow us down and it was nearly an hour before we got to the house.

'I was surprised to see it must once have been a nice

little place, old, you know. It must have been built a hundred years ago, when there were market gardens around there, and is more in the way of a cottage than a house. The building is in a sorry state now, too many people living in it, I dare say. You know how the landlords crowd them in, a family to a room. As we came to it, with all our followers whistling and making a hullaballoo behind us, a big fellow came out of the front door, a real bruiser of a chap with a cap pulled down over his ears and the top of his face. Funny thing, sir, but despite all the fuss, he never even glanced in our direction. He set off smartly down the street away from us.'

'Not anxious to meet a police officer, plain-clothes or not,' I broke in to comment.

'My mind exactly, Mr Ross. He must have a bad conscience, was my thought. Well, in we went and the crowd hung about outside. Mrs Scroggs has one little room on the ground floor to herself, as her daughter told us. If she's there on her own, she has more space and privacy than others. The room has an open, old-fashioned hearth in it. A miserable sort of fire smouldered there, under an iron pot on a trivet. I don't know what was cooking in the pot, but the smell was something horrible and I wouldn't have fancied eating it. Along the shelf over the hearth the old woman keeps her crockery and utensils. There was a little rickety table, one Welsh chair with arms and a three-legged stool. In the corner was a bed made up on a rickety bedframe. It was a very narrow bed and Scroggs will have to sleep on the floor. That was it for furnishings. There was a rope tied across the room from one side to the other and some wet washing hung on it, a man's shirt, by the looks of it. There was also a petticoat. All the wash was dripping on to the floor, making for a damp and unhealthy atmosphere. The old woman's cloak hung on a hook behind the door and it looked as if, apart from that and the wet petticoat, she'd only the clothes she wore on her back.

'You can imagine what happened when I appeared with the maid. To begin with, news of our approach had gone ahead of us. Someone had recognised Britannia with me, and run ahead to tell the old woman that her daughter was taken in charge. So Ma Scroggs was in a fair state of panic by the time we arrived. She kept screeching, "What's she done?" She followed that with, "She's a good girl and she's not done nothing!"

'Britannia told her to calm down, as she'd not been arrested. But she'd had to leave her place, and come home, as her mistress had been murdered. Well, that made things worse.

'"What?" yells the mother. "How do you mean, murdered? You mean, you ain't got no place of work? How are you going to get another, with living in and all found, like you was with Mrs Clifford? How shall I manage here without the couple of shillings a week you give me?"

'She then sank down on to the floor and put her apron over her head. She rocked back and forth, moaning and lamenting, while Britannia tried to get her to stand up. In the end, I ordered her to do so. So she did scramble to her feet, hanging on to Britannia's arm. She then seemed to see, for the first time, Britannia's bundle of belongings.

"'You can't stay here!" she shouted. "I got no room for you."

"'I got to come here, Ma," says Britannia. "The rozzers say so."

"'What d'ya mean, they say so? 'Oo? That one there?" She pointed at me. "Who's he to say I got to take you in?"

"'They need to be able to find me, Ma, if they want me. I can't stay at Mrs Clifford's house, 'cos she's a goner, I told you," explained Britannia.

'Now then, Inspector Ross, sir, there is one thing the poor fear more than anything and that is the workhouse. It's not just the place itself, you understand, but the shame of it. If you've nothing else, then keeping yourself off the parish is the last thing you cling to before you tumble into destitution. So, when I saw that Ma Scroggs was inclined to be awkward, I spoke up.

"'If it is inconvenient for you to give her a bed, madam, then I can take your daughter to the casual ward for tonight. Then, tomorrow she can apply to be taken into the workhouse itself. That is, if you can't let her stay here a couple of nights, that is, until she gets herself a bed somewhere and a new job."

"'It's going to be bad enough trying to find someone to employ me, coming from a house where murder's been done!" snaps Britannia. "Without I'd spent the night before in the casual ward. Have you seen what sort they take in there for the night? Drunks, beggars and sick people and such. Fine thing it would be for me to tell any employer! As for applying to be taken in by the parish, you can forget it. I'm not going to any workhouse. *They*'d put me to work picking oakum, *they* would. That's what the workhouse would do!"

'My suggestion did the trick. The old woman stopped moaning and declared, "No one in this family is going to any workhouse! Not unless I ends up going there myself, which is likely, if you don't get a new place, Britannia, and can let me have some money. What you give me pays my rent here. But no Scroggs has ever gone on the parish! We're respectable people."

'So, in the end, it was agreed Britannia will stay there and look for work. If she does find somewhere like her previous situation, where she can sleep in, she'll let us know her change of address. But for the time being, we know where she is.

'Funny thing, Mr Ross, I couldn't help feeling sorry for the two women, for all they nearly deafened me with their screeching. I couldn't help thinking that the old woman had had seven children and there she was in old age, with just a few shillings from the one surviving daughter to keep her out of the workhouse.'

I interrupted at this point to say, 'A man's shirt had been washed? But the old woman lives alone and does not even have a bed big enough to share with her daughter.'

Morris considered the point. 'Some workman might have paid her a few pence to wash it for him. Unless she wore the shirt as a nightgown, I suppose. Anyhow, I had to fight my way out of the place. There was a crowd of neighbours all round the door and halfway down the street. Someone threw some horse dung at me, but I didn't spot who it was.'

Morris had grown a little hoarse by the end of this narrative. I thanked him for his efforts and dismissed him. I was not surprised to hear that the sergeant and Miss Scroggs had attracted so much attention. The scene before the door of the Clifford house had shown how the cry 'Murder!' attracts a host of the curious and the ghoulish. Besides which, the populace loves the opportunity to shout abuse at the police.

I set off home, prepared for it to be my turn to be interrogated – by my wife.

Chapter Nine

Inspector Ben Ross

'OH, I am glad to see you, Ben,' Lizzie exclaimed as soon as I walked in. 'What have you done with Edgar Wellings?'

Bessie was hovering in the hall, ostensibly to take my coat but really to hear the latest news.

'I have not done anything with that wretched young man,' I said. 'Other than accompany him to the Yard and have Biddle take down his statement. Then I let him go.'

'Oh, thank goodness you don't have him in a prison cell,' Lizzie responded.

'He ought to be locked up!' said Bessie, sharing the view of the old gentleman in the bath chair.

'Haven't you something to do in the kitchen, Bessie?' I asked. 'As it happens, I don't need him in a cell. I know where I can find him. More to the point, Lizzie, what have *you* done with Patience Wellings?'

'We went to see Frank,' Lizzie said. 'And it was Patience's idea, before you say I ought to have left Frank out of it. But Patience can't leave Frank in ignorance. Frank was very good about it. He escorted Patience to

Goodge Place to tell her uncle and aunt. I came home, so I have no idea how the Pickfords took the news. Patience is very upset, as you can imagine.'

'I think we can safely assume they will have taken it badly,' I told her. 'I told the young fellow he had to own up to his family. But his sister has pulled the chestnuts out of the fire for him, after all. I really have no sympathy for young Edgar. I am sorry for poor little Patience. As for Carterton, he will manage to survive this somehow, as he always does. Only I hope he doesn't turn up at the Yard with the intention of meddling. I don't care if he does sit in Parliament. This is a police matter.' I took a deep breath. 'And, Lizzie, my dear, that goes for you, too. Superintendent Dunn is worried you will start investigating on your own.'

My wife didn't care for that, as I knew she wouldn't.

'I really don't know why Superintendent Dunn should even mention it!' she said loftily. 'Of course, I realise it's a police investigation. It's a horrible crime. I dare say Mrs Clifford was a very unpleasant person, but still, murder is never to be justified.'

Lizzie looked extremely virtuous as she said this. The expression 'butter wouldn't melt in her mouth' came to mind.

'You know how Dunn worries,' I said rather weakly. 'And you have done it before.'

'With quite some success, I should like to remind you! However,' Lizzie held up her hand, 'please don't worry. The very last thing I'd wish to do is to make difficulties for you with Mr Dunn. I shall do my best to support

Patience, of course, as that is a private matter – a family matter. In fact, I think I might call in at Goodge Place tomorrow.'

'Lizzie!' I protested.

She leaned forward, forestalling any objection I might be about to make. 'Are you forgetting?' she asked. 'Someone has to tell Aunt Parry about all this!'

I had to admit I had forgotten Aunt Parry.

Elizabeth Martin Ross

I hastened to Goodge Place the following morning. The hour was far too early for a respectable visit, but this was an emergency. I was shown into the same little back parlour where I'd met with Edgar and his sister, and which Patience seemed to have made her private refuge. As I'd thought, Patience was overjoyed to see me, running to greet me and flinging her arms around me.

'Oh, Lizzie! I am so glad you have come. Is poor Edgar locked up in a dreadful prison cell?'

'No,' I assured her. 'Ben let him go, after Edgar signed a written statement. But it is not the end of it, Patience. Edgar is still in trouble; and Ben has told him he must not leave London.'

'Do they know about it at Bart's?' asked Patience anxiously. 'They would not like it at all.'

'To the best of my knowledge, no one has informed the hospital, at least not yet.'

Patience looked relieved. 'I am so happy Edgar hasn't been in a cell all night, catching gaol fever. I was going to send Lucy out again with a note to ask you to come. It has been awful here, just awful! You can't imagine it. What's more, we'll have to go through it all again. Frank says that this afternoon we must go and see Mrs Parry. She cannot be left in ignorance. She'll get to hear of it anyway, so Frank says. She'd never forgive him if she heard it elsewhere first.'

I had already told Ben this. Although normally Aunt Parry preferred to be left in ignorance of anything that would disturb her comfortable world, this was far too important. Frank was quite right. Gossip would bring the news to her ears before long and she must be prepared.

'Frank and I,' said Patience, conducting me to a chair, 'do so hope you will come to Dorset Square with us. Mrs Parry listens to you. Frank says so. You will be able to calm her.'

'She listens, perhaps, but she also disapproves of me,' I warned.

'But Frank says you are not afraid to speak openly to her, concealing nothing. No one else does that. Even Frank has to be careful what he says to her. She makes him a monthly allowance, you know, and he does need it. Being a Member of Parliament is a very expensive business.'

This was the Frank Carterton I knew of old. He had always been adept at manoeuvring his way around his aunt. But if he thought I would be an obedient pawn on his chessboard, he was wrong. Patience appeared to have complete confidence in my powers of reason with regard to Mrs Parry; I would have to disabuse her of that, too.

As for calming Aunt Parry down when she heard of a scandal in the Wellings family: that would take more than my efforts.

'I will come with you,' I said, 'not just for your sake or for Frank's, but for hers, too. Mrs Parry again seems to be without a companion and she will need support. This is going to be a terrible shock to her. I don't know what she will do. You must not rely too much on my influence, Patience.'

'She *is* without a companion. The last one left after only a month,' said Patience, diverted. 'Frank says she's had several. They never stay.' In a lowered voice, she added, 'Frank told me one of her companions was *murdered*!'

'Yes, that's true. Sadly, the young woman in question was my predecessor. I came to London to be Mrs Parry's companion, you know.' I allowed myself a smile. 'I didn't last long, either.'

Patience sat back on her chair and folded her hands in her lap. 'What a strange place London is, people being murdered all over the place all the time.'

'Well, not all the time,' I protested.

'Certainly more than they are at home,' said Patience. 'What else did Inspector Ross say to you about Edgar last night?'

'He said only that he had not arrested him. Ben does not confide details of police investigations to me, you know. That would be quite improper.'

Patience looked dissatisfied. 'I'd ask him, if it were me.'

'Yes, I dare say you would. I admit I do, from time to

time. You would find, as I have, that I don't always get answers, or sufficient answers. Now then, tell me how your uncle and aunt took the news about Edgar.'

So Patience began her account. I was soon very pleased I had not been present on that occasion. She and Frank had agreed that Frank would open proceedings by explaining that Edgar Wellings had got into debt. This was as the result of gambling, mostly in card games. As a result Edgar had found himself financially embarrassed. Edgar was well aware how distressing this would be to his family.

'That was as far as Frank got,' said Patience. 'My uncle and aunt were so shocked that they had listened in silence to that point. But when Frank paused for breath, oh dear, there was an awful scene.' Patience closed her eyes briefly. 'My Uncle Pickford asked at once how Frank knew this; and why was Edgar not there himself to confess? Frank tried to break it gently. He said matters had escalated and Edgar was not able to be present in person, because he had been obliged to accompany the police to Scotland Yard.'

Here Patience was overcome by the memory and couldn't continue for a moment or two. Probably there had been no way Frank could have broken the news that would have made it any less dramatic.

Patience recovered enough to continue her account. She agreed that whatever Frank had said, it would not have been quietly received. As it was, Aunt Pickford had set up a wail 'like a banshee', as Frank had afterwards described it. Uncle Pickford, a man of no-nonsense manner, had promptly told her to control her distress or take it elsewhere. He then turned on Frank as if it were 'all poor Frank's fault'.

Why was his nephew at the Yard? Frank told him about Edgar owing a large sum of money to a woman in Deptford. At this point, Uncle Pickford interrupted to demand, who was this woman? And what had Edgar been doing in Deptford?

The woman was a moneylender, he was told. Uncle Pickford had turned quite purple at the news and Patience had feared he was going have a fit. Why the deuce had the boy gone to a moneylender? If Edgar needed money, why had he not come to a family member: his father or uncle? Pickford yelled this at the top of his voice. The whole house could have heard and his wife had begged him to moderate his tone.

That had not been received well, either. 'You keep quiet there, Matilda! It is enough I have to listen to this . . . incredible yarn from Frank, here. Just sit there. Patience! Take care of your aunt.'

Patience herself had ventured to speak up at this point and tell them how distressed and ashamed poor Edgar was. This was why he had not dared to confess earlier.

While Aunt Pickford whimpered in the background, and Patience administered what comfort she could, Uncle Pickford had then delivered a long speech about it being quite right that Edgar should be distressed. 'Distressed? That is not the half of it! The wretched boy should be here on his knees, begging forgiveness.'

'I do not think,' Patience added at this moment, in

comment, 'that Edgar would ever do that, however sorry he was – is. Anyway, my uncle declared that Edgar had not only brought shame on himself, his sister and his parents but on the inhabitants of Goodge Place too.'

Uncle Pickford had spluttered to a halt briefly, breathless. Frank had resumed his account to explain that, alas, the borrowing of money was not the end of it. The moneylender had been murdered. Edgar had been taken to Scotland Yard, accused of the crime by a maid employed in the house where the crime had taken place.

At this point Patience had to run at once to her aunt, as Mrs Pickford appeared to have fainted. But it was only momentary. Mrs Pickford was too determined to hear everything to pass out completely.

'Murder?' thundered Uncle Pickford. 'Has the boy lost his mind?'

Patience, still propping up her aunt, had spoken up again to insist that it was impossible that Edgar had murdered anyone. The maid in Deptford must have been mistaken. Uncle Pickford had declared that he was going to the Yard at once to demand his nephew's release.

Frank, heroically and with a splendid argument, said Patience, had persuaded Uncle Pickford he must wait until the next day.

'That is to say, today,' clarified Patience. 'I must say I am sure Frank will make wonderful speeches in the House. I don't think anyone else could have prevented my uncle rushing out and going to the Yard at once, yesterday. But he has gone this morning, Lizzie, instead.'

Oh dear, I thought, Ben must probably be fending off

Uncle Pickford right now. I glanced at the clock. Patience, however, had resumed her narrative.

'How am I to write to my brother-in-law?' had boomed Uncle Pickford, standing before the fireplace with his thumbs in the armholes of his waistcoat. 'How am I to tell him all this sorry business has taken place without my even becoming suspicious? Here's my nephew running about the place ruining himself, and the family's good name, very likely to hang as well, and I don't even notice something is amiss?'

Frank tried to calm him down by saying that there was no reason why he should have been suspicious. Uncle Pickford was then very rude to Frank, said Patience indignantly.

'How?' I asked, fascinated.

'He said, ours was a well-ordered family, or at least, he had always believed it so. Frank might not think it odd that no one had noticed Edgar had gone to the dogs. Things were done differently in London, perhaps. But where we came from, our town, people kept a better eye on things. He hoped that Frank, as a Member of Parliament, was going to keep a better eye on what went on in his constituency.

'Frank went awfully red in the face when Uncle Pickford said that,' continued Patience. 'I thought he might say something sharp. He would have been entitled to do so, but it wouldn't have helped. However, fortunately, there was a— a diversion then. It interrupted things just at the right moment.'

'How so, a diversion?' I was intrigued.

Uncle Pickford, explained Patience, had been so carried away by indignation and being rude to Frank that he had not paid attention to how near he stood to the fire. Aunt Pickford hadn't noticed either. She'd been sitting in the corner, sniffing a cologne-soaked handkerchief. But then there was a very strange smell of burning, like singed cloth.

'And smoke started going up from the tails of Uncle Pickford's frock coat! So there was a bit of a commotion, you know. I mean, there was a commotion already, but this was for a different reason. My aunt jumped up with a shriek and cried out that my uncle was on fire. Frank called out that my uncle should take off his coat. My aunt went to help him, but my uncle only got angrier and told her to keep out of the way. So he pulled off his coat himself and threw it, smouldering, on the carpet.

'And then,' said Patience with a satisfied smile, 'Frank seized a flower vase and emptied it – water and flowers – over Uncle's coat. It was very quick-thinking of him and it saved the day. But I believe Frank enjoyed doing it.'

I was sure he had. 'So, what next?' I asked.

Mr Pickford had stamped off upstairs for another coat. The maid, Lucy, had come in and collected the damaged garment.

'She was there the moment my uncle strode out of the room,' said Patience. 'I would not be surprised if Lucy had been listening at the door. Uncle Pickford won't be the only one writing home to tell them about it. Lucy is from our town and she will inform her mother.'

Frank told Lucy to ask the kitchen to send up some tea for Mrs Pickford. While waiting, Patience had comforted her aunt and fortunately the tea had arrived very quickly. Lucy brought it in, although she was not the parlourmaid but Mrs Pickford's personal maid. Clearly Lucy was trying to keep the upset 'in the family' and away from the eyes of the curious servants.

'She also wanted to stay to look after my aunt, but I told her very firmly I could do that.'

Mr Pickford had returned, freshly attired and calmer, to find them all sitting round drinking tea. So after such a bad start things had finished up reasonably well. Uncle Pickford had repeated that he would call at Scotland Yard in the morning and demand Edgar's release. It would do no harm for the wretched young man to have spent a night in a cell, meditating on the error of his ways. He, Uncle Pickford, would then write to his brother-in-law.

'I should not be surprised if the whole family doesn't come down to London!' concluded Mr Pickford.

Mrs Pickford, seeing at long last a gap in events when she could contribute something, said she would tell Cook at once to send out for extra provisions. If they were to feed more guests, the butcher must be asked to deliver at least three good joints.

Inspector Ben Ross

I knew Lizzie intended to visit Goodge Place in the morning and wondered in what sort of state she would find the family today. Edgar's uncle had been told the news the evening before, because Lizzie had left Carterton there with Patience for that express purpose. Pickford's first instinct must have been to storm Scotland Yard. It was a wonder he hadn't burst in while I was interviewing his nephew.

But Mr Pickford had not shown himself there and then. However, I couldn't hope to be spared a visit from him today and braced myself for the encounter.

Sure enough, Biddle arrived just after ten to announce: 'A gentleman is here, very desirous of a word with you, sir. He is a Mr Herbert Pickford. He says, you will know who he is. We have arrested his nephew. He is demanding to know what the devil is going on.' Biddle blushed. 'His words, sir, not mine.'

'I understand, Constable. Show the gentleman in.'

I had carried in my head an image of Uncle Pickford since Lizzie had first told me of his existence. In my mind's eye I had seen him as tall, broad, red-faced and assertive. He would be proud of being plain-spoken and as sensitive as a block of granite; much like the men who ran the coalmines I had worked in as a young child. Now the man himself was shown into my office.

Pickford was a stout person, true enough, red-faced and with protuberant eyeballs that bulged at me from beneath bushy eyebrows. Otherwise, he was of scarcely middle height. He had short legs and stood with his feet planted well apart to balance his sturdy frame.

As a result, he gave the impression of measuring the same in all directions, a cannonball of a figure. He had thinning iron-grey hair and (in compensation, perhaps, for the loss of hair on his head) luxuriant mutton-chop whiskers, matching those hedgehog eyebrows.

'Pickford is the name!' he boomed at me and stood before me with his silk hat under his arm and the skirts of his frock coat open to reveal a remarkable embroidered waistcoat. A heavy gold 'Albert' watch chain was looped across his substantial frontage.

'Please sit down, Mr Pickford,' I invited him. 'I have heard of you.'

'Oh, have you, indeed?' he retorted. 'From my scape-grace nephew, I suppose?' Before I could reply he asked abruptly, 'Where do you hail from?'

'Derbyshire,' I told him.

This was well received. The cannonball looked less likely to explode; instead he gave a nod. 'I thought, from the sound of you, you weren't a Londoner. Well, now, Mr Ross – or Inspector Ross I should call you, I dare say – what have you done with my nephew?'

'Nothing,' I told him. 'I took a signed statement from him. I warned him not to talk to his friends – or anyone else – about the investigation; and not to leave London. Then I let him go.'

'Why?' asked Pickford disconcertingly. 'That fellow Carterton told us Edgar is accused of a murder. Utter nonsense, of course. The only person he's ever likely to murder is one of his patients some day; and then it wouldn't be on purpose. You don't let murderers free to roam about the town, do you? If you suspect my nephew of such a crime, why don't you have him locked up?'

'Edgar Wellings is a junior doctor at Bart's and won't want to jeopardise his situation there,' I said. 'I am confident he won't abscond and I can find him, if I need him.'

'So can I,' said Pickford grimly. 'And when I leave here, I'll be off straight to the hospital to get the whole story out of the lad.'

'Ah, now, Mr Pickford,' I began carefully. 'May I suggest it would be very helpful to me – and, indeed, to your family – if you did not do that?'

'How so?' snapped Pickford.

'Consider what a busy hospital is like, sir, if you would. It is a large place full of people of all sorts. There are patients, nurses and doctors, naturally. But also ward cleaners, porters, visitors, accident victims brought into the casualty area and attended by friends or family. There would be no privacy to be had for you to talk to your nephew on such a delicate matter. Besides, he could not leave his duties to attend to you, without explanation. The hospital authorities would find out the truth and – this is a murder investigation, after all – he'd be suspended from duty at once. All his colleagues and the nursing staff would know. The gossip would run round like wildfire. From there it would travel outside via every visitor who left.'

'Ah . . .' murmured Pickford.

I struck a last blow. 'Quite often there is a press reporter hanging around the entrance of large hospitals, hoping for a titbit to make a lurid headline in the evening papers. This is not, I think, what you would like for something touching your family's good name, as it does.'

Pickford glared at me with those alarming orbs, but agreed reluctantly that I was correct. 'We don't want all the world and its wife knowing about it, right enough.'

'Quite so, Mr Pickford. I recommend that it would be better for you to send a note to the hospital by a secure hand, suggesting that you call on your nephew at his rooms later, when he is off duty. Better still, that he calls to see you in Goodge Place, where you would control the situation.'

The idea of controlling the situation clearly appealed to Pickford. 'Very well, then,' he said, 'I'll send one of my clerks with a letter for him, making sure he puts it into Edgar's hand.' He studied me for a moment. 'It's a relief to hear you have not charged him,' he went on. 'Do you think you will charge him later?'

'I have no idea,' I told him. 'The investigation is at a very early stage.'

'The boy's an idiot,' said Pickford, 'no denying it. I had imagined him sensible and I'm sorry to be proved wrong. Oh, he's a pleasant young fellow and has taken to his doctoring well. But, to go playing cards and losing money like some young rake with nothing better to do . . .' He gave a snort. 'Worse, to borrow from a moneylender! That is what he did, I understand.'

'That is what he did,' I agreed.

'Young fool. I am told the lender is, or was, a woman. That sounds extraordinary to me. Not a woman's business, is it, hey? Can't say I'm surprised she ended badly. No doubt of it being murder?' He pulled an alarming face. In anyone else, I'd have said he squinted at me. But his bulging eyes did not quite allow him to squint. Instead, his eyelids seemed to be struggling to meet. I wondered what happened when he went to sleep.

I wrenched myself from this entertaining speculation. 'No doubt whatsoever, sir, I am afraid. The woman was the subject of a vicious attack.'

Pickford shook his head slowly from side to side. 'I can't see my nephew doing that. Strike a woman? No, sir, he would not do it. Clearly someone set about this woman and the fellow, whoever he is, might go battering another one. I don't believe it was my nephew.'

'He does indeed deny it.'

'So, why did you arrest him, then? Yes, yes, you told him to remain available, but see here, I am looking at it as I imagine you must do. So, hey, what else is there?' Another fraught manoeuvre of the eyelids.

'There is a witness, sir, who accused him. But I wouldn't say I arrested him, exactly. I had questioned him at the probable scene of the crime. He arrived there, with your niece and my wife, while we were examining the scene. I later requested him to accompany me to the Yard so that his account could be formalised. You must admit, Mr Pickford, Edgar Wellings does have a strong motive. He could not repay the money and was terrified his father would find out. He does not deny he was at the house on the evening in question, when the crime took place. The witness I mentioned saw him there. Nor does he deny that he and the deceased argued fiercely during that visit. That is why it is important that he stay in

London. I shall certainly have to talk to him again, if only to verify certain points – or if any new evidence should emerge.'

Pickford tapped the lid of his silk hat with a stubby forefinger. 'There has to be something else,' he said shrewdly. 'If you've got a witness, I'd expect you to hold on to the boy. There must be some other reason you didn't lock him in a cell last night and throw away the key.'

'The victim's body was moved.' I did not want to reveal to him more than I had to, but Edgar himself would tell his uncle that detail. 'We do not know in what circumstances, and as yet we have no evidence to show your nephew moved it. When it was discovered it was at some distance away from the house, although still in Deptford.'

'Moved when she was dying or moved when she was as dead as mutton?' demanded Pickford.

'Oh, I think she would have been dead as m— she would have died before her body was moved. But establishing the exact time of a death in a case of murder is not as easy as many people imagine it to be. It is not impossible that she was fatally injured but still alive when she left the house. Though it seems unlikely she could have left unaided and got some distance.'

'Rum business,' muttered Pickford. 'Confound it, what am I to tell all those women?'

'Which women?' I asked, startled.

'At the moment, I must find words to calm only my wife and little Patience. But the boy's parents will come to London at once, as soon as they get my letter. They'll bring my wife's sisters with them. I don't just mean the boy's mother. She'll come, of course. But Caroline and Amelia, they'll tag along, too. There are four of them, you see: my wife Matilda, Dorothy – the boy's mother – and the other two. The Briggs sisters they were known as, when they were girls. Not by separate names, just as a matched set, always seen together, went to church together, went to our little gatherings at the Assembly Room together. Their father was an ironmonger, and did very well out of it. I married one of them. Walter Wellings married another. The other two remain maiden ladies.'

Pickford paused and looked suddenly milder, reminiscent. 'They were good, sensible girls and not bad to look at. It is a pity no one came to marry either Caroline or Amelia. I say this not only because a pair of unmarried women in a family are a responsibility to the rest of us. But I also feel it's a great pity because they would have made fine wives. Caroline, now, a young fellow did ask for her. As things turned out, the marriage never took place. It was a mercy, for I didn't like the look of him. He was a clerk employed in a wholesale business. He had an eye to better his chances and pocket her dowry, that's my belief.'

Uncle Pickford – I caught myself thinking of him thus and told myself sternly that I must take care, or in an unguarded moment I'd refer to him by that title! Mr Pickford, then, shook off his reflective moment and fixed his bulging eyeballs on me.

'As it is, they've become regular busybodies, have

Caroline and Amelia. Nothing else to thinking of but other people's business. The house will be full of women,' finished Pickford despondently. 'All weeping and fainting and then coming round to talk nineteen to the dozen, blaming me.'

'Why you, sir?' I asked in surprise.

Pickford rose to his feet and clapped his silk hat on his head. 'Because, Inspector Ross, when in London I represent the family business. That makes me, here in town, de facto the head of the family. I stand in the place of my brother-in-law with regard to his children. Little Patience is living in my house. I should have been keeping an eye on young Edgar. You cannot imagine it, Ross. Edgar has always been the apple of everyone's eye. How to tell them about all this? It is the very devil of a situation, sir!'

'You, ah, have not met Mr Carterton's aunt? Mrs Julia Parry?' I asked.

'No, heard of her, of course.' Pickford glowered at me. 'She's another of them, is she? Swooning away and shrieking?'

'I don't know about the fainting. I believe she inherited her late husband's numerous property interests; and is a shrewd woman. But she is devoted to her nephew, Frank Carterton, whom Patience Wellings is to marry. She will certainly have a lot to say.'

'That's another thing,' said Pickford gloomily. 'That young fellow, Carterton, has prospects, a career in politics. So, how is all this going to affect that marriage, eh? Will it now take place? All the women will be worrying about that!'

Chapter Ten

NO SOONER had Herbert Pickford left than I received another visitor in the person of the excitable Constable Evans.

'Inspector Phipps's compliments, sir. Harry Parker, the witness who found the body, he's turned up again. We've got him in a cell now over at Deptford. We're holding him, sir, in case you want to talk to him. Mr Phipps said to tell you that we'll keep him as long as we can. But we can't arrest him because he's not committed a crime, only left the area against orders. And we'll need the cells later on this evening, sir. There are two new ships in, one out of Bergen and one out of Hamburg.' Evans saluted me both at the beginning and at the end of this speech.

'Where did you find him?' I asked.

'Constable Barrett found him, sir. Parker was at the docks, seeking work,' Evans told me. 'He'd run out of money.'

So, I thought, if Parker took the fob watch, ring and earrings, he hasn't sold them, not even a single piece. The ring would have been the most obvious. Gold is easily disposed of. But he hasn't. Lack of funds has driven him from his hiding place. Phipps was right: Parker's home turf is Deptford and away from the place, he'd starve.

So someone else took the jewellery. I remembered how busy Deptford had been the night Morris and I had been called out there. A dozen passers-by might have blundered into Skinner's Yard, found the body, stolen the valuables and run off. No one there would have wanted to tangle unnecessarily with the police. It had been Harry Parker's misfortune that he had rushed out of Skinner's Yard into the arms of Constable Barrett. I allowed myself a wry smile. Barrett appeared to be Parker's Nemesis.

Daylight allowed me to see Parker more clearly than I had been able to do in Skinner's Yard, but it had not improved his appearance. If anything, he looked smaller, more wizened, and decidedly more nervous. He had carried into the room the odours of his dockside haunts: stale beer, oil, coal dust, tar and bilge water. Mixed in with these I caught the unexpected hint of exotic spices and tobacco. Some cargo, perhaps, he had helped unload or from which he had pilfered.

'You were told to remain available,' I told him sternly. 'Why did you run away?'

'I never run away,' Parker defended himself. 'I had to leave my lodgings, didn't I? Landlord threw me out.'

'When?'

'That same night. You told them to send a rozzer home wiv me to see where I lived. The landlord don't like lodgers brought home by the p'lice. He told me to leave, there and then, chucked me out into the street. I was too late to get a place in a casual ward and had to sleep in a doorway. The next day I went over to Limehouse to see my brother, see if he'd take me in, just for a bit. But I couldn't get work there. So I had to come back.' He sniffed and rubbed his nose with the back of his hand.

He was probably telling the truth. I asked him where he was living now. He said he had found a room locally. 'Got to share it,' he added gloomily. 'Share wiv two other blokes and I don't like the look of either of them.'

'You must tell them here where it is you are lodging. If you leave, you must notify Deptford police station that you have moved; and where you have moved to.'

Parker was gazing at me in a mixture of bewilderment and fear. 'What d'you want to know so much about *me* for? I ain't done nothing.'

'You found the body,' I reminded him.

'I didn't *want* to find her, did I?' His voice rose plaintively. 'It's like I told you that night. I fell over her. I thought she was drunk. I gave her shoulder a shake because I thought she ought not to lie there on a cold night, likely catch her death of pneumonia.'

'That was thoughtful of you,' I said drily. 'You were not looking to see if there was anything of value on the body?'

'Of course I never did!' Harry Parker attempted some dignity. 'You ain't no right to accuse me. I ain't no thief. I found her, like I said. I run out into the street and found a constable.'

'You did not have to look far for him, did you? You ran into him, as I understand it from Constable Barrett.'

'Whether I run into 'im, or whether I went and found 'im,' retorted Parker, 'it makes no difference. I told him there was a body.' He sat back and gave me a satisfied look. 'So there,' he said 'And you can't prove different.'

I could not prove differently, he was right. But I was sure there was something he wasn't telling me. He'd had time to think about his story and had made it – so he believed – solid.

'Did you recognise her?' I asked him, not because I expected him to say he had, but because I needed time to think.

Unexpectedly I had struck some vulnerable point in his story. I saw the fear flash into his little eyes before he cast his gaze down to his hands, twisting his cap.

'No idea who it was,' he mumbled.

'You knew it was a woman.'

He sounded exasperated when he replied, 'Of course I did! She wore a dress.' He looked up. 'There's no gaslight in Skinner's Yard. I couldn't see her face and I'll swear that on a stack of Bibles if I have to. You can't expect me to put a name to every woman in Deptford!'

I was thinking furiously. He had been so certain he had got his story watertight. Despite that, he'd slipped up.

'I recall you said you were carrying a box of lucifers,' I reminded him.

He gaped. 'Me? No, never. Whaffor?'

'I don't know what for. Anything!' I retorted. 'But you

told us the night the body was found that you struck a match to see more clearly what you had stumbled over.'

'Oh, yes, that's right. I forgot! Yes, I just looked to see what it was nearly brought me down. Gave me a nasty turn to find it was a body. Yes, I did just check to see if she was only drunk. But I never looked at her face, not close.' He sounded more than certain; he sounded relieved. I had asked the wrong question. A pity, I had thought it a possibility. So what then?

I leaned forward and asked him quietly, 'So, tell me, Harry, what – or whom – *did* you see?'

Now there was no disguising the naked terror in his eyes. His beady gaze flicked away from me towards the corner of the room. 'I never saw anyone,' he said sullenly, addressing the wall. 'That's why I went into Skinner's Yard, because I thought no one was there. I didn't think I'd be there more than five minutes. I'd never have gone near the place if I'd known all this was going to happen to me.'

He had regained control of himself. He turned his gaze back towards me. His little dark eyes, so like a rat's, were now unreadable. 'I never saw nothing. I never saw no one,' he said. 'And that's that.' His lips parted, showing his discoloured teeth. Did he laugh at me or did he, like a cornered feral creature, defy any further approach?

'Parker,' I said to him firmly, 'if you withhold information in the matter of a serious crime, you will find yourself in a lot of trouble. You could be accused of seeking to obstruct the police in their inquiries. After all, you have the opportunity now to tell me every detail.'

'I done that,' he replied sullenly.

'All right!' I told him briskly. 'Let us look at it a different way. If you do have information regarding a murder, and you do not confide in me – or any other officer – then that knowledge you are anxious to keep secret is a dangerous thing to carry around in your head. I suspect you know more than you are telling me; and the guilty party may suspect that also.'

Fear leaped into his eyes. But he remained obstinate. 'That's it, all I told you is all I know.'

I tried to sound encouraging. 'I can protect you, Parker, if you confide in me.'

'No, you couldn't!' he muttered.

'Ah! So there is something else, something you've not told me.'

'No, there ain't!' he shouted. 'I only meant, how could any policeman protect me unless he walked round with me all day? If there *was* anything else to tell you, which there isn't. You're getting me confused. I'm all in a muddle now.'

'Think it over, Parker,' I advised him. 'Your silence may not protect you. All right!' I held up a hand to prevent a further outburst of denial. 'Let us say, something may have slipped your mind. You may remember it later. Whatever it is, however trivial it seems, come at once to me, Inspector Ross. You understand?'

'Yes!' he said promptly, obviously deciding that agreement was the best way to end our conversation.

There was no point in continuing it now. I had to let him go, after I'd impressed on him he must leave an address where he could be found, and that he was not to go missing again. He scuttled away, relief in every move.

Inspector Phipps now decided to put in an appearance. 'Anything new?' he asked.

'Not from Parker, or not yet. I'm not giving up, There is something he's hiding. He's scared out of his wits. The unfortunate thing is that, at the moment, he is more afraid of someone else than he is of me.'

I prepared to take my leave. 'I have impressed on him that the best protection he can have is that of the police. Sadly, he has no confidence in my word.'

'He's afraid of being labelled an informer,' said Phipps. 'I can't hold him in the cells here. Much as I'd like to oblige you, of course.'

'Of course not, I quite understand. Tell Barrett well done for bringing him in.'

Elizabeth Martin Ross

As I had agreed to accompany Patience and Frank to Dorset Square that afternoon, Patience asked me to stay and lunch with the family. As soon as I accepted, she led me off to meet her aunt. Mrs Pickford was a small, pale-skinned, fair-haired woman. She welcomed me with the air of a startled fawn; and whispered something I didn't quite catch and did not like to ask her to repeat.

'Yes, Aunt Matilda,' said Patience, answering for me. 'Mrs Ross is married to the police inspector who is investigating the case.'

'Mr Pickford,' whispered Mrs Pickford, 'has gone to Scotland Yard this morning.'

'Please don't be alarmed, Mrs Pickford,' I told her. 'My husband will be very tactful.'

'Mine won't!' said Mrs Pickford simply. She made a gesture indicating Patience and then me, probably meant to indicate Patience would have to carry any conversation. 'I have to tell the kitchen we shall be one more at table, please excuse me.' She hurried from the room.

Luncheon was promising to be a difficult experience. Fortunately Frank had been invited too. He arrived some twenty minutes later, chattering in his usual cheerful way and filling the silence. Mrs Pickford had also rejoined us. In Frank's presence she brightened. Shortly after that, Pickford himself came home; and the animation that had briefly flickered in his wife's face when talking with Frank faded.

I admit I had been longing to see Patience's uncle. His arrival caused some commotion in the hall, much scurrying about of the maids and his voice booming out some criticism. But no one appeared to find this unusual. With all the recent drama in the house, Mrs Pickford had prudently supplied herself with a small vial of sal volatile, and remained in her chair, gripping the little flask like an amulet to ward off harm. I realised we were all waiting with bated breath to hear how her husband had fared at the Yard. Frank met my eye and grimaced. Then the door burst open and a short, very plump gentleman, with a somewhat pop-eyed stare, appeared framed in the doorway. I was unfortunately reminded of one of those toy theatre sets on which the paper characters, attached to thin sticks, are pushed on and off stage by hidden hands.

'My Uncle Pickford!' Patience informed me. 'This is Mrs Ross, Uncle.'

Pickford fixed his bulging gaze on me and exclaimed, 'Ross, eh? So you are the wife of that Scotland Yard inspector! I have just been speaking with your husband, madam.'

Mrs Pickford broke in nervously to suggest we talk over luncheon, as the kitchen was ready to send up the soup, so we trooped into the dining room and took our places round the table. We three ladies modestly declined the wine, contenting ourselves with water. Mr Pickford poured out generous glasses for himself and Frank. My earlier impression of a toy theatre was enhanced when the door was flung open by a maid to admit a stout youth wearing a black waistcoat with brass buttons and carrying a large soup tureen. He deposited this on the sideboard with some ceremony. The maid had followed behind. The waistcoated boy ladled out the soup into bowls and the maid bore them to the table. It proved to be a thick soup made from dried peas in a ham stock, and was very filling.

Following the soup and the clearing away of the dishes and tureen, there was a few minutes' wait during which Uncle Pickford tapped his knife handle on the table impatiently and breathed heavily through his nostrils like a heavy-laden horse. Still no one spoke.

The curtain then went up on Act II (as I could not

help but see it). The door flew open again to admit the stout youth and a pair of maids. All three staggered beneath trays, between them bearing a boiled ham and a raised game pie, together with a dish of potatoes mashed with swede, another of buttered carrots, one of Brussels sprouts and all accompanied by a gravy-boat of white sauce and a bowl of stewed apple. Pickford cheered up at the sight of the main course and ceased snorting and tapping the table. He even broke the silence.

'We keep a plain table, Mrs Ross,' he boomed. 'I can't be doing with fancy dishes. I like proper food.'

Mrs Pickford gave me an apologetic smile, whether for the simplicity of the menu or for her husband, it wasn't certain.

It was obviously not the habit in the Pickford household to make conversation over the table while eating. Mr Pickford tucked his napkin into his collar and set about his plate with gusto. His wife and niece followed suit. Oh my, I thought, if Patience is to be hostess at Frank's dinner table, she will have to learn the art of making conversation and eating at the same time! But we worked our way through the ham, game pie and vegetables in silence, broken only when Mr Pickford demanded testily, 'Are there no more carrots?'

Mrs Pickford signalled to the maid, who scurried away. She returned with the carrots and, as a precaution, more Brussels sprouts.

Eventually, Mr Pickford set down his knife and fork and announced: 'That was a fair piece of gammon, Matilda.'

Matilda Pickford looked relieved and rang for the dessert to be brought. The soup, ham, game pie, potatoes and other vegetables had left me wanting nothing more, but I suspected to refuse the next course would be regarded as an insult. Now that the serious part of the meal had been eaten, conversation was allowed.

'Now then, Mrs Ross,' said Pickford, as we waited. He mopped his mouth with his napkin and settled back in his chair to survey me.

'Your husband appears a sensible fellow,' he continued. 'I am pleased he is in charge of this sorry business. Very glad, too, that he hasn't locked Edgar up. That will be some consolation to his afflicted parents. I had intended writing a letter this afternoon, once I had verified the details of the business with your husband. But I begin to think I shall send a message by the telegraph system. Then I won't have to explain it in detail, only to have to chew it all over again when they get here. Marvellous invention, the telegraph, Mrs Ross.'

'The police force finds it very useful,' I said.

'Quite so, we must all move with the times!' Pickford nodded. 'It's of great value in business. Why, we can contact a customer in minutes – minutes, mark you! Or we can receive an order and set it in hand the same day. If you are in business, Mrs Ross, you have to keep up with the latest inventions. I am pleased to hear the police have not lagged behind.'

'If you send a message by the telegraph, my dear,' ventured his wife, 'Dorothy will think someone has died or is dying.'

'Well, someone has died: that wretched woman in Deptford!' snapped Pickford.

'But Dorothy – and Walter – won't know about the woman in Deptford,' argued Mrs Pickford, 'because you won't have told them. So they will think one of us is lying ill.'

Alarmingly red in the face, Pickford declared, 'I shall put in the telegram that we are all well, but an urgent situation has arisen requiring family consultation. There!' concluded Pickford. 'I trust that will satisfy you, Matilda. Now then, don't fuss about it and leave it all to me.'

At that moment the door opened again and the trio of servants reappeared, carrying more laden trays. I had hoped we might be served something light, some jellies, perhaps, or a blancmange. But Mr Pickford's wish for 'proper food' clearly extended to this course, as to the previous one. Displayed for our approval were a large fruit tart, a splendid tower of a steamed sponge pudding (with dates in it) and a baked custard. These were all set out on a sideboard. Lastly a pitcher of cream was set down with a flourish. The maids retired and the boy with the brass buttons remained by the sideboard, with a large serving spoon grasped in his hand.

'Which would you like first, Mrs Ross?' asked Mrs Pickford.

I asked for a small portion of fruit tart and was presented with a substantial slice by the boy. I met Frank's eye and he grinned at me. Frank had lunched chez Pickford before.

Frank now took advantage of the interruption caused

by this arrival of the third course to tell Pickford he intended to pay a call on his aunt that afternoon. 'In company with Patience and my cousin Elizabeth.'

I guessed Frank was anxious to underline that Edgar's misdemeanours were being treated as 'a family matter', even if I was married to the investigating officer.

'You are going to tell her all about this, I presume?' growled Pickford over the date pudding.

'I cannot leave my Aunt Julia in ignorance, sir. I dare say she will hear about it, anyway.' Frank hesitated and glanced at Mrs Pickford. 'I am afraid it may make an article in the evening papers. The reading public does like a murder. We can't hope the press will ignore it.'

Mrs Pickford gave a little cry and fell back in her chair. Directly in my line of sight was the sideboard with the boy in brass buttons waiting by it. He was listening with interest. This news would go back to the kitchen with the cleared dishes.

'Don't alarm yourself, madam, I beg,' urged Frank. 'The same readership so avid for a lurid story will forget about it if a new scandal or anything dramatic appears in the following day's papers.'

'Well, I suppose Mrs Parry's got to know,' grumbled Pickford. 'Yes, yes, of course she must.'

At this point Matilda Pickford met my eye across the table and I could not mistake the entreaty in her expression.

Sure enough, when the gentlemen were returning to the parlour, Mrs Pickford hung back in the dining-room doorway.

'Let us just go upstairs and tidy ourselves,' she said, nodding at Patience. Patience began to climb the stairs but Mrs Pickford made no move. When her husband's stout form and Frank's tall lean one had disappeared, and Patience was too high above us to hear, she spoke to me in a furtive whisper.

'My dear Mrs Ross, forgive the question, but this won't affect Patience's prospects, will it? Mrs Parry is Mr Carterton's nearest surviving relative, as I understand it. Patience has told me that Mrs Parry is very fond of her nephew. She has been very supportive in his political ambitions. I suppose, all being well, one day . . .'

Mrs Pickford obviously recollected that it would be unseemly to speak of Aunt Parry's will. But I understood her. Everyone, myself included, supposed that Frank was named as her heir.

'I mean,' resumed Mrs Pickford, 'Mrs Parry won't object to the wedding going ahead, now that Edgar has behaved so foolishly and caused such a scandal? It will be the almost the first thing my sister, Dorothy, will ask when she arrives. After she's inquired about Edgar, of course.'

'Frank is determined to stand by Patience and I believe that Mrs Parry will pay great attention to that,' I said tactfully.

Mrs Pickford did not look very happy at this reply, but Patience was leaning over the banister above, curious to know what we were whispering about. So we went upstairs to join her.

The respite was brief. Mrs Pickford was determined to

continue her quizzing of me. To do this, she had to remove Patience from the scene.

'Goodness, my love, your hair is all awry. Lucy! Go with Miss Patience to her room and put up her hair afresh.'

So a reluctant Patience was sent away; but not before she had given us a sharp look. Mrs Pickford chose to ignore the look and concentrate on me. 'I know *you* will be as concerned about this wretched business, Mrs Ross, as are we in Edgar's family,' she began.

'I understand you are worried, ma'am,' I assured her. 'But please don't make yourself ill fretting about it. My husband will make sure the investigation into the— the matter will be carried out very discreetly and efficiently. As for Mrs Parry, as I told you earlier, she will be guided by Frank.'

'But she does not know Edgar!' protested his Aunt Pickford. 'Frank believes we must expect there will be a story in the newspapers this evening. Worse, suppose nothing more interesting happens for a week and the press is full of nothing else but the Deptford murder? They may print some of those dreadful illustrations the artists work up for newspaper stories, so vulgar and bloodthirsty. Mrs Parry would come to quite the wrong conclusion, thinking Edgar is a rascal of the worst sort! Yet he is the dearest boy. He wouldn't, couldn't, murder anyone and the thought that he might be cast into prison—'

'He hasn't been!' I interrupted briskly. 'He quite free and engaged in his duties at Bart's Hospital; too busy, I dare say, to worry about it.'

'Well, he should worry about it,' argued Mrs Pickford. 'You have met Edgar, I understand, Mrs Ross?'

'Yes, in this house. Besides, I was there in Deptford with them when— when we discovered what had taken place.'

'So,' said Mrs Pickford firmly, 'I can tell my sisters, when they arrive, that you will speak up for the boy with Mrs Parry?'

'I will do my best,' I said. 'But I can't interfere . . .'

'My dear Mrs Ross, I wouldn't dream of asking you to interfere. But I have to say something to reassure Dorothy – the boy's mother – when she arrives. She will be distraught. Amelia and Caroline, my sisters, won't be much better.' Mrs Pickford sighed. 'It is too much to hope that Amelia and Caroline won't come to London with my sister and her husband. You may put money on it, as my husband would say.'

A look of dismay crossed her face. 'I do not mean, by those words, to indicate Herbert is a gambler. No one in our family is so profligate. Not to date, anyway. I cannot imagine, Mrs Ross, where Edgar learned such bad behaviour. I do so hope that Mrs Parry does not imagine we are all wastrels! Oh, dear, what can she think of us?'

She leaned forward and grasped my hand. 'Dear Mrs Ross, I am so depending on you to correct any false impression Mrs Parry may have had.' She beamed. 'Now let us go down and join the gentlemen.'

Later, Frank, Patience and I set off for Dorset Square by cab. Frank was, as usual, incurably optimistic.

'Well, that went pretty well,' he said, referring to our

luncheon. 'Your uncle has calmed down considerably, my dear. And Lizzie, I do declare the crusty old fellow took a liking to Ross. That's an unexpected stroke of luck! Now then, all we have to do is present our case to Aunt Julia.'

Patience gripped my arm. 'You will say you've met Edgar and he is really harmless, won't you, Lizzie? Isn't that what my Aunt Pickford was urging you to do? Do tell Mrs Parry what a really kind, generous and helpful person my brother is.'

'You'll watch out my Aunt Julia doesn't have some sort of nervous attack?' added Frank. 'You're very good at calming her down.'

Everyone, it seemed, was depending on me.

Chapter Eleven

'THE BEST-LAID schemes o' mice an' men,' as the poet described them, are apt to go wrong. We should have borne that in mind, for our sanguine plans for dealing with Mrs Parry were soon dashed. Frank had been right to warn us all about reports of the whole affair in the popular press. When Simms, the butler, admitted us to the house in Dorset Square, he had an unusually conspiratorial air.

'Mr Carterton, sir,' he said in a low voice. 'The early editions of the evening newspapers have just been delivered. But I have not yet taken them up to Mrs Parry. She is expecting you and I thought perhaps it best you speak with her first, sir.'

'Well done, Simms,' said Frank, 'quite right. Did Mrs Parry send out for the newspapers?'

'Yes, sir. That is to say, she sent a message to the nearest newsagent's shop. She asked that they should send a boy round with the early editions, as soon as they had them.'

'So,' said Frank thoughtfully. 'She's got wind of what's happened already, has she? The cat's out of the bag.'

'I fear so, sir,' said Simms sorrowfully.

'Who told her?'

Before Simms could answer, there was a rustle on the staircase and a fashionably clad lady began her descent. With sinking heart I recognised a neighbour in the Square, Mrs Belling. She was a woman of sour disposition and she had never liked me. She probably liked Patience even less, because she had at one time entertained hopes that Frank would marry her daughter, Dora. How happy it must have made her to be able to run round with the dramatic news as soon as she'd heard about it. How had she done so? I wondered. But London, for all its size and variety, often seemed no more than a village when it came to gossip.

We exchanged chilly greetings in the hall before she left and we began our own ascent to the first-floor drawing room.

'Damn it!' muttered Frank to me. 'That woman would get here first. We'll have to review our strategy, Lizzie. Let me do the talking.'

I had every intention of letting him start the conversation.

Aunt Parry was seated by the fireplace in majestic pose. It struck me that she had modelled it on our Queen Victoria. She did bear a strong resemblance to the monarch, being amply proportioned and radiating disapproval. No wonder: Mrs Belling must have taken great pleasure in telling her the news. Aunt Parry had not only been taken by complete surprise, but also left deeply embarrassed.

'How are you, Aunt Julia?' asked Frank, bowing and kissing her hand.

'You may well ask,' said Aunt Parry in a voice throbbing with emotion. Her face was very flushed and I did not think it was only from the proximity to the hearth. Mrs Belling had found revenge sweet and made the most of it. She would not have said that Frank would never have become involved in this, if he'd married Dora. But the message would have been clear to read behind the spoken words.

'What on earth has been going on?' continued Aunt Parry passionately. 'Mrs Belling has called to tell me that a member of *your* family, Patience . . .' here she turned an accusing eye on Frank's fiancée, '*your* family, Miss Wellings, has been arrested for a murder!'

At this unjust accusation I am afraid I abandoned my intention of allowing Frank to lead the conversation.

'Indeed, Ben did *not* arrest him, Aunt Parry. Edgar Wellings only went with Ben to Scotland Yard to make a statement. He was then allowed to leave. He was never – at any time – under arrest!' I burst out.

Aunt Parry turned a glacial look on me. 'Mr Morton saw him led away from the house where this dreadful murder took place, led away by your husband. If that is not arrest, what is?"

'Who the devil – I beg your pardon, Aunt Julia and ladies! – who, may I ask, is Mr Morton?' broke in Frank angrily.

'Mr Morton is a friend of the Belling family. He lives in Deptford. He is a naval architect, now long retired, and was for many years engaged on important work at the naval dockyard there. He is now a very elderly gentleman, and infirm. He only leaves the house in a bath chair. His health makes him disinclined to move from Deptford, despite some of the rowdy scenes that take place of an evening. He doesn't go out in the evening, anyway,' finished Aunt Parry.

'But how did he know it was Edgar Wellings at the house?' demanded Frank.

'Dr Wellings had been pointed out to him on a previous occasion. Mr Morton has a nephew who has also entered the medical profession. He calls regularly on his uncle. On one such a visit, he accompanied his uncle on his afternoon outing, the weather being a little milder. Passing down one street, the nephew gave an exclamation of surprise. On being asked why, he told Mr Morton that he had just seen a young doctor from Bart's walking on the other side of the street. He said the young fellow's name was Wellings and he wondered what he was doing there in Deptford.'

'When was this, Aunt Parry?' I asked quickly.

She waved a pudgy, ring-bedecked hand, 'Oh, some two weeks or so ago. Mr Morton's nephew did not hail Wellings, as he was occupied with his uncle. But although Mr Morton is an invalid, there is nothing wrong with his eyesight and his memory is unimpaired. He recognised Dr Wellings at once when he saw Inspector Ross leading a young man away.'

Just like a village, I thought again, exasperated. Even in London, you cannot be sure you won't be spotted by someone who knows you. Perhaps Edgar had believed that if he went to a moneylender south of the Thames no one would recognise him there. He had clearly been wrong.

'It must have been Mr Morton I saw in the street before the house,' I told her. 'There was certainly an elderly gentleman in a bath chair, in the charge of a maidservant. He had become very agitated.'

Aunt Parry gripped the arms of her chair. 'As well he might be with murder being committed on his doorstep!'

'It was not committed by my brother!' declared Patience, entering the conversation in such a forceful tone and manner that we all turned to her.

'Then why was he arrested?' demanded Aunt Parry.

'Aunt Parry,' I insisted, 'please understand that he was *not arrested*. Ben only escorted him to Scotland Yard so that he could make a statement.'

'I cannot see the difference. And what, pray, were you doing there in Deptford, Elizabeth?'

'Lizzie kindly accompanied my brother and myself at my request,' said Patience so loudly and firmly that her words were followed by a moment's silence.

I saw Frank look at her, a faint smile tugging at his lips. You have chosen the right girl to marry, I thought. Whatever happened in his political career, Patience would stand by him and face down his foes.

It was perhaps as well that the silence was broken by Simms, who brought in the tea things, followed by a maid with a sponge cake.

Mrs Parry regarded the sponge cake with dismay. 'Plain sponge! As if I did not have all this to worry me,

I have Dr Bruch's wretched diet to cope with! Just when I need sustenance.'

The arrival of food and drink had served to calm her, however. When conversation started again she sounded not so much magisterial as pettish. But I was still her target.

'I would have thought,' she said, 'that seeing his own wife at the scene and knowing the connection with this family, the inspector would not have marched Dr Wellings away in such an obvious manner.'

'There was a sizeable crowd of curious neighbours,' I reminded her. 'They were becoming unruly. The constable before the door had difficulty in persuading them to disperse. I am sure Ben thought it best to escort Dr Wellings through the throng, for his own safety.'

'He could have asked your brother to call at the Yard later.' Mrs Parry turned to Patience. She still sounded pettish and was not prepared to listen to any argument. 'Your brother would not have attracted so much interest if he had not been in the charge of the police.'

'I should tell you, Aunt Parry,' I said loudly, 'that amongst the onlookers making the most fuss was Mrs Belling's friend, Mr Morton, as I now know his name to be. He was shouting abuse.'

Mrs Parry studied me thoughtfully. 'Was he, indeed?' she said. She turned back to Patience. 'Why were you and your brother at that house, with Elizabeth, in the first place?'

'Dr Wellings had business there,' Frank said quickly. 'It was an unfortunate coincidence, nothing more.'

'Had he? What manner of business was that, I wonder, in Deptford of all places? Nor can I see what necessitated Elizabeth's presence.'

Patience bit her lip and flushed.

Mrs Parry had turned her attention to Frank. 'None of this, I trust, will involve *your* name? You are only at the start of your career. You cannot afford to be associated with sordid events of this nature.' She turned to Patience. 'Nor can there be any question of continuing with the arrangements for a wedding until the air has been cleared, your brother's innocence loudly declared by the police, and the whole sorry débâcle forgotten.'

Patience gasped and blanched. She threw an imploring look at her fiancé, following it with one at me.

'I am sure Ben will sort it all out,' I assured her. 'And with the utmost discretion.'

'Are you, Elizabeth?' Aunt Parry drew a deep breath. 'None of this would have happened if you hadn't insisted on marrying that policeman, you know.'

This was so unjust and, at the same time, subject to such distorted logic, that her listeners were all of us reduced to silence.

Until this point Aunt Parry had shown no indication of the nervous collapse Frank had feared. She seemed to realise that it was time to show less aggression and more frailty.

'My nerves are in shreds,' she informed us. 'And plain sponge cake won't help them. Ring the bell, Elizabeth. I am sure Mrs Simms can find something more interesting in her kitchen. Frank,' she turned to him, 'we shall not discuss this further at this moment. Come and see me tomorrow morning. Come alone. I wish to speak to you in private.'

Patience bit her lip and cast an apprehensive glance at Frank. We all knew that he relied heavily on his aunt for financial support. I guessed that it was about to be spelled out to him. Either Edgar Wellings's name was to be cleared, quickly and absolutely, or someone would suffer. At the moment, the only person vulnerable to any direct action by Mrs Parry was her nephew. She would reduce – or sever altogether – the money supply.

When we finally left Dorset Square, Aunt Parry still had not suffered any nervous collapse. But I was very worried; Frank was for once visibly downcast; and poor Patience on the verge of tears.

Later that evening I told Ben all about my day over our supper table. After we had allowed ourselves a smile over Uncle Pickford, Ben grew serious.

'I am sorry you've had such a difficult time,' he said. 'That Mrs Parry should think you are in any way to blame for anything in this is ridiculous. I do agree that, as far as Carterton is concerned, his aunt will prove a problem. He will have to placate her somehow. But, knowing him, I dare say he'll find a way!'

'It would be easier for him if Mrs Belling had not meddled,' I grumbled.

'Well, she did "meddle", as you describe it, but from my point of view Mrs Belling's account is interesting. Her friend Morton and his nephew saw young Wellings in the street where Clifford lived as recently as two weeks ago, or thereabouts, walking along in broad daylight. It supports the impression I've already formed of Wellings. He has absolutely no sense of discretion or commonsense. On the night of the murder, he admits to visiting her after dark and standing by the streetlamp so that she could see his face before opening the door. But by then he was at odds with her and she was making threats. Before that, he was in the habit of calling on her whenever he was free, even of an afternoon when he could be seen and recognised. Now we know he *was* seen and recognised! That want of discretion and judgement can lead someone like Wellings into a situation where he can lose his head completely.'

My heart sank. 'Oh, Ben, you are not ruling Edgar out as a suspect, then?'

'How can I? The young man's a fool, but a desperate fool. Desperate fools are very dangerous, Lizzie.'

Inspector Ben Ross

I was more than sorry that Lizzie had come in for criticism in Dorset Square; I was angry. I remained angry the following morning.

It wasn't difficult to concentrate my wrath on Frank Carterton. Never mind that Edgar Wellings had started the whole sorry business. The only reason Lizzie had been dragged into yesterday's embarrassing scene in Dorset Square was Carterton's request that she help him with his formidable aunt. Knowing my wife, I had to admit she couldn't be dragged anywhere she didn't want to go. But while Carterton knew that he could count on Lizzie's support, that didn't mean he had to ask for it.

Lizzie had told me that she and Patience had hidden from Carterton that Edgar had asked his sister for money. Had Carterton known, I am sure he would have been the first to say Edgar had no right to ask. It's wrong to take unfair advantage of another person's good nature, and that's undeniable in my view. Especially if that person is my wife.

But there was nothing I could do about it, at least not for the time being. I would keep a close eye on that situation and, if necessary, speak to Carterton myself.

In the meantime, I had a murderer to track down.

'We ought to speak to Britannia Scroggs again,' I said to Morris the following morning. 'She may have calmed down a little by now. She's also had time to think. She may have remembered something useful. Take me to the house where her mother lives. Britannia ought to be there.'

But Britannia was not there when we arrived. Ma Scroggs was at home in her cramped and cheerless room. Looking round, I saw an untidy pile of tattered bedding in one corner. That must be where Britannia was bivouacking, as there was no space in her mother's narrow cot. Britannia had been thrown out of her private little attic bedroom for this. She would blame the police entirely. There was no wash dripping from a line today, but there was still a damp atmosphere and a fetid smell about the place. Ma Scroggs was certainly not pleased to see us; and disposed to be sarcastic.

'What, police coming along here in twos now, are you? Not frightened of me and my poor girl, surely?'

Despite the cold day, there was no fire lit in the hearth. Morris had spoken of some kind of bad-smelling stew simmering in a pot when he had last come here. But today, although the iron pot hung on its hook in the arch of the fireplace, nothing was being prepared in it. Was it the loss of Britannia's job that had necessitated further privation in an already poverty-stricken home?

'Where is your daughter?' I asked her brusquely. 'She was told to stay at this address.'

I was not going to be draw into a bad-tempered and useless exchange with this old harridan. I'd probably have that with her daughter – when I finally tracked her down. From the corner of my eye, through the dirty windowpane, I saw a street urchin of about nine years of age running away from the house. Down the street he scampered, full pelt. I wondered if he was on his way to warn Britannia, wherever she was, that the police were back and looking for her.

'She's working,' said Ma Scroggs malevolently. 'Such work as she can get round here. She can't sit round like a lady, you know. She's got to earn some money. I can't support her. I depend on her to support me.' She glowered at Morris. 'You 'ad no business bringing her here.'

'She's your daughter,' retaliated Morris. 'And if she's been giving you money from her wages, all the time she worked for Mrs Clifford, the least you can do is give her a place to sleep now.'

She shuffled forward and peered up at him, her

wrinkled face framed with wispy grey hair escaping from a grubby mobcap. She had a shawl round her shoulders and gripped the edges together at her chest with a claw of a hand.

'She had a place to sleep,' she snapped. 'She had a perfekly good place at Mrs Clifford's 'ouse.'

'Mrs Scroggs,' I said firmly. 'You must understand that, now Mrs Clifford is dead, Britannia cannot sleep at her house. Her reason for being there has gone. Besides, it is the scene of a murder. What if the murderer returned?'

'I shouldn't think he'd do that, not with half the rozzers in London hanging about the place!' she argued.

I was beginning to understand where Britannia had learned her combative manner. 'Where is your daughter?' I demanded. 'Stop wasting my time. Where is she working now?'

'Oh, yus!' shouted Ma Scroggs at me with surprising force. 'Go there and lose her that job, why don't you? You think people like the p'lice turning up on the doorstep?'

Her words recalled Harry Parker's. He had been turned out by his landlord on the night of the murder, because Barrett had accompanied him home to check the address. Or so Parker had claimed. I must talk to Parker again; our last conversation had been highly unsatisfactory. The wretched fellow knew something and I would have to get it out of him somehow or other.

Ma Scroggs, having been as awkward as she could be, and delayed us for as long as possible, now admitted that Britannia was working at the Clipper public house.

'Where is that?' asked Morris.

I touched his elbow. 'I know where it is.' As we walked away from the Scroggs's dwelling, I added to Morris, 'It is not so very far from Skinner's Yard where the body was found.'

'Coincidence?' asked Morris.

'Could be,' I agreed. 'She needed to find work urgently and may have gone round all the public houses, asking if they required domestic help.'

We found Britannia easily enough at the Clipper. She was washing the floor of the public bar. We bid her good morning and asked if we could have a word. She sat back on her heels, wrung out her rag, and hung it over the edge of her bucket.

'Whaffor?' she demanded.

A very large man in a leather jerkin appeared. His mashed features reminded me of Wally Slater, the cabman. I guessed that this fellow, like Wally, had once graced the prize ring. The man glowered at us, and asked, 'What's up, Tanny?'

'Nothing's up!' snapped Britannia.

'Peelers, ain't you?' asked the large man of us. 'Fancy sort, plain-clothes, outa the Yard, most likely.'

'Yes,' I told him. 'And who are you?'

'I'm Jethro Smith, landlord. If you want to speak to my staff, I want to know what about.'

'It'll be Mrs Clifford's murder,' said Britannia with a hiss of annoyance. 'I already told them all I can.' She squinted up at us from her crouched position. 'Here, I still got clothes at the house. I need to go back for them. You said I could go back for them. But when I went there yesterday, the house was all barred up and there was a copper outside the door. He told me to clear off, the cheeky little— cheeky blighter.'

'You should arrange a time with Inspector Phipps.'

'Oh, him . . .' muttered Britannia dismissively. 'I gotta take meself all the way to the police station and argue with that ginger-whiskered fellow, have I? He don't like me and he's got no respect for my lawful rights. That's my property at the house and I want it! If I get him to agree, then we got to go back to Mrs Clifford's house. Like I say, if he'll let me. Like as not, he'll say he can't spare a constable to go with me and unseal the house. "Come back tomorrow," he'll say. I know his sort! I ain't got time to walk all over London, you know.'

'Here,' growled Smith. 'If you want to talk to her, you do it out back. I don't want people seeing you here. Puts the customers off. No one will come in for a pint while you're here.'

'Ever feel unwanted, Morris?' I murmured to him, as Britannia scrambled to her feet and wiped her hands on her apron.

She led us through the building and into a paved backyard stacked up with all manner of junk from broken chairs to boxes of empty bottles and stacks of empty kegs. Despite that, a watery sunshine trapped in the area made it quite a pleasant spot.

'Well?' demanded Britannia, hands on hips. My eyes were drawn to her distorted knuckles again. Washing the floors here wouldn't help the rheumatism or whatever it was setting in.

'In our experience,' I began, 'people often begin to remember details a few days after the event. At the time, with the shock, things slip the mind. So, I am wondering if there is anything you have recalled since we last spoke.'

'Like what?' retorted Britannia. She folded her arms. Perhaps she had seen me studying her hands. Now she tucked them out of sight.

I made an effort to keep calm. 'We have spoken about Dr Wellings,' I began, 'and his visit on the night of the murder. How often had you seen him at the house before?'

'Oh, *him*,' said Britannia. 'He came a few times.' She frowned. 'He started coming about six months ago, or a bit more. Full of himself, he was, when he first turned up, quite the gent.'

'He came in the evenings?'

She shook her head. 'Came all times of the day. Sometimes of an evening and sometimes of an afternoon. Once he came in the morning when I was scrubbing the front step. That didn't please me, I can tell you! I'd just got the step all nice and white and shining; and he put his big boot right on it and left a muddy print. I spoke to him about it!'

'What did you say?' asked Morris curiously.

'I said, "Oy! Watch what you're doing!" – something like that,' Britannia told us.

'You didn't mind upsetting a customer, then?' observed Morris.

Britannia surveyed him with a look of resigned tolerance that people sometimes give those who are slow on the uptake.

'He wasn't a customer,' she said. 'Not like he'd come to buy something and he'd go elsewhere if he didn't like the reception he got. He was in debt and couldn't pay. He was skint, for all his airs and graces! Not a penny to bless himself. Lost it all on cards and dice and I don't know what. He'd come to borrow and he wasn't in a position to make a fuss, was he? I'd seen his sort before, plenty of them. Mrs Clifford, she called them her "bread and butter clients". They were a regular kind to turn up, she meant. She liked them, from a business point o' view.'

'How so?' asked Morris, still playing the simple soul.

'Because she knew she'd always get the money in the end. They had family, see? Family what had money.' Britannia smiled, showing her chipped front tooth. 'Family would pay up, if she went to them. The clients was all mortal afraid of that; and their families was mortal afraid of scandal.'

Somewhere in my head a bell rang, signalling she had said something I should take note of. Not that she had said anything we hadn't known already, but, somehow, it had been set in a different context.

It must have shown in my face. Britannia uncrossed her arms.

'She didn't discuss business with me,' she said brusquely. 'And, if you don't mind, I got to get back to work. Or I'll lose this job, too.'

As we left the Clipper public house, I noticed an urchin loitering about outside, kicking stones. He looked very much like the one I'd seen running from Ma Scroggs's home. The landlord, Jethro Smith, was standing outside the door and, as we appeared, he gave us a look of dislike, then shouted out to the urchin to 'clear off, you!' The boy ran away.

'We are finished for the moment, Mr Smith,' I said to him politely.

My courtesy gained me nothing. His scowl deepened. 'Not coming back, I hope? I run a decent pub. There's never trouble here that I can't handle. I don't need police around the place.'

'You will not hold it against Britannia Scroggs that we were here, I hope?' I asked. 'We are making inquiries into the death of her former employer. You will not turn her away?'

He stared hard at me for a moment then shrugged. 'I don't hold it against her, but I don't want you coming back.'

'I am glad you are able to give her some work,' I told him. I don't know quite why I said it, perhaps just to have the last word.

But it was not to be the last word, for he leaned forward and growled, 'She's a good worker and a good girl, is Tanny Scroggs. You lot have no business persecuting her. Go ask your questions among those young swells who borrowed money from the old witch, Clifford. That's where you'll find your answers to your inquiries!'

'You have known Miss Scroggs for a while?' I ventured.

'Know the whole family,' said Smith.

'There is only Britannia and her elderly mother, I understand?' I suggested. 'A small family, at that.'

'Used to be more of them!' snapped Smith.

'You knew them, the younger Scroggs children? The boys, for example, the one who fell off a cart and was killed and the other one, the elder one, who went to sea?'

'Billy,' said Smith. 'We were pals as kids, me and Billy. He was a big youngster and I reckon he could've been useful in the prize ring. But he had a mind to travel, so he signed on a clipper ship as cabin boy and went off to sea.'

'His mother and sister believe him drowned,' I said, anxious to keep him talking about the family.

He turned his bloodshot gaze on me. 'There's a lot of them go to sea and end up on the bottom of the ocean with the fish nibbling at them!' He looked away again. 'I don't know what became of Billy. Likely his ma is right. I knew the sister, too, the one as died in childbed. They've had enough bad fortune, have the Scroggses, without more of it now. They don't need trouble and they don't need you hanging about them!'

With that, the landlord turned and stomped back inside his premises.

'Surly blighter,' I observed to Morris, as we turned to leave. 'But he could be right. We should be questioning anyone we can find who borrowed money from Clifford or knows someone who did. If only we had those IOUs! Wellings was there that night; we must not overlook that. A late hour to call and do business.'

'Well, sir,' observed Morris. 'If that young fellow, Wellings, came all hours of the day, it could be because he couldn't choose when he visited. He was needed at the hospital most of the time.'

'Quite so. I keep thinking about that robbery, Morris.'

'Yessir?' Morris eyed me with interest.

'Items stolen from the house fall into two groups. One group is the cashbox and any loose cash lying about. The second group of stolen goods comprises the missing IOUs. Let us suppose that the killer was primarily after the IOUs. That would suggest one of Clifford's clients, desperate to recover a document to which he'd put his name. That could well be someone normally regarded as completely respectable.'

'Like a doctor,' said Morris drily.

'Like young Wellings, quite. Whoever it was, he was astute enough also to take the cashbox; to make it look like an ordinary burglary. That all went horribly wrong when the house owner disturbed him.

'However, now let us suppose that he was not a client, like Wellings, but an ordinary burglar or thief, who was set on taking the cashbox from the first? He might have been clever enough to take the IOUs to confuse the issue and make it appear the deed was done by one of Clifford's clients. Our suspicions would rest either on Wellings, who called that evening and was seen by Scroggs from the attic window; or someone who came later, after Wellings left, and was not seen by Scroggs. Remember, the kitchen door was not forced. Clifford had apparently let the murderer into the house.

'Now, if we continue to suppose the killer was not a client, and only after the cashbox: he sees the IOUs in the desk. He realises what they are, and also realises they'd be worth a fortune in the hands of a blackmailer. But he's a common thief. He might not attempt the blackmail himself. He wouldn't know how to go about it, so he takes them to sell on to someone more accomplished in that line of villainy.'

'Then, if it was a common burglar, how did he get in?' demanded Morris. 'Clifford would only have admitted a known client at that time of night. That girl *had* to have let anyone else in. You should arrest her, sir. Once in custody, it would easier to break her story. She'd panic.'

'I admit that she is the one person, other than Wellings, that we know for certain was in the house that evening. But only consider, Sergeant. You have met her mother and seen the poverty in which she lives. You have talked with Britannia. Is she the sort of housemaid usually employed in a respectable household? No, she is a maid of all work of the most basic sort, employed normally for rough duties only. Working for Mrs Clifford may not have been enjoyable. But she lived in, her own little room, and all food found. Her modest wages allowed her to pay her mother's rent. She even had a little status. Not a skivvy! She could claim to be a housemaid. Now she has lost that position and her only work is washing the floors of a public house. So it will be for the rest of her life. She is not pretty enough even to take to the streets. When you first visited old Mrs Scroggs, you say, there was a fire of sorts in the grate, is that so?'

'Yes, sir, that's so. It wasn't much of a fire, but there was one,' agreed Morris stolidly.

'Now there is none. Her employment by Mrs Clifford gave Britannia Scroggs a home, food, a regular wage. Why would she jeopardise all of that?'

Morris grunted agreement. Then he asked, 'If I may speak, sir?'

'Go ahead,' I invited him.

'All you say is true, sir, and I don't deny it. But there are things going on here we don't know of. Fact of the matter is, Mr Ross, that, dying or dead, the Clifford woman was taken from the house and left in Skinner's Yard. Until we know why, we shan't get to the bottom of it, and that's my view, sir. With your permission,' Morris concluded.

'Fair enough,' I conceded. 'Well, Britannia will not leave the area. Like Parker, she belongs in Deptford. Her elderly mother, who depends on her, is nearby. That landlord, who knows the family – knew the siblings when they were all young – he will employ her. So long as she sticks to her story, we shall have the devil of a job to break it, if she is lying or concealing something. We have all the pieces, Morris, but we are not yet assembling them correctly. I agree with you that we must find out how and why the body was moved to Skinner's Yard.'

'Perhaps the killer just wanted rid of it,' said Morris simply.

'In Skinner's Yard, sooner or later, it would be found.' I hesitated, because I knew Morris would be sceptical, but then continued. 'Wellings was telling me of badly injured accident victims who arrive at the hospital on their own two feet, including a man with a knife in his head. Let us suppose someone offered to take Clifford to get medical attention. But she collapsed and died before they had got very far. No one wants to be found with a dead woman at his feet. The body is dragged into Skinner's Yard and abandoned.'

'Who robbed it?' demanded Morris. 'What happened to her fob watch, earrings and wedding ring?'

'Parker denies robbing the body and, although at first I suspected him, I am inclined to believe him now. However, Parker is afraid of something – not just being accused of robbing the body. No, no, he heard or saw something – or someone. We must call on Inspector Phipps right now. He must send a constable to bring in Parker again.'

We were not to know we were already too late.

Chapter Twelve

IT WAS impossible to find a hackney cab in this poor part of London, so Morris and I made our way to Deptford police station on foot. Sometimes walking is the quickest way to reach your destination in the crowded streets; particularly as we were so quickly identified as representatives of the Law. The throng parted before us as the Red Sea before the Israelites. We got some curious looks but not much abuse, just the occasional catcall, which we chose to ignore.

Our ears were assaulted with all kinds of noise. They were building an iron-clad vessel in one of the private yards along the Thames and the clang and thud formed a continual background. I knew there were problems with building the bigger vessels in the Thames yards; as they had found out ten years before when the launch of the SS *Great Eastern* had proved so difficult. How long before the private yards followed the great naval dockyard into history?

The merchant ships Evans had told me of had spilled their crews into the streets. There were numerous foreign seaman with faces tanned to the hue and texture of old oak from wind and weather. Different languages echoed in the air and I couldn't identify them all. Now I caught a Scandinavian lilt, now something I thought was Russian. Then a few words I recognised as German. No doubt that evening the new arrivals would fill the drinking dens and brothels; and the usual rowdy scenes would break out, keeping Phipps and his men busy. We passed a busy warehouse taking delivery of a load of timber. The air was thick with the not unpleasant resinous smell; and for a moment we might have been standing in some thick forest in the far north, with snowflakes drifting down through the boughs above, and perhaps, in the distance, the howl of a wolf. The warehousemen manhandled the heavy planks, muscles straining and sweat running from them. The air, in addition to a chilly November dampness, had a curious aroma to it. In patches it was misty. I suspected the fog was forming and by tonight we might be in for a real 'pea-souper'. But for now these brawny fellows had stripped to their tattered shirts. At the end of the day they, too, would make for the nearest alehouse.

Aloud to Morris, I mused: 'With all this activity, who is to notice any detail in the crowd, however odd? What if one of these men, tired and thirsty, were to pass a woman, staggering and apparently drunk, being guided along by a man – or even two men? He would think nothing of it, and very likely not even take any heed of it. As for the foreign crewmen, it would be of no interest to them. They would be seeking drink and available girls.'

'There's enough of *them* hereabouts,' said Morris,

indicating a pair of young prostitutes already out and scouting for business.

They were dressed in cheap finery and their youthful faces were already hardened, their eyes both watchful and predatory. I wondered how old they were. Fourteen, fifteen? There were houses of refuge run by charities that took in such girls. They tried to help them, offering them a basic education, trying to curb their wild ways, and training them in domestic work, or a trade such as seamstress. They provided them with medical care and advice and tried to give them a better future. But very often the girls did not stay long in these houses. They did not like the strict rules, or they behaved so badly, fighting among themselves and subjecting the staff to abuse couched in the foulest of language, that they were ejected. Sometimes, too, the pimps came and took them away. These two girls had already spotted us and correctly identified us. They slipped away into the crowd.

I remembered Daisy Smith, whom I'd encountered on Waterloo Bridge one foggy night, and who had told me of the 'River Wraith', who preyed on the street women. I wondered where red-haired Daisy was now, if she was even still alive.

We arrived at the police station to find the reception area unexpectedly busy, not with raucous clientele, but with uniforms. Inspector Phipps had emerged from his den, and stood before the desk with Constables Evans and Barrett. A stout, red-faced custody sergeant stood behind the barrier, propped on one elbow, and listening with interest. A middle-aged navvy, clearly the worse for drink even at this early hour, had been brought in. Presumably the custody sergeant should be booking him. But the lively discussion had interrupted normal procedures. The sergeant watched the show. The drunk, temporarily forgotten and content to be left in peace, had fallen asleep on a chair in a corner.

As I appeared with Morris, heads turned towards us. There was a moment's startled silence and then Phipps stepped forward.

'Good heavens, Inspector Ross! Are you a mind-reader? I was about to send a constable to fetch you.'

'What has happened?' I asked with sinking heart.

'We had a report from Wapping of a body taken from the river this morning. It was later delivered to the mortuary there for the reception of such corpses. A lighterman saw it bobbing about, apparently, and hooked it aboard. He was fully laden, so did not want to turn back or put ashore. He stowed the body among his cargo, and carried it with him to his destination. He only called in to deliver it to the mortuary on his return journey. Apparently, he did not mind having the corpse aboard, as he knew who the dead man was.' Phipps grimaced.

'He identified the drowned man?' Morris asked with a frown. This was very unusual. Bodies floated down the Thames frequently, but could seldom be identified so quickly.

'So he claimed.' Beneath his ginger moustache, Phipps twisted his lips into a rueful grimace. 'And it is bad news for us. The lighterman declared the body to be that of Harry Parker, whom we know from present on-going investigations into the death of the woman Clifford. Because, according to information given by the finder, Parker had been a Deptford resident, the mortuary superintendent sent word to us that they held his body, and asking what we wanted to do about it.' Phipps gave a grim smile. 'I'll send someone to the address Parker gave us before he left here, but it's a lodging house and they won't know anything about his family, or whom to inform.'

There was a silence. My heart sank. Whatever it was Parker had seen on the night of the murder, or knew, it was lost to us for ever.

The silence was broken by the sleeping drunk, who fell off his chair with a resounding crash and lay on the floor face up. His eyes opened and he gave us all a bleary stare. 'God bless your honours!' he greeted us in a soft Irish brogue. Then he went back to sleep again. The custody sergeant came from behind his desk and, with the help of Constable Evans, manhandled the fellow to his feet and dragged him off to a cell.

'Parker told me he had a brother in the Limehouse area,' I said. 'That, according to him, is where he went when he disappeared temporarily from here. He may have been speaking the truth.'

Phipps brightened. 'Then it's not up to us to find his next of kin. Let Limehouse do it.'

'The body is still at Wapping mortuary?' I asked, reflecting that Inspector Phipps seemed always ready to pass his problems to another division.

'As far as I am aware,' said Phipps in an off-hand way. He no longer cared.

'Then we'll go there and try and find this lighterman.'

These were not the circumstances in which I'd wanted to
meet up with Harry Parker again. I gazed down at his
lifeless corpse. He looked as rat-like in death as he had
done in life, and even smaller.

'You have a name for the lighterman who brought in
the body?' I asked the officer in charge of the mortuary.
'His address?'

'We do, sir. He is name is Frederick Midge. But he'll
be back at work on the river and you will very likely not
find him again until this evening.'

'Are there any marks of violence on the body?'

The man consulted his paperwork again. 'None
recorded, sir. Most likely, he fell in when drunk.' He
leaned forward and pointed. 'There is a mark here, on
the shoulder. The skin is not broken: it is more in the
nature of a graze. It was probably caused postmortem
by collision with debris in the river – or by contact with
the lighter when the body was dragged aboard.'

'If anyone comes to claim him, let us know at the
Yard,' I requested. 'There is some reason to believe
he has a brother living in the Limehouse area.'

'They'll have to claim him quick,' said the officer. 'We
can't keep him here for long. You can see for yourself
we don't have the space. We'll post information of
his death in local news sheets. If no one comes forward
to claim him, either he'll be given a pauper's funeral
by the parish, as soon as the coroner has declared his

findings, or the body will go to a medical school for dissection. The coroner will rule "accidental death", you may believe me.'

'We'll go to the address given for the lighterman this evening,' I said to Morris as we left. 'If he's not there, we'll leave a request that he report to the Yard.'

'If we find him, he'll have nothing to tell us,' said Morris lugubriously.

'Probably not, though it might be interesting to discover how Midge knew Parker. The Thames boatmen and lightermen are professionals and a tight-knit community. How would one of them know of Parker, a casual labourer in the docks?'

I could only put the wretched Parker out of my mind for the time being until we had a chance to speak to the lighterman.

In the meantime I discovered, when we returned to the Yard, that another visitor awaited me.

'A gentleman to see you, Mr Ross,' said Biddle in impressed tones.

'Mr Pickford again?'

'No, sir, not the pop-eyed— not Mr Pickford. A very fashionable gent, sir.'

I could easily guess who that would turn out to be. I had been bracing myself for when Mr Francis Carterton, MP, came to call. And here he was.

He rose to his feet to greet me, a dapper, almost dandyish, figure, in a well-tailored blue frock coat and lavender-grey trousers. He held a silk top hat and a silver-headed cane in his hand.

'I hope this is not an inconvenient time to call on you, Ben?' he asked cheerfully.

Try as I might, I cannot help being irritated by Frank Carterton. It isn't just because I know he chased after Lizzie before she married me. Or because I know Lizzie harbours a chaste affection for him. Or because, through Carterton's engagement to Patience Wellings, Lizzie has become involved in the Deptford murder investigation. Or, again, because Frank persuaded Lizzie to go with him to see his Aunt Parry and talk her round with regard to the Wellings family's troubles. Or that Lizzie, as a result of Edgar Wellings's stupidity, has become a sort of confidante of Miss Patience's; and now feels a responsibility to look after that young woman. So, you see, I have quite a list of grievances.

Chiefly, above all of these things, Carterton has the knack of annoying me, at any time. Now, for example, he had hailed me familiarly as 'Ben' at my place of work. I don't mind him calling me 'Ben' on the few social occasions when we meet. (Though he usually calls me 'Ross' even then.) But his visit here today was in relation to a police investigation that I was heading: business, in other words. This was Scotland Yard and not a rich woman's drawing room.

And if he thought by buttering me up I would tell him something I would otherwise not normally divulge, he was wrong.

'I hope you have not been waiting long, Mr Carterton,' I said formally, shaking the hand he proffered. (Expensive grey suede gloves! But, socially correct as always, he had pulled off the glove on his right hand before he had extended it to me.)

He did not trouble to hide a grin. 'I should have called you "Inspector Ross", eh? Well, well, I suppose I should. My sincere apologies, my dear fellow.'

Only Frank Carterton could apologise so gracefully and manage to make things worse. Now I knew I must have sounded pompous.

'Come into my office,' I growled at him. 'We can talk privately.'

I showed him into the large broom cupboard designated as my office and invited him to take a seat. If I hadn't made the offer, he'd have sat down anyway. He looked around him as he did so, noting every detail of the cramped workaday surroundings. Well, this is not the House of Commons, Mr Carterton!

'You'll know what I've called about,' said Carterton. He folded the suede gloves and put them carefully into his upturned hat.

'I have been expecting you,' I returned brusquely. He made me feel the Derbyshire pit boy I'd once been. What of it? There is no shame in honest labour. Though I had not hewn the coal. I'd been a child, a 'trapper', sitting for hours in the dark depths of the mine to open and close the doors that controlled the flow of air. Lizzie's father had rescued me from that and paid for my schooling.

Carterton was studying me with a casual elegance. I had the horrid suspicion he knew exactly what was going through my mind. Irritating fellow though he was, he was no fool. I might even, were it not for his connection with

Lizzie, have liked him. Well, tolerated him, anyway.

'You have come about Edgar Wellings,' I said.

'Yes. You have already received a visit from my fiancée's Uncle Pickford, I understand?' Carterton suddenly grinned. 'Amazing old fellow, isn't he?'

I struggled with the memory of Pickford and then had to return the grin. 'What is often called "a character", I believe,' I said. 'But I dare say a shrewd man of business.'

'My word, yes!' agreed Carterton. 'And worth a pretty penny.'

I sensed him grow serious. 'What do you intend to do with young Edgar?' he asked.

'I have no plans at the moment for Edgar Wellings. He has been told to stay in London, and be available for interview if needed.'

'Oh, he'll stay in London, all right,' said Carterton. 'He's terrified of going home. Although home is shortly to come to him. The whole family is about to descend on Goodge Place. That will include his parents, of course, but also a pair of maiden aunts, his mother's sisters. So Edgar won't be able to avoid facing them.' Carterton leaned forward. 'See here, Inspector Ross, Edgar is often heedless, sometimes foolish. But I can't see him turning to violence. Do you suspect him of this foul murder?'

'I cannot rule him out as a suspect,' I told him. 'Though I have no reason to arrest and charge him at the moment. Our investigations are ongoing. He was there, at the house of the victim, that evening. There was a witness who heard a quarrel. Wellings himself does not deny it. He had borrowed money from the woman and couldn't repay. He was a desperate man. She was, by all accounts, an unpleasant person to deal with. So, you see, I cannot say it's impossible to believe that Wellings lost control.'

'But the body was not found at the house, I understand?' Carterton's tone was challenging. 'She left the house, possibly injured, but by her own efforts.'

'We cannot know that. She left, I agree, but aided by someone else at least. Even if still alive, she had to be very fatally injured and dying. I know Edgar can give examples of seriously injured persons arriving at hospital all alone, but I don't think so in this case.' In a deliberately casual tone, I added, 'Someone might have sought to take her to a place where she could get medical care, but abandoned her when she collapsed and died.'

Carterton paled. 'You do not think Edgar did that, surely?'

'How do I know?' I countered.

He sat back and sighed. 'I do not want to sound selfish, but you will appreciate how embarrassing all of this is for me personally.'

I nodded. 'You want to avoid a scandal. It would do your career no good.'

'No, it wouldn't. As it is, my marriage to Miss Wellings is delayed until matters are sorted out, one way or another. My aunt, Mrs Parry, insists.' He looked up and met my eye. 'But do not mistake me, Ross. I shall stand by Patience. We shall be married, whatever happens.'

'And your career as a politician?' I asked.

He gave a wry smile. 'If Edgar goes to the gallows, then that will be the end of me as a Member of Parliament.

The shadow of scandal, you see . . . A wife with a murderer for a brother! But, so be it. If I have to find another career, I shall do so. I have done it before.'

I had an urge to ask him why he had abandoned the diplomatic career he had followed before giving it up to stand for Parliament. But I did not really want to know; I had enough complications to deal with.

'Carterton!' I said firmly. 'I don't like my wife being involved in this. That is not only for personal reasons. It threatens to compromise my position as investigating officer. If you take her with you again to Dorset Square, I shall have to report this to my superior; and no doubt he will take me off the case. Do you understand?'

'Perfectly,' he replied. 'And I apologise for taking Lizzie along with us to see my aunt. It was unwise. It was just that Lizzie is good with Aunt Julia – and Patience is so grateful for her support. As am I,' he finished.

There was a moment's silence. 'This is difficult for Patience,' Carterton went on and then paused again. 'I do not want you off this case, Ben. I trust you. You will be thorough. You will get to the truth of it. You will not give favours and I won't ask any. I will not ask Lizzie to come with me again to see Aunt Julia. You have my word.'

'Thank you,' I said.

He met my eye. 'I cannot prevent Lizzie going to Dorset Square of her own volition. That's up to you.'

'Yes,' I said awkwardly.

He knew, as well as I did, that trying to persuade my wife not to do something she was decided on was well-nigh impossible.

*

Around five that afternoon, the fog began to gather. We had been free of it for more than a week and it was only to be expected. The mist started forming mid-afternoon and thereafter thickened quickly. The temperature had dropped. Condensation formed on the windows and trickled down so that trying to look through the panes was like staring into some heavily patterned lace curtain. It was already dark and the gas lamps were lit.

Morris and I set out for the home of the lighterman, Midge, by cab. But when conditions worsened, the cab rocked to a halt. The cabbie appeared at the door to advise us that he did not want to drive on for danger of collision.

'Not so much with other road traffic, sirs, but for fear of running down a pedestrian. People must try and get across the street as best they can. They can hear us, it's true, but not see us until we are upon them. It is difficult for them to judge how far away we are. We can neither hear nor see 'em. I can drive you on if you wish, but it will be at a walking pace; and, to be honest with you, gentlemen, you'd make better progress on foot.'

So we descended, wrapped our mufflers well round our faces and began to make our cautious way forward. Other walkers were stumbling along as blindly as we were. We bumped into one another, grunted our apologies and carried on as best we could. The shops were lit, but the light only made a paler patch in the fog before their premises and did little to show up the detail. At one point Morris gave a yelp and swore hoarsely.

'What is it?' I called.

'I walked into something, sir, something horrid! Oh, my lawd, it's a dead body a-swinging . . .'

I made my way to him and reached out. My fingers touched a solid form that swayed beneath my touch. Above the sulphurous, bad-egg smell of the fog I caught a whiff of dead flesh. I pulled off my glove and ran my hand down it. It was cold to the touch, smooth and bare. Then it came to an abrupt end with a small, protruding funnel-like shape. I felt bone and gristle and withdrew my hand with a gasp.

At the same moment a shout reached us from beyond, inside the building.

'Oy!' It was a man's voice. 'Who's there? You keep your thieving fingers off my meat!'

'It is a side of beef or pork, Morris!' I exclaimed in relief. 'We must be passing by a butcher's shop. There are others. They are hanging up in a row.'

A dark outline loomed up. 'Clear off!' it shouted at us.

'Police!' I called back. 'Are you the butcher?'

'I am. Joseph Perkins, purveyor of quality meats and game,' was the suspicious reply.

I suggest you take these sides of meat indoors, Mr Perkins. We have just walked into them.'

'Just about to do it!' retorted the shape of Mr Perkins. 'I'll get the boy.'

We carried on. More ghostly forms passed by us, coughing and wheezing like a ward full of consumptives. Eventually, after what seemed an age, we found ourselves in Wapping's narrow streets and alleys.

There, after several false turns and much inquiry, we found ourselves before a small house and rapped at the door.

A voice within shouted through it to ask who we were. When we identified ourselves, the door was pulled open and a gust of warm air and bright light engulfed us. A stocky figure stood there, peering at us.

'You come about that body?' he asked hoarsely. 'You don't look like ordinary peelers.'

'We are from Scotland Yard,' I told him.

'Blimey,' he said. 'We're going up in the world! Best come in. The fog's getting into the house.'

We stepped gratefully into the warmth and soon found ourselves in a neat, if tiny, parlour. There we were seated like guests of honour on the two best chairs, while Mrs Midge and her eldest daughter bustled about in the kitchen behind us; and a gaggle of small children crowded in the doorway to stare and giggle at the visitors.

'You don't want to take no notice of them,' said their father, waving a hand at his brood. 'Selina! Come and take these kids away!'

A female form appeared and swept the infants off. The door shut.

'Mug of ale?' inquired Mr Midge hospitably. 'I'll send one of 'em down to the pub with a jug. It's just at the corner.'

'Thank you, but no,' I told him. 'I wouldn't wish to send one of your children outside on such a foul night. We cannot stay long and must make our way back again in this fog. I understand you retrieved a body from the river this morning, Mr Midge.'

'Yus,' he said, nodding. 'And if the fog had been like it is this evening, we'd never have seen it. But it was as clear as crystal early this morning when I set off downriver.' He eyed us. 'Never knew Scotland Yard take an interest in a drowned docker before.'

'We understand,' I said, ignoring the clear invitation to take him into our confidence, 'that you recognised the drowned man.'

'That's it. It give me a nasty shock. There I was, going about my business, when the boy yells out that there's a drownded body in the water. Well, to tell you the truth, I thought it would only be some jetsam. The foreign ships coming upriver, they sometimes chuck their rubbish overboard and leave it to float ashore, or out to sea when the tide turns. I've seen all sorts of things bobbing alongside of me as I've been going downriver. Empty crates, bottles wiv foreign labels . . . every bit of rubbish pumped outa the bilges. It's not always rubbish, mind! I saw a top hat once. It was good silk one like a gentleman might wear. It was bobbing along all on its own, and didn't look as though it'd been in the water for long. So I fished that out. My wife cleaned it up a bit and I kept it for funerals.' Mr Midge added reminiscently, 'I've been to more funerals wearing that hat than I can recall. It makes a great impression, does a silk topper.'

'So you went to see what had attracted the boy . . .' prompted Morris restlessly.

'I did, but young Sammy had already thrown out a grappling iron and hooked it. It was a body, right enough.

So we pulled it close in and hauled it aboard. We turned him over and bless me, I recognised the feller!' Mr Midge slapped his knees and looked pleased at this turn of events. "That's Harry Parker!" I shouted out. The boy said, "Go on, it's never!" I told him, yes, it was. I'd bet my granddad's gold watch on it.'

'How do you know Parker?' I asked.

'He'd done a bit of work, casual labour, loading cargo, for me. Done it a couple of times. He was a funny little fellow, Harry. He'd pop up all along the river, looking for a day's work. Everyone knew him. Well, what to do next, eh? I had a full load and only so much time before the tide turned. I had to go on, couldn't heave to anywhere. So I laid him out decent and put a tarpaulin over him to keep the gulls from pecking at him, and took him along with us. It seemed the civil thing to do, seeing as I knew him.'

'If you hadn't recognised him, would you have thrown him back in the river for someone else to find?' asked Morris dourly.

'Ah!' returned Mr Midge with a wink. 'That'd be telling, wouldn't it?' Then he added virtuously, 'O'course not! I knows my Christian duty and my responsibilities as a citizen. Five generations of lightermen I come from. You learn to respect the river and all that happens on it. Finding drowned creatures: dogs, cats, a donkey once . . . that's all in the way of things and no need to worry about them. But a yooman being – you can't ignore that, can you?'

There was nothing more to be learned here. We thanked Mr Midge for his help, advised him to go back to Wapping station to ask about a finder's fee, and refused a renewed offer to send one of the nippers down to the pub with a jug.

Outside, it seemed colder, danker, and foggier after our brief time in the Midge family's cosy parlour. There were few people about so that the street was unusually quiet. Nevertheless, my ear caught the scrape of a boot against a cobblestone and a rattle, as if the stone had been dislodged and rolled away. The sound seemed to come from opposite the Midge house.

'Did you hear that?' I asked the sergeant quietly.

We both stood still and strained our ears. Ribbons of fog swirled past. In among it, I thought a shape moved, large but formless. I whispered to Morris to ask if he'd seen anything.

But he said he hadn't. 'Fog plays tricks, sir,' he said. 'You could imagine we had ghosts all around us, if you had a fancy.'

'Not a ghost, too solid,' I returned. 'Is there anyone there?' I called.

But another wait of a few minutes in the cold dank air rewarded us only with silence. I sighed.

'There is nothing more to be done now, Morris. Let's go home.'

We set off again, apparently alone in our foggy world, but twice I paused and looked back, peering into the dense grey mass.

'Somebody following, sir?' whispered Morris.

'It's just a feeling.'

'Know what you mean,' said Morris. He, too, had

more than once in his career experienced that tingling between the shoulder blades and at the back of the neck that tells a trained officer there is someone tracking him.

We proceeded onward, stopping once more to no avail.

'He's a clever fellow,' murmured Morris. 'When we stop, he stops.'

'But he's there,' I muttered.

'Aye, sir, he's there,' agreed Morris.

We had reached the parting of our ways. 'This will confuse him,' I said. 'I'll see you in the morning, Morris.'

There were more people about now, distorted forms dodging one another or colliding if they weren't alert enough. The air was filled with muttered apologies and curses. If the stalker had tried to follow either Morris or myself now, he'd have given up. He, too, had probably set off home.

Elizabeth Martin Ross

It was a little before five that afternoon. Bessie, bringing in the coal scuttle from the yard, had set it down with a clang on the kitchen floor to announce, 'The fog's coming up, missus.'

I glanced at the window. Already the backyard had a misty veil hanging over it. It was too dark indoors to work by; but I did not want to light the gas mantles yet. Instead I lit a paraffin lamp and placed that on the kitchen table to enable us to set about the vegetables for that evening's supper. Bessie had fired up the kitchen range and the atmosphere was cosy. I hoped Ben would not be delayed and would be able to get home before outside conditions deteriorated.

At that moment, startling us both considerably, there came a rattle and knock at the kitchen door. Bessie and I looked at one another. We had not heard the creak of the door from the alley that gave access to the yard, nor any footsteps approach across the paved area.

'Who's that?' grumbled Bessie. 'I've just been out there and there was no one about!'

I went to the kitchen window and peered out. I could see no one. The knock came again at the kitchen door, more insistent. It also came from very low down. Bessie took up the poker from the range and held it ready as a weapon. Then we both approached the back door and I pulled it open.

A swathe of mist drifted in. But I still saw no one. Then, giving us both a shock, a voice spoke at the level of our knees.

'Good evenin'!' it piped.

We looked down and saw the figure of a small child, well wrapped up against the chill.

'Hullo!' said Bessie. 'Who are you, then? What do you want?'

'You got any rags?' demanded the childish treble. 'Any old clothes what you don't need no more?'

More and more thick mist was entering the kitchen and the pleasant warmth was fast evaporating.

'You had better come inside,' I said to the child.

Bessie gave me an 'old-fashioned' look and, turning to the infant, demanded, 'You ain't on your own, are you? Who are you with and where is he?'

'Our granddad,' said the child.

'Where is your granddad?' demanded Bessie again.

'Going down the 'ouses on the other side of the road,' said the little girl, as we now saw the speaker to be.

Reluctantly Bessie stood aside to allow the caller into the kitchen, and shut the door behind her. We surveyed our visitor.

She was so bundled up in a mixture of clothing and shawls that she resembled nothing so much as a parcel of rags herself, with overlarge boots at one end, and a pale, grime-streaked face, framed with tangled fair hair, at the other. The whole figure was topped by an adult woman's hat of felt, with a broken feather in it.

Bessie was still suspicious. 'How did you get into our yard? You're not tall enough to reach up to the latch on the door.'

'I stood on me box,' said the child immediately.

'Box? What box? I don't see no box!' snapped Bessie.

'What is your name?' I interrupted Bessie's inquisition.

'Sukey,' said the infant. Then, returning to her purpose with a businesslike determination, 'We need old clothes, anythin'. Rags is better than nothing.'

Bessie, still holding the poker, had gone to the window and was peering into the evening gloom. 'He might be out there,' she said warningly, to me. Then, to the child, 'We've got nothing for you. You clear off!'

'No, wait!' I put out a hand to stop Bessie, who was

making to open the back door again and eject the visitor. I had remembered what Ben had told me of the old clothes' dealer he'd encountered recently, with a young child among the rags on the cart. Of the child, I asked, 'Your granddad wouldn't be known as Raggy Jeb, would he?'

The child scowled at me and didn't reply.

'It's all right,' I assured her. 'My husband knows of your granddad.' I turned to our maid. 'Bessie! Go upstairs and fetch down those two old shirts of the inspector's.'

'I was going to cut them up for polishing cloths,' objected Bessie.

'If the child was sent out to collect, she will be in trouble if she goes back to her grandfather empty-handed,' I whispered.

'Oh, all right,' said Bessie ungraciously. She handed me the poker. 'But you keep tight hold of that while I'm gone, missus. She could be sent in ahead as a decoy. Thieves do that, you know! I'll bolt this door here, so no one can rush in, once you're on your own.'

'Yes, yes, Bessie. Just go and get the shirts. It won't take you more than five minutes. You sit down on that chair by the range and warm yourself, Sukey,' I added to the child.

Sukey clambered on to the wooden chair and sat there, with her short legs swinging, the over-large boots incongruous. Still the little businesswoman, she said, 'Shirts is all right. Lace is better. You got any lace?'

'No, Sukey, I don't have any lace. I do have some fruitcake. Would you like a piece?'

Sukey's eyes gleamed in her grimy face. 'Yus,' she said simply.

I cut a slice of cake and handed it to her. She grabbed it from me with a muttered, 'Fanks!'

'It is a very cold night for your grandfather to bring you out!' I said. 'If he is around, I shall tell him so.'

'It's all right,' said Sukey indistinctly through a mouthful of cake. 'I always goes wiv our granddad.'

'How old are you?'

Sukey considered the question. 'I think I'm six,' she said. She frowned. 'I might be five but I think I'm six. Anyway, I ain't a baby.'

No, I thought with a sigh. She wasn't a baby. She was a child of the poor and the poor cannot have a childhood. As soon as they are able, they are put to some work. Ben, at six, had been sent down a coal mine. There were households aplenty where the women earned money doing 'piecework', such as hemming plain handkerchiefs or sewing sets of buttons on to cards. Little girls no older than Sukey were set to help add to the day's quota. As the day grew late, and the child tired, she would often be 'tied up'. This meant attaching her to the furniture in a standing position so that she could not fall asleep over the work.

Sukey was carefully picking up cake crumbs that had fallen on to her lap and transferring them to her mouth. She was such a frail little thing that I wondered when she had last had a proper meal. She would grow up stunted and old before her time, I thought sadly. But her grandfather probably did his best to take care of her, even if he did take her out on such a cold and clammy night as this.

'My husband says your granddad lets you ride on his cart,' I said. 'He said you were tucked in under the old clothing when he met you both.'

'S'warm . . .' mumbled Sukey through the last crumbs.

'I would have thought it might be a bit fusty – smelly.' I didn't know if 'fusty' was in her vocabulary.

Sukey looked at me, clearly perplexed. She was used to the smell of the old clothes and thought nothing of it. 'Well, it is kind of him, anyway', I said hurriedly. 'Is he a kind man, Sukey?'

'Yes,' said Sukey. 'He looks after us when my pa is away.'

'You have brothers and sisters?'

'I got one brother. I had a sister but she took a fever and died.'

'I'm sorry. Where does your papa go when he – er – goes away?'

I suspected he answer might be that he went to prison from time to time.

But Sukey said, 'He goes to sea.'

'That is hard for your mother, to have him away so much.'

'It *don't matter*,' said Sukey patiently, 'Because we got our *granddad*.' Perhaps to underline that I was worrying about nothing and her grandfather was adequate in all circumstances, she added, 'He give a drunk woman a ride the other night, on the cart.'

'So you had to squeeze in with the . . . drunken lady?'

'No,' she shook her head. The movement dislodged her hat and she put her hands to straighten it. 'Granddad sent me off to the pub to wait for him, while he helped the drunk woman.'

'The poor woman had no friends to help her?'

Sukey frowned. 'I fink she was on her own. She must have had a skinful if she couldn't walk. Pa had to give a hand. I didn't see her,' she added regretfully. 'I heard Pa telling our ma about it later.'

'And do you have a grandmother, too?' I asked.

Sukey scowled. 'I don't see her much. She's our pa's ma. Pa takes us to see her sometimes, when he's home, but she asks him for money and he don't have any – and she never has cake!' she concluded with a wistful look at our cake tin on the kitchen table.

I took the hint and cut her another slice.

Bessie clattered back downstairs as Sukey was finishing this second helping. She was carrying the old shirts bundled in her arms and also two small items in a colourful pink.

'What are those?' I asked.

'Woollen mitts,' said Bessie defiantly. 'I knitted 'em for myself but she can have them.' She turned to Sukey and held up the pink mittens. 'Here, see these? These aren't for your granddad, they're for you, understand? They will be a bit big, but you can put your hands in and pull them up over your sleeves. They'll keep your hands warm.'

Sukey obediently held out her hands for Bessie to put the mittens on them. I have to admit, I was hard put not to laugh, for the poor child was already such a mix of clothing that the mittens added a final incongruous touch.

I was reminded how, in winter, children will put an old hat on a snowman, and stick a clay pipe in its mouth.

'Now then,' said Bessie briskly. 'You can be off back to your granddad. I'll see you out!'

She opened the back door and pushed Sukey ahead of her into the gathering murk. I heard the slam of the door into the alley. Moments later, Bessie was back.

'She has got a box,' she announced. 'It's only a cardboard one and not very big. But it's strong enough to support her weight. She's dragging it down the alley and stopping to climb on it at every back gate, so that she can reach the latch.'

'Poor child,' I said. 'It was kind of you, Bessie, to give her your mittens.'

'They worked up too small for me, anyway,' said Bessie gruffly. 'Now then, let me get on with them carrots.'

Much later that evening, after supper, Ben and I sat before our parlour fire and he told me of his day.

'I have lost Harry Parker. He was a valuable witness and I was remiss in not questioning him more closely.'

'So you are sure it is not an accident he was in the river?'

Ben hunched his shoulders. 'There is such a thing as coincidence, but in murder investigations it doesn't show up often. I have my own theory. Someone saw Harry as a threat or a serious problem. Parker was very short of money. Let us suppose he had seen something, or heard or knew in some way of something. Instead of keeping dangerous knowledge to himself – or telling the police – he went to another person; and asked that person to pay a price for his silence. Perhaps we'll never know.

'I thought, if I insisted, he'd stay tight as a clam. If I waited, he might either get careless and let slip a piece of information; or so frightened that he would come to me rather than risk his chances alone. But through waiting I missed my chance, and gave a killer his. So, there it is.' He heaved a sigh and added quietly, 'He is out there, Lizzie. He watched Midge's house while we were there tonight. He followed us when we left. Morris agreed.'

I shivered at the image of the two officers walking through the fog-bound streets, knowing that someone tracked them, unseen.

To dismiss the uncomfortable thought, I said, 'Speaking of coincidences, you recall you told me of Jeb Fisher, the rag-picker?'

Ben looked up, surprised. 'What of him?'

I related Sukey's visit.

Ben looked annoyed. 'I meant to fix a stronger bolt on that alley door. But no bolt, however strong, is any good if it's not used. Tell Bessie, that door is to be bolted on this side all the time.'

'Yes, I'll make sure it is. But, Ben, it was such a sad thing to see a little child out on a night like this, dragging a cardboard box along to stand on.'

'There are children her age in worse circumstances. She has a family and she lives with them in some sort of hovel. Others are out sleeping in doorways. I believe her grandfather looks after her in his own way, and probably loves her. You say he cares for the family when her father goes to sea?'

'So she says. There is another grandparent, her father's mother and not Raggy Jeb's wife. I gather this grandma isn't so popular in the family because she doesn't help out. Quite the opposite! She asks Sukey's father for money whenever she sees him. Sukey told me Raggy Jeb took a drunken woman on his cart the other night, so it seems he is a kindly soul, and not just within his family.'

Ben looked up sharply. 'A drunken woman? Which night?'

'I have no idea. Her father had to help put her on the cart, so he must be home from his latest voyage. Sukey didn't see the woman. She was sent off to wait in the pub.'

Ben tapped his fingers on the table in thought. 'A drunken woman, incapable, possibly unconscious . . . Not, in fact, unlike . . .'

With a burst of enthusiasm he said, 'Suppose some conveyance like that were used to move Clifford's body? It wouldn't be difficult to find one in that part of town. There must be handcarts and barrows of all sorts around, used during the day by costermongers, fish sellers, and scavengers like Raggy Jeb. The owners wouldn't be plying their trade at that hour of the evening and their barrows and carts would be available to borrow.'

A silence fell; during which Ben was lost in his thoughts until, suddenly, he looked up. 'You gave her my old shirts? What was wrong with those shirts? They had plenty of wear in them!'

Chapter Thirteen

LATER THAT evening, after I had persuaded Ben that the shirts really had been too frayed for an inspector of police to wear, we fell to talking of the Wellings family again. More specifically of Frank and Patience; and Ben's request that I would not go back to Dorset Square – or not for a while.

'It puts me in a difficult position, don't you see, Lizzie dear?' he asked anxiously. 'There is Superintendent Dunn telling me you must not interfere—'

'I have not interfered!' I had interrupted, annoyed at the unjust accusation.

'No, of course not! But, Lizzie, it is enough that Carterton seems to believe he can waltz into Scotland Yard whenever he feels like it, and quiz me about an investigation. At least that is direct, unlike his using you, which was underhand.' He raised a hand to stem my protest. 'Yes, it was. He has not the right to employ your help, either to learn anything about police business, or to act as his accomplice with regard to your Aunt Parry.'

I still had my mouth open to deny Frank had manoeuvred me. But then I thought to myself that, probably,

Frank had done just that. It was ever Frank's way to make use of others. So I only said, 'Mr Dunn would not object to my visiting Patience in Goodge Place? That is a family matter. Frank is to marry her, after all.'

'No, no, go to Goodge Place, by all means,' said Ben. But he added, 'If that young fellow, Edgar Wellings, shows his face while you are there, take good note of anything he says, won't you? Or let me know of anything at all that you should hear or notice while you are there. Anything you think might be of interest to me.'

Aha! I thought. So Frank Carterton is not the only one seeking to make use of me. I am to spy on the Wellings family on behalf of Scotland Yard.

By the following afternoon the fog, which had begun lifting in mid-morning, had completely dispersed. The London fog is like that: sometimes it can last two or more days and the world seems to have come to a halt. But now, though it remained cold and dull, it was dry and as clear as London air ever is of a wintertime when every chimney is putting forth smoke. I had been wondering how Patience was managing under the strain. It seemed a good idea to take advantage of the better conditions and what daylight was left before the early dusk fell. I dressed in my best and set out for Goodge Place.

I found the household in a great to-do. Patience's parents and her two aunts, Amelia and Caroline, were due to arrive at any moment.

'This is not a good time for me to call,' I apologised.

'But it is! I am so glad you are here, Lizzie,' said Patience. 'Do come into the back parlour.' She seized my arm and towed me towards the room. In a conspiratorial whisper, she added, 'We are less likely to be disturbed here, although my Aunt Matilda is running all over the house, fussing about the arrangements. One moment she is upstairs making sure the beds have all been aired. The next moment she is in the kitchen conferring with Cook about the dinner. She has twice sent round to the butcher for extra meat and to the baker for white bread. I am sure we could feed an army, not just my family.'

I could hear Mrs Pickford's voice for myself, echoing from upstairs. 'But there must be enough towels! Lucy, do go and look in the cupboard. No, no, not those. They are worn and whatever would my sister Wellings think?'

'What about Edgar?' I asked, when Patience had shut the door. 'Will he be coming today, or is he too busy at the hospital?'

'He says he is too busy at the hospital. But he will have to come this evening and dine with us all.' Patience gazed at me in despair. 'And then, oh Lizzie, then it will be a time of reckoning. As soon as dinner is over, Papa and Uncle Pickford will take Edgar into the study and, as my uncle says, "sort the matter out, once and for all".'

'Edgar must be expecting that,' I said. 'He can't be surprised. He has got himself into this scrape, after all. At least the financial worry will be taken care of, won't it? Your father will settle his debts?'

'Oh, yes,' said Patience. 'He will do that. It isn't the money that is worrying Edgar now – although he will get a terrible lecture on his ways. It will be mortifying for him. But far worse will be news of the murder investigation.

You see, my parents have not yet been told *any* of that. Learning that Edgar has been gambling, that he has run up debts and been borrowing money; all that will be bad enough! But they must also be told that Edgar was marched off to Scotland Yard by Inspector Ross.'

'Ah, I see,' I said. It would be a horrifying shock to the Wellings family. I wondered how they would cope. One thing did occur to me. 'Patience, my dear,' I said. 'Please do try and prevent your father going to Scotland Yard and demanding to see my husband. It is enough that your Uncle Pickford went. Ben is very busy with this case and it doesn't help to have people bothering him for information that he really cannot give them. Frank has been to see Ben, you know. I don't think Ben can do with any more interruptions.'

'I will do my best,' said Patience dolefully. 'But they pay no attention to me, you know. When they find out that Edgar is being treated as a suspect in a murder inquiry . . . when they learn all about his having gone to a moneylender . . . when they learn about the awful thing that happened to Mrs Clifford . . . My father's first instinct will be to rush to Scotland Yard for information. My mother will be utterly distraught. My aunts will be in hysterics. They will all insist that Papa do something.' Patience fell back in her chair and gazed at me in despair. 'Whatever shall *I* do?'

'My dear, other than persuade your father not to trouble Ben, *you* don't have to do anything!' I told her firmly. 'It is Edgar who is in a pickle, not you.'

'But I am!' Patience sat up with a start and waved her

hands. 'A different pickle, if you like, but it has to do with Edgar's problems. My parents must be told that my marriage to Frank is delayed because of it. Mrs Parry insists and, you know, Frank has to listen to her. Until the murderer is found and Edgar's name cleared, there can be no wedding. My poor mother will be so worried and upset. Papa, too. On top of the debts, the murder, Scotland Yard's involvement, now the wedding uncertain, oh, it will be too much for them. How I wish my aunts weren't coming, too. They do interfere dreadfully and always have such a lot to say about everything. And it really isn't their business, you know.'

'Are neither of them married?' I asked.

'Neither of them,' said Patience. 'Aunt Caroline was engaged but her fiancé was sent by his company to India, to oversee some business there, and he went down with a fever and died. Aunt Caroline has worn half-mourning ever since.'

'That is very sad,' I said.

'Well, yes, at first it was,' agreed Patience. 'But it was all twenty years ago; and to keep on wearing mauve and grey, or purple when she wants to look grand . . . I believe she does it to draw attention.'

'I see. Will Frank be here to dine this evening?'

'Oh, no,' said Patience. 'It is to be a family conference. Frank isn't exactly family because he and I are not yet married. Perhaps,' added Patience, tears coming to her eyes, 'we never shall be!'

'Frank is a man of his word, Patience,' I told her firmly. 'I do not say that Frank doesn't have his . . .

shortcomings. But he says he will stand by you and he will. Of that you can be absolutely certain.'

'I do believe it,' said Patience in a small voice. 'Dear Frank is so loyal. He is the kindest, sweetest man. But, do you see, he has a fine career to make and he cannot make it if my family's troubles drag him into a scandal. If Edgar— if Edgar were to get into even more trouble, I should be obliged to release Frank from our engagement. I cannot let him ruin his life because of me.'

'Pull yourself together, Patience!' I ordered her. 'This is no time to go to pieces.'

Nor was it; for a tremendous hubbub broke out.

'They are here!' cried Patience, running to the parlour door and throwing it open.

The house seemed to be full of people; not only that, but their luggage, too. There was a quantity of it: trunks and hatboxes, various mysterious bundles and a picnic hamper. The stout boy with the brass buttons and two maids were busy gathering up the luggage to take it upstairs. Outside the house, through the window, I glimpsed two four-wheeled cabs trotting off.

Some of the party had already spilled into the drawing room, but remaining in the hall were two amply proportioned ladies, one clad in a virulent shade of violet. They were divesting themselves of bonnets and shawls. This revealed both of them to be laced as tightly as could be into their corsets. That, combined with the effort of travel and the emotion of reunion, resulted in both of them being very red in the face, and perspiring. They mopped their brows as they chattered of their journey, talking over one another and not waiting to hear if anyone replied.

Otherwise, they bore a striking resemblance to one another. They had round, good-natured faces framed with false curls. I was secretly glad that I had been warned of Caroline's taste for mauve and purple, as it would enable me to remember which of the sisters she was. Neither of them was very tall but both were vociferous.

'Such a throng of folk on the station! You would never believe it! The smoke from the engine came right into the carriage, and we had to veil our faces to shield ourselves from it. When we reached London, I swear, we never saw so many people running up and down the platforms. And the noise! You never heard the like. Well, how are you, Matilda love? How do you manage with all the crowds in London? We were terrified to see so many cabs and carriages, omnibuses and folk walking, well running . . . everything so helter-skelter . . .'

'My aunts,' whispered Patience unnecessarily.

But we had been spotted. With cries of delight the two ladies descended on Patience and embraced her. Then they turned their attention to me.

'This is Mrs Ross,' Patience introduced me. 'She is Frank's cousin. Lizzie, allow me to present my Aunts Briggs. This is my Aunt Amelia and this' (turning to the lady in violet) 'my Aunt Caroline.'

'Bless me,' exclaimed Aunt Amelia. 'Dear Frank's cousin! We are pleased to meet you, aren't we, Caroline?'

'We've not met any of dear Frank's family, have we, Patience? It's lovely to make your acquaintance, Mrs

Ross,' gushed Caroline. 'Frank is such a splendid lad, and so clever, and we are so looking forward to seeing him married to our Patience here. We tell her all the time what a lucky young woman she is, don't we, Amelia?'

'I am also very pleased that Frank and Patience are to be married, Miss Briggs,' I told her. It was not for me to tell them of Mrs Parry's objections.

'Now, Mrs Ross,' declared Amelia, 'you must come and meet our sister Dorothy, Patience's mamma, and her husband, Walter.'

'I am looking forward to meeting them both,' I told them. 'But to tell you the truth I was just about to leave. I have another call—'

'But you cannot go without meeting Dorothy and Walter! They are in the drawing room, come along.'

So I was borne along into the drawing room, wedged between the two ladies, Amelia in front of me and Caroline behind. Both wore full crinolines so there was no other way of proceeding. Patience followed at the tail of the procession. In the drawing room I found Mr and Mrs Pickford, with a lady and gentleman. The man was tall and rather distinguished-looking. This must be Mr Wellings. An anxious-looking lady of faded prettiness, and slighter build than her sisters, must be mother to Patience and Edgar.

Introductions were made and much more chatter followed. Eventually, Mrs Wellings asked if my husband and I were to come to dinner that evening with, perhaps, Frank and others of his family?

At this, such consternation showed on the faces of Mr

and Mrs Pickford that I had to speak up loudly and insist that, alas, my husband and I were unable to come to dine that evening. But I was sure we should all meet again. In the meantime, I really had to leave . . .

They all expressed regret. As I was ushered out into the hall by Patience, I heard Walter Wellings ask, 'Well, now, brother-in-law! What has happened that we must all of us come running down to London, eh?'

As the front door closed on me, I heard, from the street, a sudden outbreak of female shrieks and wails. Anyone else passing by would have thought all the ladies in the house under attack – or that a fire had broken out. I guessed the news had been broken that the marriage was delayed. How they would all react when told of Edgar's debts and the murder, I dreaded to think.

Inspector Ben Ross

I was pleased to see the fog lift by midday. It interferes with business of all kinds and with police work in a dozen ways. The morning was quiet. Dunn called me in and asked how the investigation was going. I told him that we had unfortunately lost a prime witness, the man who had discovered the body.

'Drowned, eh?' grumbled Dunn. He scratched his head of thick, stiff hair. Even the damp air had not made it lie flat. It was as much like a brush as ever. 'Foul play?' he asked abruptly.

'Impossible at the moment to say, sir. There are no marks upon the body other than what one might expect.

It's a fortunate thing for us that the lighterman, Midge, recognised the dead man when he and his assistant hauled him aboard.'

'I don't like coincidences,' growled Dunn.

'There is nothing against Midge,' I said. 'I had Biddle check our records. Besides, Morris and I visited the man in his home last night. He appears a decent, hard-working fellow. He has a family. The house is as neat as a new pin.'

'Yes, yes . . .' said Dunn, waving away my description of the Midge family household. 'Well, then, let us say that coincidences do happen. But how did Parker come to be in the water, eh? He was an important witness. You told me you thought there was more he could tell you, that he was holding something back. Is that what killed him?'

'It is possible someone wanted to stop his mouth, sir. In fact, I feel that is the case, but I have no proof of any kind to set before you, or the coroner. To tell you the truth, I have a fancy someone watched Midge's house while we were there. It could have been a curious neighbour. It was too dark and too foggy to make anything out. But whoever it was followed us for quite a way when we left. We couldn't see him, you understand, but Morris felt his presence, too.'

Dunn nodded. He understood.

'The fellow in charge of the morgue is confident it is a simple drowning; and he's seen any number of bodies taken from Father Thames.'

'But you are not?' Dunn squinted at me.

'My instinct, like yours, sir, is that there must have been foul play. To lose Parker now, when I had renewed my interest in him? I don't think it's a coincidence. Nevertheless, there are other possible explanations and I know I mustn't dismiss any of them out of hand. It could be a straightforward accident. He could have drunk too much and stumbled into the water on his way home. Also, he expressed concern to me, regarding his room-mates. He was obliged to share lodgings with two others. He said he did not like the look of either of them. But if they had set about him, I would expect to find more injuries on the body. Inspector Phipps has sent a constable to the lodging house in question. He does not expect to learn anything of interest.'

'If the police have come asking questions, Parker's roommates will have vanished,' Dunn said. 'Now, then! About young Edgar Wellings. We should be seen to be doing more about him. The public does not expect an obvious suspect to be going about his business without any hindrance from us. What's more, I do believe that the hospital authorities, when they do find out, will be angry they weren't told at once that one of their doctors was in such serious trouble. They must be informed, Ross. There is a prima facie case for charging him.'

'With respect, sir, it is weak when it comes down to detail. If we arrest him it will be, frankly, because we have no other suspect. If only we had the missing IOUs. That would give us a list of likely persons! All of them would have wanted to be free of Mrs Clifford.' I paused.

'The entire family is about to descend on Goodge Place. I do not envy young Wellings. He will probably be wishing we had arrested him and locked him in a cell where his furious relatives can't reach him.'

Dunn snorted. 'Perhaps, so. But I shall be contacting the hospital. They will wish to suspend him from his duties, pending our investigations, I dare say. But he can expect no less.'

I had hoped to avoid this; but I had to agree that the superintendent was right. We had not found another suspect. Bart's must be told that the shadow of a violent crime lay over one of their young doctors; not a man to have treating the sick and vulnerable until he was completely cleared of all wrongdoing. The world, however, cannot always wait. It would not have surprised me if Bart's dismissed Wellings outright, here and now.

'He has still not been charged, sir!' I protested. 'His behaviour has been reckless in the extreme and foolish. But he claims that when he left that house, Mrs Clifford was alive. She was found nearly half a mile away. How could he have transported her, dead or dying, to Skinner's Yard?'

'He could have attacked her and then bitterly regretted it. He saw she was alive, but injured and in need of medical help. He could have set off with her to seek assistance.'

'He is a doctor, sir!' I clung to my defence of the wretched Wellings. 'He could have treated her there himself at the house. Called on her maid, whom he must have known slept in the attic, and between them they could have got the poor woman to her bed. Then he could have sought help.'

'And, when she died, he'd have found himself charged with causing her death and not a jot of defence. Caught with her blood on his hands!' snapped Dunn. 'Come, come, Ross, he's lucky not to be sitting in a cell as we speak. That uncle of his was right to be surprised we hadn't arrested the fellow and locked him up. That, by rights, is what we should have done. The longer he remains free to wander about at will, and no one any the wiser in the hospital where he works, the more indefensible our lack of action appears. Especially following the death of the witness, Parker. If the gentlemen of the press find out we have a suspect and have not charged him, I can imagine what they will do with that!'

The press would have a field day, anyway, I thought to myself, once the news gets out, as it must when Bart's becomes involved.

Dunn had been watching my face and read my misgivings. 'I will take care of it, Ross. If Mrs Ross complains, refer her to me,' he added.

'My wife will understand,' I told him. It was true; she would do so. But she would not like it.

Chapter Fourteen

Elizabeth Martin Ross

WHEN BEN came home that evening he was downcast. The investigation had stalled. Worst of all, from my own personal viewpoint, Superintendent Dunn intended to inform St Bartholomew's Hospital that one of their junior doctors, Edgar Wellings, was a prime suspect in a case of murder. Patience would be sure to call on my support at once. It would not just be Patience who would be distraught. I could find myself with the whole family on my hands.

'But you don't think Edgar pushed Harry Parker into the river, surely?' I protested.

'I don't know who is responsible for that. I am certain in my own mind that Parker's death is suspicious, even without the physical evidence of a fatal blow.' A thought apparently struck Ben because he clicked his fingers and added, 'See here, if I had locked up young Wellings, he would be completely out of the picture with regard to the death of Parker. Now, unlikely though it seems, we can't discount him. I was remiss in not keeping him under my eye. The wretched fellow is completely unreliable. I should have ignored the possible embarrassment to Carterton and just done as I would with any other suspect.'

'Oh, this is ridiculous!' I protested.

We had squabbled about it until bedtime. Then, as it is a point of honour with us not to end the day with cross words hanging in the air between us, we called a truce. We even found something we could agree on.

'That fellow Wellings is a troublesome rascal,' said Ben forcefully. 'And I wish he had gone to follow his medical studies somewhere other than in London, the further away the better. Edinburgh, I believe, has an excellent school of medicine.'

That made me smile, despite my worries. 'Why not send him to Europe, to study in France or in Germany?' I asked.

'Even better!' said Ben.

We could not know, when Ben left for Scotland Yard the following morning, that Edgar had not yet done with causing everyone problems, not least himself.

It had begun to rain. Bessie and I were set to make a weekly trip to the markets. We had drawn up a list of what was needed, supplied ourselves with baskets, and dressed in suitable outdoor wear, with galoshes over our boots, and were all ready to go. Then came a thunderous hammering on the front door as someone attacked the knocker with such vigour, I wondered the brass did not jump off and fall to the ground.

'Who's that?' demanded Bessie, setting off in the direction of the summons. 'We're not all deaf here, are we? Oy!' she yelled. 'Stop that! I'm coming!'

I had run into the hall behind her; because such a summons must mean bad news in some form. I admit my heart was in my mouth, because I am always afraid, as any police officer's wife must be, that some misfortune has befallen her husband. But when Bessie pulled the door open and prepared to confront the impatient visitor, we saw, standing in the rain outside, Patience Wellings. Behind her was a hansom cab, its driver hunched on its perch enveloped in a waterproof cape.

'Oh, you are here, thank goodness!' said Patience, seeing me. She turned and waved to the cabman, who whistled to his horse and clattered away.

'Whatever is the matter?' I asked her, pulling her into the house.

'Oh, Lizzie,' Patience began wildly, 'you will say, I know, that I ought not to have come alone in a hansom cab because a lady shouldn't, but there wasn't a closed cab to be had, and I had to come at once!'

'Let me take your wet cape, miss,' said Bessie, ever practical.

Divested of her cape, Patience entered our parlour still in a state of disarray. Her hair had become unpinned beneath her hat and tumbled in curls either side of her flushed cheeks. She did look very pretty and animated.

'You had no problem coming here?' I asked. 'No, er, no one tried to hail your cab or call out?'

Patience frowned. 'In fact, twice gentlemen did. One

man waved his cane at the cab and called out "Halloo!" as they shout when hunting a fox. It was very odd, because clearly they could see the cab had a fare.'

I was not surprised that any gentleman walking alone, and seeing the open-fronted cab bowl past with just the one unescorted pretty young female in it, had gained the wrong impression. I persuaded her to sit down and calm herself before beginning to tell me what was wrong.

'Edgar has gone. He is missing!' Patience threw her arms out wide.

My heart sank. 'When? How? Are you sure?' I asked all three questions in quick succession.

'Absolutely sure. He can't have gone very far, Lizzie, because he has no money and, oh Lizzie, I am so afraid he has been driven to do something terrible and we shall find his dead body in the river!'

'Pull yourself together, Patience. Edgar would not do anything so foolish. Just wait a moment,' I told her. I went to the kitchen to ask Bessie to make tea and found the kettle was already boiling.

'What's the young gent done now?' asked Bessie in a stage whisper.

'I don't know. I don't think we shall be going to the market today, somehow.'

'Tea is coming,' I assured Patience on my return to the parlour. I sat down, facing her across our hearth. The fire had not yet been lit, but there was residual warmth in the room from the evening before, and it was not too cold. Patience, in any case, would not have noticed if there had been icicles hanging from the ceiling. 'Tell me the whole story from the beginning,' I urged her. 'Or from the time I left Goodge Place, following the arrival of your family.'

Patience drew a deep breath. 'Well, after you went, my Uncle Pickford told Papa and Mamma – and my aunts – that a difficulty had arisen. Of course, they all wanted to know in what way. My Aunt Pickford managed to get in an answer before my uncle, for once, and said they should not be unduly alarmed, but although Edgar would be joining us all for dinner, Frank would not. The engagement was still on, but the wedding preparations must be delayed. Edgar had found himself in some difficulty and as Frank's position as a Member of Parliament was very important and public, he could not be involved in any scandal.'

'That was when they all started shrieking,' I said. 'I heard them from outside, on the pavement.'

'They all went quite mad,' said Patience simply, 'or so you would have thought. It was the word "scandal" that caused the most trouble. Uncle Pickford was cross and shouted, "See what you have done, Matilda! I told you to let me handle it."

'Then he took Papa into the study to explain the situation to him. Aunt Matilda and I stayed in the drawing room; and my aunt had to explain it, anyway, to my mother and Aunts Briggs. I don't know which bit was the worst. The gambling had them throwing up their hands in horror, then came the borrowing of money from a moneylender. At that point we had to stop and fetch smelling salts to Mamma. But the worst was yet to come;

and Aunt Matilda couldn't bring herself to speak of it. I had to tell them – about the murder, I mean. And Edgar being obliged to go to Scotland Yard and make a statement. Aunt Caroline fainted right away. Aunt Amelia burst into tears and my poor mother was struck dumb. She sat, frozen, unable to speak or move. We feared she'd had some sort of stroke. But after we had rubbed her hands and bathed her forehead with cologne and administered more smelling salts, she finally spoke, in a whisper. She asked, "Where is he?"

'Aunt Matilda and I assured her that Edgar would be coming to dine that evening. He was not locked in gaol or anything like that. That did calm my mother and aunts considerably; and both aunts said they were sure Edgar would be able to explain what was clearly a terrible mistake. Oh, Lizzie, I wish now that Inspector Ross *had* arrested Edgar, because at least we should know where he was, and now we don't.'

I thought wryly that that was just what Ben had said the previous evening. Had Edgar been locked in a cell, he couldn't be suspected of more wrongdoing; nor could he have vanished as he apparently had done.

'When did you discover he was missing?' I asked. 'Really missing and not just failed to show his face.'

'The first indication was when he didn't arrive at the house to dine with us, last night,' sobbed Patience, her self-control completely dissolving.

Fortunately the tea arrived. Bessie and I managed to comfort her and she stilled her tears. After some minutes, and two cups of tea, she managed to continue, occasionally dabbing at her eyes and nose.

'We waited for him to join us, as arranged. Of course, we all talked of nothing else while we waited. But he still didn't come. Uncle Pickford consulted his watch and said it was very poor form for the boy to be late. We women all made excuses for him. We said, perhaps he had had difficulty finding a cab.

'We waited some while longer. Aunt Matilda began to fret about the dinner. Uncle Pickford grew very red in the face and Papa had turned very pale. My father is not a man who says a great deal, you understand. But he feels things deeply. I could tell how worried he was when we still received no message to explain what the delay might be. As you will understand, we all began to fear the worst. Aunt Caroline said she was sure Edgar had met with an accident in London's traffic. Aunt Amelia said perhaps the police had arrested him, after all, and he was in Newgate Prison, where he was sure to catch a fever. Mamma began to weep.

'At last Uncle Pickford declared that clearly Edgar had not the courage to face us all. That, and nothing more complicated, was the reason he had not shown his face. Uncle Pickford apologised to Papa, and said he (my uncle) should have foreseen the possibility. But really, he had not thought Edgar would let him down like this. He now regretted not bringing Edgar to the house that morning, and locking him in a room until the family arrived.

'Papa said Uncle Pickford could not have been expected to do that and ought not to blame himself. Eventually, Uncle Pickford sent out for a cab and took himself off to Edgar's lodgings. It is a place for young professional gentlemen. When he came back, it was to tell us that the landlady had not seen Edgar all evening. She took him up to Edgar's room, and all his things were still there. He had not packed or anything, and he must have returned from Bart's earlier because his stethoscope was lying on the table. But no one had seen him go out again, so he must have just slipped out and vanished. Uncle Pickford asked the other people in the house. No one had any idea where he might be.

'Mamma and the aunts asked what was a stethoscope, please, and was it decent? We explained it is a device used to listen to people's hearts and lungs. It is like an ear-trumpet but with a rubber tube attached to make it flexible. Aunt Caroline said that must be a great improvement on a doctor placing his ear on a lady's bosom. That was a very questionable business. Aunt Amelia agreed and said she'd never permitted any medical man such a liberty. It was high time someone invented another way to do it.'

Patience hissed in exasperation. 'It was ridiculous, Lizzie. I thought they would all fall to discussing modern medicine. So I called out, "What shall we do? Shall we tell the police?"'

'How was that received?' I asked.

'Very badly,' admitted Patience.

'"For G—d's sake, leave the police out of it!" cried Papa. He never uses profane language. I'd never heard it, and he was always saying to Edgar that he must mind his words when ladies were present. So he was clearly dreadfully upset and worried.

'Eventually, we all went into dinner without Edgar. No one felt like eating, not even Uncle Pickford. The roast was cold and the vegetables and the gravy had turned solid, but nobody cared, except Aunt Matilda who was in tears. In the end, we ladies all went up to bed. Papa and Uncle Pickford stayed downstairs talking for a long time. I fell asleep eventually, but woke very early this morning before it was properly light. I had heard wheels outside. I hoped it would be Edgar, coming to explain where he'd been all night. But when I looked out of my window, I saw Uncle Pickford and Papa getting into a four-wheeler, so they must have been going to look for Edgar again, probably to see if he'd returned to his lodgings.

'Breakfast was a miserable affair, like dinner. Worse, because only we women were there. Mamma was crying and the Aunts Briggs lamenting; and poor Aunt Matilda just didn't know what to do. She kept asking me how many I thought would be at home for lunch! In the end I suggested she have Cook prepare a cold collation, with perhaps hot soup. Then those who felt like eating could take what they wanted and, if Papa and Uncle Pickford were not there, nothing would spoil. Aunt Matilda cheered up a little at that and went off to consult with Cook.

'Then, my father and uncle returned. Edgar had not been at his lodgings all night. They had no news from him. So, Papa and my uncle set off for the hospital, hoping that he might be there. Even if he had decided he could not face us all the night before, if he was needed at work, he would go. Edgar is very conscientious.'

Somehow, 'conscientious' was not the word that leaped to my mind when I thought of Edgar Wellings, but I only nodded and asked, without much hope, 'And was he? At the hospital?'

'No,' said Patience miserably. 'But a very senior police officer was there, a Mr Dunn.'

'Superintendent Dunn? I know the gentleman,' I admitted. But my heart was sinking. So Dunn had stuck to his intention, described to Ben, of going to Bart's and telling whoever was in charge of junior doctors that Dr Wellings was in a spot of bother.

'Papa said that Dunn appeared to be a very decent fellow, but had to do his duty, and had done it, in telling the hospital about Edgar's involvement with a case of murder. So Edgar is suspended from work at the hospital; we don't know where he is; everyone is prostrate with grief and worry at Goodge Place; and I have come here, Lizzie, to ask you what we should do.'

'Well, it seems as though your father and uncle have done all that can be done,' I began.

Patience interrupted me. 'No, no! I mean what *we* – you and I – should do.'

'But what can we do?' I gasped, taken aback by her complete confidence that I would have the answer to the problem.

'Well, find Edgar, of course! And tell him to go to Goodge Place to apologise and explain himself. At least so we should all know he is safe, not drowned or . . . or done anything else desperate, like take poison.'

'Poison!' I exclaimed. 'Where would he find poison?'

'Anywhere!' said Patience firmly. 'It's not hard to find, is it? They put it down for mice and rats. Anyway, he works in a hospital. The dispensary there must be full of bottles of poison.'

There followed quite a long silence during which I racked my brains to find some ideas and Patience sat watching me hopefully. Finally, when I had worked out a plan that – though almost certainly doomed – would satisfy Patience for the moment, I spoke.

I began by explaining the difficulty of my own position in this. 'Through that meeting between your father and uncle and Superintendent Dunn at the hospital, Mr Dunn now knows that Edgar is missing. That means that time is not on our side, because he will almost certainly alert constables on the beat to look out for your brother. He would not be pleased to find out that you and I are conducting our own search. You see, Patience dear, Superintendent Dunn has already spoken to Ben, spoken very firmly, about the importance of my not interfering.'

'We're not interfering!' interrupted Patience. 'We're helping. We're going to find Edgar and bring him to his senses.'

'I agree with you. Anything I've ever done in the matter of an investigation has been done with discretion and to help. Unfortunately, what you or I would describe as "helping" is just what Mr Dunn will call interference in a police matter. He dislikes my "playing detective", as he calls it; and there is no reasoning with him. He is particularly sensitive on the issue because, though I say it myself, I have had some success in the past. Men do not like it, you know, when a woman has been able to do something they couldn't.'

'I wish I were as clever and practical as you,' said Patience wistfully. 'But, if we find Edgar, surely Mr Dunn will forgive you. In any case, neither you nor I need go to Scotland Yard in person. We just need to take Edgar to the door and watch that he goes inside. No one, neither Mr Dunn nor your husband, need be any the wiser. We'll tell Edgar that he must say he decided himself to come to the Yard. There!' Patience smiled at me with that serenity and confidence that I was, privately, beginning to find rather irritating.

'Perhaps,' I replied. 'Things seldom work out so well. Besides, I really don't have any idea where to look for your brother. He is at none of the places he ought to be: his lodgings, the hospital, Goodge Place. My only suggestion is that you and I return to Deptford and try and find some lead—'

'Lead?' interrupted Patience, puzzled by a technical term.

'Some clue, as to the identity of the real culprit. But we must be very, very careful, my dear. We cannot arouse the interest of Inspector Phipps at Deptford police station. That means we must not go near any constable, if we should see one. You must promise me, Patience, that you will follow my instructions. That is the condition on which I will go with you to Deptford and ask a few questions.'

I had no idea of whom I would be asking these questions. But Patience expected me to do something; and I would have tried. Then, when we failed to find any clue to where Edgar might be, or who might have killed Mrs Clifford, Patience might leave me in peace.

I saw, through the window, that it had stopped raining and even that a watery sun had emerged, which I decided to see as a blessing on our adventure. I went to tell Bessie to go up to the railway station and return with a four-wheeler cab. The money I had set aside for that week's groceries would now be spent elsewhere.

Sadly, Bessie did not find Wally's cab. But the cabman who came conveyed us to Deptford in good time. I asked him to set us down by the shops, as I didn't want to be seen arriving at the scene of the murder. The area was crowded; but no one took much notice of the two of us. I asked a respectable looking woman if she could direct us to the street. Fortunately she was able to do so.

As we walked there, Patience bubbled with enthusiasm and disastrous ideas. We should knock on every door in the street and ask if anyone had seen visitors, other than Edgar, to the Clifford house, that was the first of them.

Certainly not, I told her firmly. To begin with, the police would already have done that. Secondly, we should raise so much interest and gossip that Inspector Phipps would be sure to hear of it.

Well, then, suggested Patience next, how about if she should pretend to be taken faint and I knocked on a door to ask for a glass of water?

243

'The householder would suspect a criminal ploy,' I said. 'She would think some bullyboy lurked nearby who, once she had opened the door to admit us, would rush by her into the house, seize some valuables and rush out again.'

'Goodness,' said Patience in awe. 'Is everyone in London so suspicious?'

'Yes!' I said firmly, although I realised I had not taken my own advice when admitting little Sukey to my kitchen when she had come knocking at the door on that foggy night.

'Or,' I continued, 'the householder might think you and I are a brace of thieves, wheedling our way indoors.'

'We don't look like thieves,' protested Patience.

'Confidence tricksters don't look like criminals,' I retorted, 'or they would find no gullible marks.'

Patience was so impressed by my knowledge of criminal slang that she fell silent until we had almost reached the street. Then I saw something that made me stop and grasp her arm.

'See there!' I gasped.

On the other side of the street, someone else had been tempted out by the unexpected sunshine. A wheeled invalid chair was being propelled along the pavement by a young maidservant. The occupant of the chair was very elderly and well swathed in rugs. But both of us recognised him.

'That old gentleman,' whispered Patience, 'was in the crowd before the door of Mrs Clifford's house when we were there, with Edgar, asking to be allowed in.'

'It is Mrs Belling's friend, Mr Morton, it must be,' I told her. 'You remember. It was from him that Mrs Belling learned about Edgar leaving the scene of the attack, with Ben.'

'Yes, he wanted to hang poor Edgar!' said Patience indignantly.

I put my hand on her arm because I thought she might march across the road and harangue the old gentleman. 'Let me speak, say nothing!' I warned her. 'We might just learn something.'

I approached the old gentleman with some trepidation, conscious of Patience following close behind me. The maid, no doubt glad of a moment's rest, stopped propelling the chair immediately she saw my interest. The occupant looked up in surprise.

I saw that he was indeed a very sharp-looking old fellow. He must once have been very handsome, a Regency buck. His hair, though silver, was still thick, and his features lean, with a hawk nose. It put me in mind of pictures I had seen of the Duke of Wellington.

'I beg your pardon, sir,' I began. 'But I believe you are Mr Morton? Mrs Belling, whom I believe you know, mentioned you to us when we were visiting Mrs Parry in Dorset Square. I am Mrs Ross. Before my marriage I lived briefly with Mrs Parry and know Mrs Belling from that time.' I hoped I hadn't made an over-complicated explanation.

'Indeed, ma'am?' he returned. He did not sound discouraging exactly, but his gaze sharpened even more.

'Sir,' I pressed on, hoping I did not sound too

desperate, 'I understand – from Mrs Belling – that you have a nephew who is in the medical profession. This lady . . .' I extended my hand to bring Patience to the fore. 'This lady is Miss Wellings and she has a brother who studied medicine, I believe, with your nephew.'

The old fellow continued to survey me with his unsettling gaze as I set out my case. An awkward silence fell.

'Ross?' said the Mr Morton thoughtfully. 'That rings a bell.'

I realised that Mrs Belling, during the conversation she had had with Mr Morton about the murder, must have told him she had met a Scotland Yard detective by the name of Ross. It was quite likely that Mr Morton, for all his apparent isolation in Deptford, knew a great deal about me.

'There was a murder committed recently nearby here,' I continued. But that was as far as I got.

'Indeed there was, ma'am,' snapped Mr Morton, suddenly energetic. 'A dreadful business and shocking that it should happen here! I remember when Deptford was a very different place to what you see now. And,' his voice rose triumphantly, 'and I remember *you*, Mrs Ross! You called at the house, the scene of the crime, while the police were there. I was before the house and saw you there myself!' He shook his forefinger at me triumphantly.

'I was there, too, sir,' burst out Patience, unable to keep silent any longer.

Mr Morton turned his eagle eye on Patience and his manner softened. 'Bless me,' he said, 'so you were, my dear.' Then he grew stern again. 'It was no place for a young girl! And the murderer was with you, upon my soul, yes, he was. A young fellow! I knew him, too. My nephew had pointed him out to me on an earlier occasion.'

'But my brother is not a murderer!' she protested. 'Oh, sir, my brother has been wrongfully accused. He didn't do that dreadful thing!'

'Is he in Newgate?' demanded Mr Morton with interest.

'No, sir, he has not been arrested.'

'Why ever not?' cried Mr Morton, growing agitated again. 'Bless my soul! Does the police force of our capital not protect honest citizens? I thought that was Peel's idea in setting up the whole system? I had my doubts at the time, I remember. We managed very well before without them. The Bow Street Runners were very good fellows. There was proper punishment for criminals, too. More often than not they went to the gallows. I remember being taken, as a boy, to see a highwayman hang. That is the way to get it into a young lad's head that he must not commit crimes. Take him to watch a rogue kick at the end of a rope. Then he learns the lesson!'

Mr Morton had grown so overwrought I wondered if he would suffer some kind of apoplectic fit. Fortunately he now became more subdued, though he still clung to his argument, adding regretfully: 'They hang no one now except for murder, unless he is a proven traitor. And does the public feel any safer for it? No, ma'am, it does not!'

The system of law enforcement in his youth, described with such approval by the old gentleman, was indeed the very imperfect one that had led Sir Robert Peel to found our police force. But not everyone can be brought to accept modernisation.

His tirade had proved all too much for Patience, who now manoeuvred me aside and tackled the quarry directly. 'But what do you do when it is all a dreadful misunderstanding, as with my brother?' she demanded.

'That, my dear child, is why we have courts of law and judges. They decide on the matter.'

'But you would put an innocent man in the dock and let his reputation be utterly ruined?' Patience was clinging to her argument as fiercely as Mr Morton clung to his.

Short of seizing her arm and physically pulling her back, I was helpless to stop her now. The pair of us wrestling in the street in an unladylike manner would not impress Mr Morton. There was nothing I could do but let Patience have her head. We were by now beginning to attract attention. People slowed their footsteps as they reached us. A few had gathered some yards away, an urchin among them who was taking a particular interest. As Ben had often said to me in exasperation, Londoners love a free entertainment. If we stayed here much longer, we'd have a crowd.

'And now my poor persecuted brother is missing!' wailed Patience. 'We need to find him most urgently, sir. We would like to ask your nephew if he might have some idea where to look for him. My father and uncle have looked in all the obvious places and are asking all his friends and acquaintances. I cannot remain idle!'

'The obvious place to find him,' said Mr Morton

unkindly, 'should be in a gaol. That, Miss Wellings, is where your brother should be.'

'Oh, no, sir!' Then, to my astonishment, Patience sank gracefully in a cloud of billowing skirts to kneel at his side, and reached out her hands in a manner that was pure theatre but immensely impressive. The onlookers murmured their appreciation. The maid in charge of the invalid chair was entranced.

'Mr Morton, sir!' begged Patience. 'You will not refuse to help me? You surely wish to prevent a monstrous miscarriage of justice. Please, sir, I must find my brother and establish his innocence!' Tears started from her eyes and rolled down her flushed cheeks.

I did not know then, and don't know until this day, whether the tears fell unprompted, or whether Patience had, as the saying goes, 'turned on the waterworks'. But the effect of the sight on Mr Morton couldn't be ignored. There was this elderly man – no doubt a bit of rake in his young day – unexpectedly faced with a very pretty girl, with curls in charming disarray framing tear-stained cheeks. Holding out her hands to him in supplication, she was begging him to be her knight errant. He, who had started out today on his usual constitutional, round the familiar streets, expecting nothing more than the occasional salutation of a passing acquaintance.

'Good heavens, my dear!' he exclaimed. 'Now, now, this will never do. Dry your tears. Anything I can do, although I fear there is little . . .' He then caught sight of the growing crowd. 'We cannot discuss the matter here. Watkins!'

'Yes, sir?' replied the maid in charge of the bath chair.

'Take us home! Come along, my dear ladies. We shall discuss this in more suitable surroundings.'

So we set off in procession, much to the crowd's disappointment. The urchin tagged along with us until Watkins became aware of him, and told him sharply to 'Clear off!'

'Patience,' I whispered. 'Whatever you do, don't mention Frank.'

Mrs Belling had spoken of Mr Morton's house being one of the better residences in Deptford. It stood in a quiet side street, a fine, double-fronted, early Georgian building with a pillared portico. I saw a movement at a downstairs window as we arrived. Someone had been looking out for the master's return. Sure enough, the front door was opened to reveal a plump housekeeper in a frilled mobcap. She bustled forward to help her employer out of the chair and indoors. A sturdy footman arrived to manhandle the chair. Watkins, the maid, begged us to come in.

'The ladies will stay to lunch, Hammond,' Mr Morton informed the housekeeper.

I thought this must cause alarm in the kitchen where a meal for just one elderly invalid had been prepared. But the housekeeper merely said, 'Yes, sir.'

'Would you care to come with me, ladies?' asked Watkins.

She led us upstairs to a small bedroom, obviously not in use but equipped with a dressing stand and a mirror. Watkins relieved us of our outdoor things and spread them carefully on the bed. Then she waited while we peered into the mirror and straightened our hair, collars and cuffs. Finally, we were led away downstairs to a dining room.

It was at the back of the house and overlooked a long narrow garden where a statuette of Diana the Huntress presided over a winter scene of bare twigs and a carpet of wet leaves. Indoors, there had been some fast work on the part of the staff, and the table was already set for three.

'My doctor,' said Mr Morton sadly, 'does not permit me wine. But I can offer you both a glass of sherry.'

We assured him we would be more than happy with water. The luncheon menu was as might be expected in an invalid's household. There was a clear chicken broth, followed by poached fish with plain, boiled potatoes, and finishing with a baked rice pudding.

During lunch, Patience told her story in greater detail. She explained how her brother had been an excellent student, praised by all, and had passed his medical examinations with flying colours. Sadly, he had been led astray by some companions, something he now bitterly regretted. So came the gambling, the loss of money, the disastrous attempt to remedy matters by going to a moneylender.

Mr Morton listened attentively, only remarking that he'd seen many a family fortune lost at the gaming tables.

Edgar had not lost the family fortune, Patience assured him, only run up large debts. He had been unwilling to admit this to his father, and so had tried to make things right himself. She did not mention Frank Carterton at all, as I had warned her not to do. It was certain that the next time Mrs Belling visited her old friend Mr Morton she would hear an account of today's adventure. In turn, she would go straight back to Dorset Square and Mrs Parry to pass it all on. Aunt Parry's chief concern was that Frank should be kept out of any scandal. That was the important thing, as far as she was concerned; and the reason I had warned Patience not to mention his name.

It was bad enough that Aunt Parry would be displeased with me for taking Patience to Deptford to make inquiries. Aunt Parry disapproves of my detecting activities as much as Superintendent Dunn.

Luncheon was over and we retired to a small parlour to take tea. Mr Morton had now made his decision.

'Well, my dear ladies, I can give you the name and address of my nephew. He is Dr Henry Morton, the son of my late brother. He is in practice, as junior to an established colleague, in Egham.'

'Egham?' asked Patience. She turned to me. 'Where is it? Is it far away from London?'

'It is in Surrey and not so very far,' I told her. 'And we can take the train there from Waterloo.'

'I will give you a letter to take with you,' said Mr Morton. 'I will tell him I have spoken at length with you both about the matter and your inquiries have my approval.'

'Dear sir,' said Patience, grasping his hand. 'You have been so very kind and I am – my entire family – will be so grateful.'

'Well, well,' said Mr Morton who, by now, was looking pink-cheeked and cheerful. 'Anything to oblige! But I do not know if you will learn anything from Henry.'

Neither did I. I thought the whole expedition to Egham would prove a wild goose chase. But it helped Patience to think she was doing something in Edgar's cause.

When we were ready to leave, we came to say a final farewell to our kind host, and thank him. He, in turn, handed me the letter of introduction he had addressed to his nephew.

Mr Morton then cleared his throat and addressed me somewhat diffidently. 'Ah, Mrs Ross, the train journey to Egham will involve some pecuniary outlay . . .'

'Oh, I have plenty of money with me!' said Patience, overhearing. 'Please don't worry about that, sir. I made sure to bring enough because I did not know what might be involved in our search today.'

She held up her arm. From her wrist dangled a satin reticule, with bead embroidery, attached to her by a silk cord. I had noticed it earlier but assumed it held only a handkerchief and a phial of smelling salts, and perhaps some small coins. I assumed that anything more valuable would be safely stowed somewhere about her person.

Mr Morton and I gazed at her, equally appalled. 'Dear child!' cried Mr Morton. 'Have you been walking around London streets with large sums of money in that – that flimsy object?'

'Oh, yes!' Patience told him. 'To have it if needed, you know. I wanted to be sure.'

'Sure . . .' Mr Morton gasped. 'Sure to lose the lot to some cutpurse! Oh, dear, oh, dear. Well, no question about it, I shall send my footman, Bunce, to Egham with you for protection.'

We began to protest, but he was adamant. 'If I were a younger man, and fitter, I would escort you both myself. Alas, my health and years do not permit it. But Bunce will go with you, I insist.'

Chapter Fifteen

OUR EXPEDITION into Surrey began with Bunce, the footman, being sent out with orders to return with a clean four-wheeler cab.

'Examine the interior carefully, Bunce!' ordered Mr Morton. 'We cannot have ladies ruining their clothes on dusty seats.'

Bunce and a cab duly returned. Having been assured by the footman that he had examined the interior of the 'growler' with care and it was clean, Patience and I were permitted to take our leave of our host.

The first stage of our journey was by the cab back across the river to Waterloo Station. Bunce was a dark-haired fellow of about thirty with a cast in one eye. He said nothing on the journey; but one eye or the other seemed always to be on us. Under this double scrutiny Patience and I could not converse freely, so the whole trip passed in silence.

On the concourse, Bunce asked us to wait and disappeared.

Patience was nervous, fidgeting with the silken cord attaching the reticule to her wrist. Bunce was soon back, with return tickets for us all. Mr Morton, it transpired, had provided the money for these, despite – or perhaps because of – Patience's assurance that her reticule was full of cash. He had probably not wanted her to open it in a public place.

There were plenty of trains to take us. Patience cheered up a little and became more relaxed, despite her worries about her brother. I understood that she felt we were doing something, even if we failed to learn anything in Egham. It relieved her frustration at her own helplessness. She gazed from the window at the passing houses and countryside, chattering animatedly. I spent it mentally composing a speech to make to Dr Henry Morton, explaining why we felt we could involve him in Edgar's troubles. On our arrival, Bunce again instructed us to wait while he went to find a cab.

'Do you know where Dr Morton lives?' I asked him, as he was about to go on his errand.

'Yes, ma'am. But you will not be able to walk there. A lot of it is uphill.'

So away marched Bunce and in due course was back with a request we follow him to the cab.

'You know, Lizzie,' whispered Patience. 'It is so much easier with Bunce here to run these errands and look after us both. I feel we are being quite spoilt!'

'He is being very helpful,' I replied with less enthusiasm. My own feeling was not that we were being spoilt, but that we were being very efficiently monitored. Bunce would report back to his employer with details of every move we made.

'It's such a pity, Lizzie,' said Patience next, 'that I do find it so difficult to look him in the face.'

'Bunce?' I asked curiously. 'Because we are seeking your brother?'

'No, because I am not sure which eye to look at.'

The cab took us to a large pleasant house set back a little from the road. Bunce told the man to wait for us. When I protested, Bunce politely, but firmly, pointed out that we should not easily find another cab to take us back to Egham station. By now I was feeling more than a little annoyed with Bunce. It was not his fault. He had his instructions from old Mr Morton. But I am accustomed to make up my own mind when making inquiries, as I like to call my investigations. Nor do I like being watched.

A plaque on the front of the house by the entrance door announced the names of two medical men: Dr Ernest Appleforth and Dr Henry Morton. I asked the middle-aged woman who opened the door to us if Dr Morton were available; and if it would be possible to speak to him.

'It is not a medical consultation,' I hastened to explain. 'It is a private matter. I have a letter of introduction for him. If he is here, would you give it to him, please? We have come from London, so I do hope we can see him.'

The woman looked at me a little doubtfully, but picked up a silver tray from a side table. I placed Mr Morton's letter on it. We were then shown into a small parlour. The woman, some sort of housekeeper I supposed, left bearing the silver tray with the letter. The limpet, Bunce, had at last detached himself and disappeared, probably to the kitchen for refreshment. For the first time since leaving Deptford, we were alone.

'Well, now, Lizzie,' said Patience, seating herself on one of the chairs lined up against one wall. 'Is this where the patients wait to see the doctor, do you think?'

'It probably is,' I told her. When I had been a girl and my father alive, he had been in a medical practice in a small town. Our house had a parlour reserved for just such a purpose and this one resembled ours. It was furnished with more straight-backed chairs than normal. A small table in the centre of the room offered reading matter by way of a newspaper and a copy of *The English-woman's Domestic Magazine*. A very small fire struggled to survive in the grate. The modest heat it generated was enough to take the chill off the air, but not enough to warm the visitor and make him or her relax. If you were really ill, it would not worry you. If you were a time-waster, it discouraged you to linger. The only thing to look at, if you didn't want to read the newspaper or the magazine, was an amateurish watercolour painting on the wall depicting Windsor Castle. Otherwise the only thing a patient could do was study any others waiting; and conjecture what might be wrong with them. It was very quiet and even Patience became subdued and silent.

The silence was broken by the rapid approach of heavy footsteps and the door flew open. A gentleman stepped into the room and closed the door behind him. This must be Henry Morton. He held his uncle's letter of introduction in his hand. Morton, a young man, perhaps a couple of years older than Edgar Wellings, was of middle height, stocky in build, with reddish fair hair. He had the sort of pink skin that sometimes goes with such a hair colour. His eyes were very blue and his lashes the same blond as his hair, which made them almost invisible.

He glanced quickly from one to the other of us and then fixed his gaze on me. 'I have the honour to address Mrs Ross?'

'Yes,' I told him, and indicated my companion. 'This is Miss Wellings.'

'Yes, yes! A pleasure to make your acquaintance, Miss Wellings.' He pulled out one of the chairs and sat down facing us both. I thought he seemed embarrassed. He fidgeted on his chair in a boyish way, as if uncertain how to begin. 'How may I help you?' he asked at length, looking very much as if he'd rather not know.

'I believe you are acquainted with my brother, Edgar, sir,' said Patience. She leaned towards him. 'We are hoping you can help us find him. He is missing. You should know he is in something of a scrape.'

'Yes, I do know, Miss Wellings,' he told her. Hastily he added, holding up his uncle's letter, 'My uncle has written here about it.'

The hesitation had been almost imperceptible but my ear had caught it. The letter was not the first time he had learned of Edgar's predicament.

'We are hoping, Dr Morton,' I said, 'that you might have some idea where we might find Edgar. You see, he has become involved in a police investigation.'

'Quite innocently, of course!' burst out Patience. 'He hasn't done anything wrong. Well, nothing criminal, you understand. He did lose a lot of money gambling.'

'Edgar was always fond of a game of cards,' said Henry Morton awkwardly.

By now I was quite sure we had done right in coming here. The doctor could tell us something. A suspicion had also crossed my mind. Edgar had told Ben that he had originally gone to Mrs Clifford on the recommendation of a medical friend. Henry Morton's uncle lived in Deptford and he visited him there. He might well have known of a local moneylender; perhaps even have used her services himself? If Morton were a gambler too, and had a losing streak, he would no more have gone to his irascible uncle than Edgar had been prepared to go to his father or Uncle Pickford.

I was careful to keep my thoughts from showing in my face even as my mind was abuzz. Was all this trouble down to this pleasant young doctor? I thought I could detect a touch of embarrassment, even an awkward defiance, in his attitude. But perhaps I was being fanciful.

'He has panicked and run away!' explained Patience. She was sticking to the matter in hand and not worrying about what had happened to bring the present problem about. 'Such a silly thing to do, but Edgar was afraid . . . not just of the police, you know, but of having to face my family. They have all come to London to discuss his debts.'

'Yes, quite, so I imagine,' said Henry, transferring his gaze to Windsor Castle, and studying it as if he had never seen the picture before.

'I think it is possible you can help, Dr Morton,' I said.

His gaze jumped from Windsor Castle to my face. He looked both startled and guilty. 'Well, I, of course . . .'

'You see,' I continued, 'the police now know that Edgar cannot be found. It has made them even more suspicious because they had ordered him to stay. If he is not back in London by tonight, they will begin hunting high and low for him. Indeed they are probably doing so already. The newspaper reporters might get to hear of it. The police went to the hospital looking for him, and reporters do hang about the hospital, don't they?'

'Vultures,' said Henry Morton succinctly, 'blood attracts 'em.'

'Edgar is in a serious enough situation,' I added. 'This is making it so much worse. He must go back as soon as possible, tonight at the latest.'

Henry Morton heaved a deep sigh and stood up. 'I see you have a growler waiting at the gate,' he said.

I wondered if we were about to be ordered to leave.

'I'll take you to him,' said Henry.

'Oh, Dr Morton!' gasped Patience, jumping to her feet. 'That's wonderful! Where is he?'

'At my lodgings.' Henry waved a hand to indicate the room generally. 'This house belongs to the senior partner, Appleforth. I have rooms nearby.'

He gave us a stern look. 'I must make one thing clear. He's not my patient. He didn't come to consult me on any medical matter, so I am not breaking any confidentiality. But he did come to me because he needed time to think things over. He expected, wrongly, no one would look for him here. I don't know how you tracked him down, ladies?' He paused and waited.

'By purest chance,' I told him. 'We were seeking news of him in Deptford, and happened to see your uncle making his daily outing. A friend of your uncle is a Mrs Belling and Mrs Belling is a friend of my aunt, Mrs Julia Parry—'

Henry waved his hands to stop the flow of information. 'Well, it's probably just as well. Edgar was – is – in a bit of a state. He confessed he was hiding from his family. But if the police are seeking him, he must of course return at once. I'll just go and let them here know that I am going out for an hour.'

When Patience and I stepped out into the hall, we found Bunce had reappeared as if by magic, ready to resume observation duties.

Henry did not look best pleased to see the footman. 'Ah, Bunce,' he said. 'My uncle sent you with the ladies?'

'Yes, Mr Henry,' said Bunce in a voice that managed to be both obsequious and unmoving. 'He asked me to look after them special. Those are his wishes, sir.'

Morton took a deep breath. 'Very well, then, let us not waste time.'

The four of us set off together in the cab.

It took only a few minutes to reach the house where Henry Morton had rooms.

'If you would wait down here for a moment, ladies,' Henry said to us in the hall. 'It is going to come as rather a shock to Edgar to see you here. Also, I need to explain to him that I did not contact you. You found him yourselves.' He turned to the hovering Bunce and ordered sharply, 'Wait here with the ladies!'

Bunce looked discomfited, but I was pleased to see Henry had also identified the footman as his uncle's spy; and had no intention of letting the man witness Edgar's reaction on learning he had been discovered.

We waited a few minutes during which we could hear the murmur of voices above our heads. Then came a sudden shout of '*What?*'

'That is my brother's voice,' declared Patience. 'We have found him!'

A clatter of feet on the stairs heralded the return of Henry Morton, even pinker in the face than earlier.

'If you would like to go up, ladies?'

Patience and I climbed the staircase while Henry remained tactfully in the hall. Bunce skulked in the background, 'his nose out of joint' in the popular parlance.

The door to a small first-floor sitting room was open and we entered to find Edgar, in shirtsleeves and with tousled hair, facing us in a defiant attitude. He opened his mouth and began, 'Patience – Mrs Ross – now, see here . . .'

But that is as far as he got. At the sight of her brother, Patience's fears that he had come to harm were dismissed. From a very worried young woman, she was transformed into a small package of fury. She flew across the room, seized his arms and shook him.

'Edgar! How could you? You have behaved despicably, do you hear? You left me to cope with Mamma and Papa – and both aunts! How could you abandon me like that?

It is your entire fault, anyway, that the whole family is in a dreadful state. You didn't think of me for one minute, did you? My wedding to Frank is postponed until I don't know when. Perhaps we'll never be married now! The police have been to the hospital looking for you; and you are suspended from working there until everything is sorted out. Mamma is in floods of tears, the aunts keeping fainting, Aunt Matilda is mad with worry trying to cope with them, and Papa used *strong language* in front of the aunts and me!'

Edgar's defiant attitude had crumbled. 'Sorry, Patty,' he mumbled. 'I just needed some time. I wasn't ready to face them all.'

'Did you think you would never have to face them?' demanded his sister. 'Did you think it all right to leave me to try and find excuses for you? I see now, Edgar, that I have made excuses for you all my life. Well, that is at an end. You are coming back with us now, straight away, do you hear?'

'Yes, yes, of course,' Edgar promised. 'Just let me explain to Henry—'

'That's another thing!' Patience was adding to her list of accusations. 'You have involved Dr Morton, who had nothing whatsoever to do with it until now, and Mrs Ross. They are innocent parties, Edgar, and you have dragged them into the— the sordid muddle you have made of things.'

'Well, I didn't think you would find me here,' protested Edgar weakly. 'I know I shouldn't have troubled Henry—'

'We shall wait for you downstairs!' declared Patience,

cutting short his excuses with an imperious gesture. She turned and swept out of the room.

'I am truly very sorry, Mrs Ross,' said the crestfallen Edgar to me. 'Will you explain to your husband? I wasn't running away. It doesn't mean I'm guilty. Oh, Lord . . .' His words tailed off in a groan.

'I'll do my best,' I told him. 'But you must go straight away to Scotland Yard and explain yourself. They will be looking for you by now, you know.'

'Perhaps Ross will lock me in a cell?' A sudden note of hope entered Edgar's voice. 'Then I won't have to face the family.'

Oh, dear, I thought. The wretched fellow is incapable of good judgement. When all this is over and settled, he will get into another scrape; Ben was quite right about him. Frank and Patience will have to worry about him all their married lives. I told him I would wait downstairs with his sister.

'The cab will take you all to Egham railway station,' said Henry Morton to us when we had all gathered before the house. 'I'll walk back. It isn't far. I walk it every day.'

'I am much obliged to you, Henry,' said Edgar, shaking his hand. 'And I apologise most profoundly.'

'Not at all, my dear chap!' Henry clapped Edgar heartily on the shoulder. But there was distinct haste in the way he bundled us all into the cab and called out to the cabbie, 'Drive on!'

'Yes, he came,' said Ben, in answer to my anxious question when he arrived home that evening. 'Turned up at the Yard with a feeble apology and expected me to sympathise with him. I soon disabused him of that!'

I had parted from Patience and her brother at Waterloo, where they had found a cab to take them to Scotland Yard, and I had walked home. Bunce had accepted the modest tip I gave him and reluctantly taken himself off to make his report in Deptford. I did wonder what version of events he would give his employer.

'Edgar knows he's behaved foolishly and selfishly,' I said to Ben. 'He was afraid of facing the whole family, all telling him how badly he's let them down.'

'Well, he has let them all down,' said Ben unsympathetically. 'He let me down, as well. I accepted his word that he would stay in London. I hope, when Uncle Pickford and all the rest of them see him, they give him a terrible time – all of them, individually and together.'

'When they see him?' I asked. 'Oh, Ben, you haven't . . . ?'

'Yes, I have!' said Ben. 'Don't look so reproachful, Lizzie. The fellow was practically begging me to lock him in a cell and keep him from his relatives. I was more than ready to oblige. A night in the cells will teach him a lesson, and concentrate his mind far better, than one sleeping on Henry Morton's sofa. So that's where he is tonight. It's all right; I'll turn him loose tomorrow – if Dunn agrees. My locking up Wellings is about the first thing I've done right in this matter, in the superintendent's view!' Ben hesitated. 'So far your name has been kept out of it. Dunn is under the impression Wellings returned of his own volition. But if Dunn asks more questions about

Wellings's stay in Egham, well, he may find out you and Miss Patience had a hand in things. Not,' added Ben with a sigh, 'that he'll be surprised.'

'Honestly, Ben!' I protested. 'I do think Mr Dunn and you might both of you be a bit more grateful for all my hard work tracking down Wellings – and Patience's part, too, for making him come straight back to London with us.'

'Dear Lizzie,' said Ben. 'Believe me, I am very grateful indeed. If I had lost Wellings, I think Dunn would have reduced me to sergeant! It was very clever of you, sweetheart.'

'Thank you,' I said.

'And you know,' said Ben, 'Dunn makes a great fuss about your interference, but he has the highest regard for your abilities. He's told me so, more than once.'

So much praise all at once was too much. I was reduced to silence.

Inspector Ben Ross

Superintendent Dunn had been delighted to know Edgar Wellings was in a prison cell. My difficulty the following morning was to persuade Dunn to authorise his release.

'He has wasted police time!' thundered Dunn, marching up and down his office, scratching his crop of bristly hair. 'That is an offence and by rights he should be charged with it. My time, your time, the working hours of half the constabulary on the beat, notified to look out for him, when they ought to be looking out for wrongdoers of every other kind! As if I had not enough problems to deal with that day. As I had told you, Ross, I had decided the hospital must be informed of what has been happening so I went in person to explain things to senior staff there. Can you imagine how they reacted when learning that one of their young doctors had become caught up in a murder inquiry? And then there was the matter of his gambling and his debts . . . He is suspended from his duties there, of course. I shall be surprised if they ever have him back again, supposing that he is cleared of any part in the murder of Mrs Clifford.'

'Yes, sir, I do understand,' I assured him.

Dunn wheeled round as if he were on parade and jabbed an accusing finger at me. 'Then, while I was at the hospital, the wretched fellow's father and uncle appeared, seeking him. That was how I learned he was missing. Not by any official communication, oh no, but through a chance encounter! On top of everything else, we had lost him. I was made to feel a complete fool.'

I protested, 'No, sir, not at all—' But I was not allowed to finish.

'Did you know he'd taken himself off?' asked Dunn accusingly.

'Well, I didn't, not until – not until you came back from the hospital.'

This feeble reply rightly elicited another outburst from the superintendent.

'You see? The Yard was made to look ridiculous by that worthless scamp. If that is *all* that he is! He might well be our murderer. And, now that we at last have him locked up safely, you would let him go again? Are you out of your mind, Ross?'

'I am sure,' I urged, 'that his family will keep a close eye on him and not allow him to do anything like that again.'

'The family? They are as bad as he is! Would any of them have come to the Yard and told us he had absconded, if they had not run into me at the hospital, and been obliged to admit it? I tell you, Ross, they would not. That whole family was determined to keep us in the dark. For what? For fear of some scandal in their home town – and a wedding!'

When Superintendent Dunn is in a mood like this, there is nothing to be done but let him work off his rage. However, I did eventually manage to persuade him to authorise Edgar's release, upon the guarantees of his father and uncle.

'If you do this again, Wellings,' I told the wretch, 'you will find yourself in Newgate, and I won't be asking for your freedom! You have gravely embarrassed me. If my wife and your sister hadn't tracked you down, I might have finished back where I began my police career, pounding the beat.'

He was almost grovelling when he left.

About an hour after Wellings had gone and I was beginning to recover my peace of mind, Biddle appeared.

'Someone very desirous of seeing you, Mr Ross, sir.'

Biddle is a well-meaning youth and shows promise; but ambition has led him to study books on self-improvement. I know this from our maid, Bessie, with whom Biddle is 'walking out'.

'You are a police officer, not a butler, Biddle,' I told him testily. 'Do you mean a member of the public or one of the Wellings family? Not Mr Carterton, I hope?'

'No, sir, a member of the public, sir.' Biddle cleared his throat. 'His name is Smart, sir, Joseph Smart. He is in business as a pawnbroker, sir, in Greenwich.'

'Then show him in, Biddle.'

A pawnbroker? Had Mrs Clifford's watch and jewellery turned up at last?

Smart was an elderly man wearing a pale-grey frock coat over pepper-and-salt tweed trousers. Because of the cold weather he had swathed his neck in a woollen muffler, twice wrapped around and then knotted in front; so that his head sat atop it with no visible neck. He had the wan complexion of someone who spends most of his time indoors, much of it by artificial light. Now that he had emerged into the day, he sat blinking at me. But his eyes were sharp. I felt I was being 'sized up', assessed for likely value as security for a loan or as goods for sale. I almost expected him to name a price.

He leaned forward slightly, but with his shoulders only, as if his shop counter stood between us. In a curiously soft voice he said, 'I deal in quite a bit of jewellery.' This sentence might have been some secret code, for he then looked at me with the air of one waiting for a prearranged response.

I found his manner and his presence unsettling; and had to force myself to be brisk and businesslike. After all, he had come to me. I was not about to offer him my watch or wedding ring.

'I imagine that you do, Mr Smart.' I didn't know if this was the right reply. It sounded weak to my ears. But he accepted it with a little nod.

'Some of it is what you might call run-of-the-mill,' he went on in that soft tone. 'Very little actual value. Gold, of course,' he added thoughtfully, 'that always has a value, depending on the degree of purity. Stones, now, they vary a lot. Some people know very little about their own jewellery. Some get it absolutely wrong. You would be surprised, Inspector Ross, how many people come in to my shop and tell me they have a diamond ring, for example, and offer it as security against an exorbitant sum. They think a diamond must be of great value.'

He uttered a curious sound I couldn't quite identify and then, with a quiver of distaste, I realised he was laughing.

'But there are diamonds, Mr Ross, and there are diamonds, eh? And then, again, things aren't always what they appear to be. I'm speaking of paste. A lot of them bring me paste jewels. They don't like it when I tell them. They don't want to believe me. They can turn quite nasty and accuse me of trying to cheat them. I tell them straight away, you go elsewhere. See what another pawnbroker will tell you. Sometimes they do, you know.'

When Biddle had told me a pawnbroker was waiting to see me, with information, I had felt a surge of excitement and hope that the missing items had at last surfaced. Now I just wanted this man out of my office as quickly as possible.

'I am a busy man, Mr Smart,' I said. 'As I am sure you

are, too. What has brought you to me today?'

He searched in the inside pocket of his coat and produced a sheet of cheap printed paper. 'This,' he said simply, and placed the paper, lettering uppermost, on my desk so that it was the right way up for me to read. I saw that it was one of the leaflets we had had printed and distributed, showing Britannia Scroggs's drawings of the missing valuables, with the description she had given us.

Trying to keep my voice from betraying my excitement, I asked, 'You have been offered some of these items?'

Mr Smart rubbed his hands together, the palms making a dry rustling noise. 'Ah, now, that's the thing,' he said. 'Have I or haven't I? That's the question, isn't it, as the Bard wrote?'

The unexpected foray into Shakespeare disconcerted me. 'Which?' I asked sharply.

Mr Smart was not disconcerted. 'Just so,' he said, and nodded.

I realised that he had not been making idle conversation about the jewellery. He had brought me something – but there was a problem.

'Here's a constable,' said Smart.

I thought for a moment he meant Biddle, but it was his way of telling his tale, setting the scene and introducing the dramatis personae. Perhaps Mr Smart did like to attend theatrical performances.

'An officer of the law,' he continued, just to make things quite clear. 'He comes into my shop. Now then, when that happens, it's very likely that he'll be asking about stolen items. A pawnbroker has to be very careful, you know. You get to judge a customer up, very quick. When they'll settle for the first sum of money you offer, and want to be in and out the door at once, that's a bad sign. I send that sort away! And, sure enough, the constable has this sheet of paper here,' he tapped the leaflet, 'with a nice set of drawings and description. Earrings, see . . .' Smart reached out and rested his forefinger on the earrings illustrated by Britannia. His hands were very small and neat. 'Rubies, gold setting, pendant style, stolen goods. So I tell the constable, I'll watch out.

'Now then, sometimes my wife helps me out in the shop. After the officer had left, she came in to the front. She'd been busy in the back, see, but she'd been listening. She always listens out, in case there's trouble. I don't get a lot of trouble. Not in Greenwich. But you never know, do you? So in she comes. I show her that leaflet. "I took in a pair of earrings like those," she says, straight off. 'Just the other day. I showed them to you," she says.

'"But, my dear," I says to her, "they were not rubies, as those illustrated here. They were sapphires." And indeed they were and very nice stones, too.

'"Joseph!" says she. "Perhaps the stones are different, but the earrings, they're the same!" And, Mr Ross, you can see for yourself, the setting is identical. My wife, Mr Ross, is a woman of very fine judgement.'

With that he foraged in his pocket again and produced a small velvet bag. He shook it over the leaflet and a pair of earrings slid out. 'If you would care to examine them,' he said politely, as if I might make an offer for them.

Then he cleared his throat, delved in his pocket again

and produced a small powerful magnifying glass of the type used by jewellers and generally called a loupe. He handed it to me.

I straightened the earrings, side by side, and examined them carefully. Then I took a long careful look at Britannia's sketches. I fancied my heart beat more quickly. The settings were identical to the maid's drawings. Surely, they had to be the missing earrings?

'These are good quality, you say?' I asked cautiously.

'Very good, oh, my, yes. Made, I would say, in a workshop in India, and by a skilled man.' Smart, satisfied he had my interest, leaned back in his chair and folded his hands.

'They are oriental? You can tell? Of course, I suppose you can.'

'I might be wrong,' said Mr Smart with the calm air of someone who knows that he isn't. 'But there is a distinct style to pieces made in the Orient, you know. The colour of the gold, too. The gold in these is twenty-two carat. That is very high quality, as you will know. I think,' Smart nodded, 'yes, I fancy they represented an investment on the part of their owner. I don't mean the fellow who brought them to my place of business. I mean, their original owner.'

I thought it, too. Clifford had laid out her money shrewdly. Perhaps she had not altogether trusted banks. I picked up the little black velvet bag. 'And they came in this bag?'

He shook his head regretfully. 'Ah, no. They came loose, that is, wrapped in a bit of paper. I put them in that bag to protect them. Besides, you should respect a good stone. You don't go wrapping it up in a piece of paper like you would a cod's head!'

I realised that Mr Smart was not without a sense of humour – of a type.

'Biddle!' I called out. 'Just step along to Mr Dunn's office and give him my compliments. Tell him, I'd be obliged, if he has a few minutes, if he'd come and look at these. Oh, and if you see Sergeant Morris, ask him to come along, as well.'

It made for quite a crowd in my small office when both Dunn and Morris arrived, and Biddle squeezed in to observe.

'Well,' said Dunn, when he had also examined the earrings. 'They do resemble the items in this illustration, to a remarkable degree, in fact. But the stones are wrong.' He placed the loupe on the drawing and turned to Joseph Smart, who had sat watching us complacently. 'Now then, Mr Smart,' said Dunn. 'Do you have a name and address for the customer who brought these to you? If he pawned them, you must have the details.'

'But he didn't pawn them, Superintendent,' said Smart in that same soft voice. 'No, no, he wanted to sell.'

'And you asked for no name or address?'

'William Jones,' said the pawnbroker with a sad smile. 'My wife did ask, even though he wanted to sell not pawn. We always ask when they come in off the street like that, poor folk but with a valuable to dispose of. I tell them it's because I need to write it on the receipt. A tradesman needs to be careful! They always give an everyday name of that sort. It might be right or it might not. To tell you the truth, they are unlikely to give a correct name even if the deal is above board. It makes them nervous, you see, because they might owe money elsewhere; or they just don't want neighbours to learn they are so hard up. In my experience, colours are very often given as the name. I've had Browns, Greens, Greys, Blacks and Whites come in to my establishment. I set no store by any name. But the address, now, was a different matter because it was one known to us. It is that of a lodging house for seamen. Nothing permanent about it, of course, so he didn't mind giving that. They come and go at such rooming houses, sirs, come and go. Very likely he's left by now.'

'He was a seaman?' I asked quickly, interrupting this account of the hazards of a pawnbroker's life. 'Did he tell your wife that he was? Or did your wife judge him a seafaring man?'

'Indeed, she did, sirs. Otherwise, she might not have taken the items in. She didn't care for the look of him, that's a fact. She described him as a hulking, rough-looking fellow, though not badly dressed in the way seamen like to dress. He wore a thick pea coat, sirs, and a cap with a peak. He was not a naval man, not the Royal Navy, in a uniform. No, she judged him off a trading vessel. Some of those crewmen are a very tough sort of bullyboy, gentlemen. They need to be, for it's a desperate hard life. They sail dangerous seas and put into all manner of wild foreign ports.'

Morris had joined us to hear what the pawnbroker had

to say and, at this description of the customer, I saw a sudden gleam in the sergeant's eyes. But this was not the moment to inquire why.

'Yet your wife was persuaded to accept the earrings? I don't understand,' I said. 'Or was she just afraid of him and did not dare to refuse?'

The little pawnbroker appeared slightly embarrassed.

'She saw they were of Indian manufacture, or somewhere in that part of the world,' he explained, 'and worth a fair bit. So she asked Jones, that being the name he gave her, where he got them. On the island of Ceylon, he told her. Well, gentlemen, Ceylon is a place renowned for sapphires, so my wife was encouraged. The man said he was there as deckhand on a tea clipper. He and some others sat gambling the whole of one night in the monsoon season. Raining like you can't imagine the whole time; and no one wanted to be out in the open. The way it went, when morning came, the game finally broke up and he was the winner. The other gamblers paid up, but the fellow who lost the most, he couldn't pay, not cash or gold coins. But he offered these earrings, took them out of an inside pocket of his jacket, where he had them wrapped in a bit of silk. Jones saw they were good and he accepted them, though the scrap of silk wrapped around them got lost.

'Now, gentlemen, you might think that's a fanciful story. But seafarers, they bring back all sorts of trinkets and jewels from foreign parts, often of more value than they know. How they came by them, well, that's not something you can verify, not as a pawnbroker. But it's not an unlikely story. It could even been true – or very nearly.'

'So how much did your wife give him for the earrings?'

'Five pounds,' said Smart defiantly. 'It was a fair price because he had come in off the street. But my wife believed him when he said he was a sailor. It was not just because of his complexion, burned by the sun and wind, or his attire. When he reached out to push the earrings across the counter, the sleeve of his coat rode up . . .' Smart paused and demonstrated, pushing up the sleeve of his own coat so that his forearm showed.

'He wore no shirt, sirs, but a knitted jersey, and that rode up too, so she saw the skin – and the tattoo. Now, seafaring men are rare ones for a tattoo. This one was a heart and a name. They very often have a heart tattooed. Generally there's a girl's name to go with it, wife or sweetheart. This one, though, it was a bit different. Instead of a name, it just had the word "Ma".'

'Ma?' Morris and I exclaimed in unison.

'Yes, gentlemen. That seemed to indicate, so my wife thought, that he wasn't such a bad fellow, not if he had a heart and a fond name for his mother tattooed on his arm.'

'Sir?' murmured Morris. I turned to him. 'It strikes me, Mr Ross,' Morris continued, 'that Mr Smart's description of his customer matches pretty well with that of the fellow I saw leaving Ma Scroggs's home, when I took her daughter there.'

'A seaman,' I said, 'Raggy Jeb's son-in-law is a seaman and he's ashore here at the moment because he gave

Raggy a hand to move a drunken woman . . .'

Morris and I gazed at one another. '*Ma* . . .' I repeated, my voice sounding hoarse.

'Well, I never!' said Morris.

I turned to Superintendent Dunn, who was looking from me to Morris and back again, in surprise.

'Billy Scroggs,' I said simply. 'Not William *Jones* but William *Scroggs*! Known to his family as Billy. He who, according to his sister, Britannia, went to sea twenty years ago and never reappeared. Supposed drowned.'

'Well, it looks like he's back now,' said Morris.

'He's been coming back after every voyage to his own wife and children. Raggy Jeb, his father-in-law, has a handcart, Mr Dunn,' I explained to the superintendent. 'His little granddaughter told my wife how she had to wait in a pub while her grandfather and father "helped" a drunken woman who couldn't walk. That is how Mrs Clifford's body got to Skinner's Yard!'

Chapter Sixteen

WE GAVE the pawnbroker, Smart, a receipt for the earrings, explaining we must hold them as possible evidence. They would be returned to him if that should not prove to be so. He looked doleful as he left us. Our thanks were poor compensation for his probably being out of pocket. I would suggest he be given some small reward, if they led us to the killer. It makes good sense to encourage such men as Smart to come forward. I didn't doubt the earrings were worth far more than the five pounds Mrs Smart had given for them. Smart might easily have decided that, as the stones were not the rubies described in the police leaflet, he could safely keep them. It was probably fear that they would be traced to him somehow, if we captured Scroggs for example, that had induced him to come to us. We would mark him down as a fence for stolen property. Then we should be appearing on his doorstep regularly and his reputation be gone.

'I will take Morris,' I said to Dunn, 'and go to the mother's home. I don't expect to find Billy there, but either his mother or his sister must know where he is. There is a possibility, of course, that he has signed on as crew on another ship and may even have sailed already.'

'We must be very careful, Ross,' warned Dunn, suddenly cautious. 'These may not be the earrings that are missing. Yes, the setting looks the same but there remains the question of the stones. You say the maid, Scroggs's sister, drew them for you. She, surely, would know that rubies are red. She would not have told you sapphire earrings were rubies, I can't believe it. Is she simple?'

'On the contrary,' I said grimly, 'I am beginning to think that Britannia is pretty sharp. But we must interview Billy Scroggs, sir. At the very least, we must do that.'

'If you are right, and he was the sailor who brought the earrings to the pawnbroker, we may have broken the case.' Dunn shook his head in doubt. 'But what, really, do we have? A tattoo, Ross, and a general description: that is all you have to go on by way of identification. All men have mothers, Ross. How many other seafarers have some sentimental tribute to their mothers tattooed on their arms? I would wager you several hundred of 'em. As for Morris's sighting of a burly fellow in a pea coat and cap, leaving the home of Mrs Scroggs . . .'

'Mr Dunn,' I said firmly, 'this has been a very strange case from the very beginning. Inspector Phipps has been inclined to disbelieve the maid from the start. I am very much afraid that it begins to look as though he may have been right, and I was wrong.'

'Then Miss Scroggs has told us a very confused, contradictory and strange story,' said Dunn.

'She has indeed,' I muttered.

'Take a cab!' said Dunn suddenly. 'It will be allowed against expenses.'

'You will allow me to express a view, sir?' asked Morris, as we jolted towards the Scroggs abode.

'Of course, go ahead, Sergeant.'

Morris folded his hands, pressing the thumbs together. This, I had noticed before, signified Morris had been thinking. 'That girl Britannia,' said Morris, 'is as artful as a cartload of monkeys, there's no denying.'

'I agree.'

'But we're like those oriental fortune-tellers you see in fairgrounds, sir. We're tossing the evidence in the air, like they do with pebbles, or ivory sticks, and watching to see how they fall. We have earrings, but they are set with sapphires, and we have been told the missing ones are set with rubies. We have a seafaring man with a tattoo that reads "Ma". I saw a bullyboy in a seaman's coat and cap quitting the mother's hovel. There is a tale told by a child of six to Mrs Ross, of a drunken woman loaded on to a handcart; and I don't think a jury will place much reliance on that! What we don't have, Mr Ross, is any real proof to convince a judge. Lots of theories tossed in the air– like the ivory sticks – and the only knowledge is what we read into them.'

'Of course, you are right, Sergeant,' I agreed. 'But someone has been trailing us around London, either in person or using a street urchin. I believe every move we've made has been observed by, or reported to, that person. It is the same person whom Parker feared so much; who watched Midge's house the night of our visit; someone everyone is reluctant to speak of, even a tough fellow like Jethro Smith. Remember, too, the man's shirt you observed dripping on the old woman's washing line. *He* has been there all the time, Morris, and I am determine we'll meet him face to face!'

Our arrival, and by cab, caused a stir around the cottage where Ma Scroggs lived and something of a crowd, including the usual small boys, gathered around us as we descended. I went to pay the cabbie and saw he was looking around him nervously. He snatched the money from my hand. My request for a receipt was met with a scowl.

'I don't want to hang about here,' he said. 'So don't go asking me to wait for you. I don't like the look of those brats. Like as not, they will start throwing stones at the horse's legs.'

'I must have a receipt,' I said sternly. 'Our business is official.'

He drew a stub of pencil and a crumpled piece of paper from his greatcoat pocket and scribbled on it. 'Good luck to you, if you mean to arrest anyone in there. This lot will start throwing stones at *you*!'

He was probably right but a faint heart would not save us now. 'Come along, Sergeant,' I said briskly to Morris and we marched into the building.

Obviously, the interest outside had warned anyone indoors that we were on our way. Billy Scroggs, if he had been here, had now had ample time to scuttle out some back exit and make off into the maze of lanes. But we threw open the door in determined fashion and entered.

There was no wet wash strung across the room; but it was in a disordered and unswept state. There was a smell in the air I couldn't for the moment place although it seemed familiar. Not wet laundry; yet something damp and fetid. I had smelled it the last time I'd been here.

Both women were there – but, as I'd feared, no one else. Despite the fact that both mother and daughter had been alerted by the commotion outside, both chose to scream.

'Oh, my dear Lord!' cried Ma Scroggs. 'Whatever is it? I do believe it is that there p'lice sergeant as came before with you, Tanny, and frightened me half to death.'

'It's him all right, Ma,' confirmed Britannia, belligerent as ever. 'And he was too scared to come on his own.. He's brought the inspector with him!'

'Good day to you both,' I said. 'You remember me, Mrs Scroggs? I am Inspector Ross.'

'I remember you,' retorted Ma Scroggs, taking her grimy apron by the corner and wiping it over her face. 'Not likely to forget you, am I? Or the other fellow. Why don't you lot leave my girl alone?'

'We have not come here seeking your daughter, Mrs Scroggs. Where is your son, Billy?'

Both women gaped at me and this time the reaction was genuine. Even Britannia was silenced for a moment. Then the volcano erupted.

'Billy?' shrieked Ma Scroggs. 'Oh, my poor dead son! It's not enough that they come tormenting the living, but these rozzers have come seeking the dead!'

'We have reason to believe your son, Billy, is alive,' I told her sternly.

'Oh? Have you?' shouted Britannia. 'Well, we don't, do we, Ma? He left this house when he was a boy, not fifteen, was he, Ma? Left here and never seen again in more than twenty years. If you want to speak to my brother, Billy, you'll have to ask the Angel to blow his trumpet and summon him up from the dead.'

'Not fifteen,' agreed Ma Scroggs and burst into tears. 'Oh, it's too much! I shan't be able to bear it, indeed I won't.' She clasped a hand to the bosom of her dingy gown. 'My heart is going like a steam train, I swear. It will burst! I will drop down dead on this very floor! Tanny, just help me over to that chair, my pet.'

Britannia did look slightly startled at being addressed so affectionately; by the parent who had refused at first to take her in. However, she rallied to play her part. She threw her brawny arm around the old woman's shoulder and guided her to the chair. Ma Scroggs dropped into it in a heap of crumpled garments and tangled grey locks. She wrapped her arms around herself and began to rock back and forth.

'Oh, my, it's too cruel, it is, I swear. Seven children I had . . . seven of you there was, weren't there, Tanny?'

'Seven of us!' snapped Britannia, glaring at us. 'And now she's only got me, ain't you, Ma?'

'Only my dear girl here,' confirmed her mother. 'This here is my one child left to me out of seven, who has looked after me and kept me from the work'us.'

'And how am I going to do that now?' demanded

Britannia. 'With you p'lice turning up at every place I work and putting the frighteners on anyone wanting to employ me?'

'Burst into my own home without so much as a by-your-leave,' lamented Ma Scroggs. 'Come here and ask to see my poor dead boy. Oh, he was the first to go, wasn't he, Tanny? He signed on as cabin boy when he wasn't fifteen. Oh, he was so young to go sailing off to foreign parts and be among savages, as very likely ate him.'

Morris had had enough. 'Don't talk rubbish!' he growled. 'Of course he wasn't eaten by cannibals!'

'They has cannibals in some places,' insisted Ma Scroggs. 'They eat missionaries, so why wouldn't they eat my poor boy? And if it wasn't head-hunters got him, then he perished in some awful storm. Shipwrecked and drowned. Or he might have got a fever. Anyhow, my poor son is dead and gone and I know it.'

'You were officially informed of his death?' I asked.

'Of course we weren't!' snapped Britannia. 'He wasn't in the Royal Navy. He was aboard a merchant vessel.'

'Then we can research its fate by consulting Lloyd's List,' I told them. 'What was the name of the ship? If it went down with all hands, its loss will be recorded there.'

They replied promptly and in unison.

'I forgot!' said Ma Scroggs.

'I never knew it,' said Britannia. 'I was only a kid myself when he left.'

'I know my poor son is dead,' declared Ma Scroggs magnificently, 'because I am a mother!' She sat up straight in the chair and struck her fist against her heart. 'Here, that's where I know it! If he had lived, he'd have come back to see us when he returned to port. He'd have let us know somehow he was well. He'd have written. He could write. I sent all my children to Methodist Sunday School, didn't I, Tanny? And you all learned your letters there and to read your Bibles.'

'And do you still read your Bible, Miss Scroggs?' I couldn't help but ask.

For once, Britannia looked briefly disconcerted. Then she rallied. 'When have I got time to read anything? I work my fingers to the bone, don't I?' She held up her distorted hands.

I admit to a feeling of shame for the moment. But I quelled it. 'See here, Britannia,' I said to her. 'We suspect that your brother is alive and is – or was until very recently – in London. We suspect he came to see you at Mrs Clifford's house and you let him in. He set about robbing the house, either with or without your prior knowledge. He was disturbed by Mrs Clifford, and killed her.'

'Oh, the wickedness of it . . .' whispered Ma Scroggs and did turn so pale I was worried she might pass out.

But Britannia's reaction to my accusation was quite different. 'Oh, you do, do you?' She placed her hands on her hips. 'Well, you must be desperate, Mr Inspector Ross, that's all I can say. Can't you find no one else? What about that young fancy fellow that came calling on Mrs Clifford that evening, what about him, eh? He admits he was there, doesn't he? He owed her money, didn't he? He and her had a yelling match, didn't they? Why don't you go and arrest him, eh? Go on, lock *him* up! But you don't, do you? Because he's got airs and graces, and friends you don't want to offend, I dare say. So you're looking around for someone else. Well, don't come harassing a respectable poor working woman and an old lady who has lost all her children, excepting the one, and lives like this!' She flung a hand out to indicate the poverty-stricken surroundings. 'We haven't even got the money to buy food or firewood or coals. If I'd robbed a house, I'd have money.'

I gambled a last throw of the dice. 'We think the earrings, Mrs Clifford's earrings, have turned up.'

Britannia narrowed her eyes. 'What, them ruby ones what I drew for you?'

'Some earrings identical to the ones you sketched for us – but sapphires. You are sure Mrs Clifford's earrings were rubies?'

'Of course I'm sure,' snarled Britannia at me. 'I ain't an idiot!'

During all this exchange, Morris had been moving slowly and methodically around the room. Now he came back to stand beside me. 'First time I was here,' he said to Britannia, 'there was a cooking pot on a trivet over there, in the hearth. I don't know what your mother was cooking but it smelled something awful.'

'She couldn't afford best cut of beef,' said Britannia sourly. 'What did you expect?'

'I expected to see the pot and trivet still in place,' said Morris calmly. 'But I see it's gone.'

'We had to sell it,' said Ma Scroggs sadly from the chair. 'I couldn't afford to buy nothing to put in it and it was a good iron pot. I got four shillings for it.'

We could do no more here for the moment. Morris had been right to have misgivings. We had been indeed tossing pebbles in the air; and they had fallen badly for us.

The crowd outside had waited to see what would happen. When we emerged, they jeered and followed us to the end of the road, shouting abuse all the way.

When we were finally free of them, I asked Morris, 'What was that about the cooking pot?'

'It wasn't there,' said Morris simply. 'It could be that they had to sell it. They've got precious little else to sell. It's just that, Mr Ross, I can't put the smell of that meat, or whatever it was, out of my mind. It really stank. I thought at the time, I couldn't imagine eating it.' Morris sighed. 'Sorry, sir, but I think I missed something there.'

'In what way, Morris?'

'If they had something to hide, sir, something small – say jewellery – or even a packet of a papers, like those missing IOUs, if it was well wrapped in an oilskin cloth . . .'

'They could have put it in the bottom of the cooking pot and then stewed something so disgusting on top of it, that a policeman might not investigate.' I slapped my hands together. 'Confound it, you may be right, Morris!'

'I missed it, sir, I missed it on my first visit,' said Morris gloomily. 'I should've asked them to tip it all out.'

'You had no search warrant from a magistrate, Sergeant. You only went there to take Britannia to her mother. You could hardly have asked them to volunteer to throw away their dinner, on the grounds it was unappetising and smelled foul.'

But Morris was not to be consoled. 'I missed it,' he repeated. 'Billy was there and gave the loot to his mother to hide. I saw him leave with my own eyes! I should have stopped that fellow and asked him why he was so shy.'

'Well, we missed him again today, I fancy,' I said. 'We are a good quarter of a mile from the river here, wouldn't you say?'

'Easily, sir,' agreed Morris. 'Nearer half a mile, I'd reckon.'

'Yet there was an odour of Thames mud in the place. Perhaps not as bad as the stench of the stew you spoke of, but bad-smelling and pervasive, all the same. He was there, Morris, just before us. He heard us arrive and he fled, but he left the odour of Father Thames behind him; a man who lives on or near the river. Deckhand Billy Scroggs, visiting his sister and dear old ma, I'd wager my last penny on it!'

When we returned to the Yard, we found that officers sent to look for the man who had given the seamen's hostel as an address to Mrs Smart had had no more luck than us. The sailor who brought in the earrings had given the name of Jones. Not surprisingly, there was no Jones in the register at the hostel, nor, for that matter, had anyone registered in the name of Scroggs. The man who ran the place had obligingly turned back the pages for the whole of the previous month, but no Jones or Scroggs graced the page. Well, that was no surprise. The hostel was run by a charity, dedicated to the welfare of seafarers.

The register had probably been an accurate record.

'We should not be surprised sir,' I said to Dunn. 'The customer gave that address to Mrs Smart because she could see he was a seaman; and he knew she'd recognise the name of a well-known hostel. As hostels go, it's respectable. Mrs Smart would have been encouraged. Wherever he was staying in London, it was somewhere else.'

Elizabeth Martin Ross

Ben came home that evening more depressed than I had seen him about a case in a long time. When Bessie had cleared the dinner dishes, Ben and I sat before the parlour fire. From the kitchen came the noise of Bessie clashing the crockery together. Ben was staring moodily into the flames. He was tired, I could see that, and angry, and above all frustrated that he could make no progress. From time to time he rubbed a hand over his forehead, tousling up his hair. It was still as black as ever without a sign of grey. Perhaps, I thought, he will be one of those lucky people whose hair never whitens, only fades to a duller shade.

I said, only to break his introspection, 'It's a wonder we have an unchipped plate left.'

'What?' he raised his eyes to my face and frowned.

'Bessie is washing up,' I said.

'Oh, is that what she is doing? I thought she was practising juggling with the dishes.' After a pause, he said, 'Fairgrounds.'

'What about fairgrounds?' I asked. 'I don't think Bessie is intending to run away and join the circus.'

'Morris was speaking of fairgrounds this afternoon. He said we were like the fortune tellers you sometimes see in such places, reading the future from cards, or casting pebbles or, Morris's favourite, ivory sticks.'

'You are no further forward?'

'Not a jot. Every step of progress we make is almost immediately reversed.' He leaned forward, his hands loosely clasped. 'Listen, Lizzie, perhaps you can untangle some of this puzzle.'

'I can try.' I could not help adding demurely, 'If you think Superintendent Dunn would not mind.'

'Don't tease me, Lizzie, I beg of you! I was never more serious about a case in my life. Yet, this is not a victim one can pity. She was a hard woman plying a heartless trade of usury. But Mrs Clifford lived in a city we like to think we police, and keep safe. She should not have been battered to death in her own home, or left in that dismal, dirty yard. But she was; and so far we have been able to do nothing about it.'

'And that is what troubles you? Professional pride?'

'That and the sense that I am being made a fool of.' Ben went on to describe the visit he and Morris had paid to Mrs Scroggs and her daughter. 'I cannot understand Britannia Scroggs, Lizzie, that's the heart of it! I feel sure she has told a pack of lies. No, that's not correct. I think she only lies when necessary. Otherwise she has twisted the truth. I believe she has misled us, taking us down all sorts of alleys and by-ways. What evidence we have comes to us largely courtesy of Britannia, what she reported – beginning with the disappearance of her employer and the discovery of blood on the carpet – and the detailed drawings she made of missing items of jewellery. She is apparently very helpful. Yet, when we examine it, that evidence is not what it seems.

'When we think we have some of the missing items, the earrings, they cannot be the same earrings, because the ones we have are set with sapphires and the ones Mrs Clifford wore, says Britannia, were rubies. She insists she knows the difference between the two. But if she meant to mislead us, by describing the wrong stones, why make such a detailed, and apparently accurate, drawing of the settings?'

'I remember you telling me of that,' I told him. I sat for a moment puzzling it through. 'Ben, didn't Britannia say she had practised drawing at Sunday School, creating religious pictures using wax crayons?'

Ben gave an unwilling smile. 'Yes, she was very proud of having been told by the teacher that she had "an eye".'

'She is not pretty, I think? No, she isn't, for I saw her myself briefly at the house.'

'Not pretty at all. If she ever had a sort of girlish charm, it's long gone. Hard work, I suppose. Her hands are swollen and the joints distorted from so many years scrubbing floors, washing dishes . . .' Ben paused. 'Lizzie, I would not wish our Bessie to finish up like that. It is a wretched life.' He looked worried.

'I do help Bessie in the kitchen. No, Ben, what I want to say is, I don't suppose Britannia ever received much praise in her life. She has no looks, no particular skills, no chance to improve herself. But once, when she was a child, a Sunday School instructor praised her drawing talent. She has savoured that praise ever since. Believe me, I am sure of it.'

Ben was listening carefully, his dark eyes fixed on my face. 'Go on.'

'Yet, even if she does have that one skill, she has never since those childhood afternoons at Sunday School had the chance to repeat her little triumph. No one since had ever asked her to draw a picture until you did. She could not resist drawing the earrings as accurately as she could. It was a point of pride with her, do you see? To show you she still has "an eye".'

'I do understand that,' he said. 'But why, then, make such a stupid error as to describe blue stones as red ones? Just to confuse us? It is a clumsy lie, if so, and Britannia, to use Morris's description of her, is as artful as a cartload of monkeys.'

'Ben, you saw Mrs Clifford's clothing at the morgue, didn't you? What colour was her dress?'

'She'd worn a skirt and fitted bodice, both dark blue.'

'Then we can be sure Mrs Clifford liked that colour. So why with so much blue clothing would she wear red earrings? No, she would wear blue earrings.'

Ben leaned back in his chair and thought for a few minutes. Then he said, 'Are you saying I should have been suspicious from the first? Britannia was angry with me when I told her we had found the earrings, but they weren't rubies. She accused me of calling her an idiot, who did not know the difference.'

'She was embarrassed, Ben, and she was panicking. When you told her the earrings had been handed to a pawnbroker; and the stones were not the ones she had told you about, she was very frightened, I am sure. She realised she had made a stupid mistake in drawing the earrings so accurately but falsely claiming them to be set with rubies. She had probably been comforting herself with the thought that, if you found the items and the stones were different, you would not think they were Mrs Clifford's earrings.

'I am sure Britannia is as artful as you describe. But it is artfulness developed because she has no other weapon to outwit the police. When that artfulness conflicted with her vanity – her drawing skill – her vanity won. She is not particularly intelligent, you see, but she is quick-witted. She thinks on the spur of the moment, as needed. She does not think ahead. There is a difference, you will agree. She also underestimates the intelligence of others. In this case, of the police.'

Ben sprang up from his chair and began to pace up and down our small parlour with such energy I thought he must start to wear a track in our carpet.

He said, with a brief grin at me, 'Britannia was good at drawing donkeys. Her uncle was a costermonger and kept such an animal. She told me that, too.'

'Exactly. She could draw outlines and tiny detail with great accuracy. But when it came to colouring in the donkey, I wonder what colour she gave the poor beast? Perhaps she let her fancy roam and made it pink!'

Ben laughed and came back to his chair by the fire. 'I have to find Billy Scroggs,' he said. 'But my fear is he has already fled the country aboard some ship bound for halfway across the world. Britannia and her mother, of course, are insisting that he is dead.'

He frowned. 'That first day when Phipps and I went to the house, Britannia told us that she was the only one of seven children left to care for their elderly mother. Billy, the eldest had gone to sea and they saw no more of him. The others died in one way or another. The father of the family had been killed in a dockyard accident and that is probably the truth. But Billy's departure for a seafaring life was buried amongst all the other information about the family.'

'She did not actually state, at that time, he was dead? I asked. 'That it was a proven fact, I mean.'

Ben hesitated. 'She indicated she and her mother *believed* him dead. She claimed he'd gone to sea at age fifteen, and had never come back or written. Thus they supposed him drowned. But that snippet of information was mixed in with the undisputed and recorded deaths of her sister in childbed, of another brother falling under the wheels of a cart and of the little ones perishing from diphtheria. So, it was presented as an established fact, even though there was no way of checking it. She gave us to understand she was the only survivor of her mother's brood of seven offspring; and we accepted it. Or,' Ben added wryly, 'I did!

'Jethro Smith, the publican, who knew Billy as a boy, was a close friend, also became uneasy when I suggested the man had drowned. He would not confirm it, nor did he deny it. But he would know if Billy was alive or dead. He knew the whole family; and it was to Jethro that Britannia went when she needed work.

'Phipps was right. He said Britannia told us a great deal but none of it was what we might want to know. I am guilty of allowing a small rivalry to exist between the good Inspector Phipps and myself. I should have paid more attention to his comments. He knew the people among whom he worked, after all. But he had called me in, across London, at great inconvenience to myself and to Morris; and I did not intend to have him seize back the reins of the investigation.'

At this point, Bessie appeared in the doorway and asked, 'Do you need me any more, missus?'

'No, Bessie,' I said. 'You can go up to bed.'

Bessie looked wistful. She would have loved to be a party to our discussion and contribute her pennyworth, as they say. But she bid us goodnight and we heard her climbing the stairs.

'The Scroggs family have sought to buy time,' Ben said when we were alone. 'That's the explanation of all the apparent contradictions in this case. They wanted time for Billy to get well away, to find a ship ready to sail but in need of crew.

'With Clifford dead on the carpet, any sign of what has happened must be removed. The dead body must be moved elsewhere. The lock on the kitchen door is not broken. Britannia can give absence of suspicious evidence, and her employer's obsession with privacy, as reasons for delay in going to the police. Billy gains a few precious hours.

'I must find Raggy Jeb Fisher! I don't know how Fisher was persuaded to help move the murdered woman, and risk his own neck, but I'd bet my last penny that is what he did.'

A knock at the parlour door made us both jump. Ben went to pull it open and there stood Bessie, in nightgown and shawl, with a mobcap on her wiry frizz of hair, and holding a tray with cups of tea on it.

'As you and the missus was talking late, Inspector, sir,' she said, 'and it being a cold night, I came down to brew up a cup of tea for you.'

'Thank you, Bessie!' I called to her. 'But I hope you have not been listening?'

'Of course not, missus,' denied Bessie.

I relented. 'You may come in and sit down over there – but don't interrupt!'

'Yes, missus,' said Bessie promptly and scuttled to a chair in the corner of the room, well pleased.

'So,' said Ben. 'Let us say that Billy and the rag-picker set off with Clifford on the handcart, covered in old clothes. Where would they be going?'

'To the river,' suggested Bessie from her corner. Then she clapped her hand over her mouth guiltily. 'Sorry!' she added.

I frowned at her. 'I will send you back upstairs if you do it again,' I warned.

'She could be right,' said Ben. 'They set off for the river. Bodies are taken from the river regularly. With luck, the tide will take it some distance before it is found, as was the wretched Harry Parker's. So, they set off for the river, with Clifford's body on the handcart, but before they get there, they must change their plan. We don't know why; but I suspect it is at this point that Parker comes into it somehow. Did he see them? Did he recognise them? If only the wretched little fellow had told me what he saw, he would be alive today.'

The coals of the dying fire fell in upon one another with a rustle.

'Well, there is no more to be done tonight,' Ben said with a sigh.

'Yes, Bessie,' I told our maid. 'Now you can go up to bed.'

Chapter Seventeen

Inspector Ben Ross

IT WAS Saturday, the twenty-eighth of November. As if to remind us that we would soon be nearing Christmas with all its festivities, a hand-propelled barrow passed us as we made our way out of New Cross railway station. We had chosen to come by train from Charing Cross. I was beginning to think that Superintendent Dunn would question any more requests for a refund of the expense of a cab. The barrow was laden with live turkeys, packed into bamboo cages. They must have been sent up from further down the line, destined, perhaps, for a poulterer's shop. The wretched occupants stared at us with resentful misery in their red eyes, as if they knew the fate that awaited them. Somehow, they reminded me of Britannia. It did not make me feel any better.

Morris and I stood in the pale winter sunshine and watched as the man in charge of the barrow wrested it on to the steep cobbled slope outside the station and began to trundle it away down the street. It was no easy matter for the load was heavy, the cobbles uncertain and slippery.

Cattle had earlier been driven down the street towards the nearby slaughterers and market. They had left ample traces of their passage. The angle of descent was perilous. The man's boots scraped on the surface, the barrow's primitive braking system was frequently applied with varying success; and the turkeys gobbled and cackled louder than ever.

'Mrs Morris and I,' said my sergeant. 'We always buy our turkey country-bred. We go down into Kent for it. Mrs Morris is of the opinion that a country-bred bird tastes better – and cooks better – than these town-bred ones. There's no telling what these town birds have been fed on. Country birds are generally better reared.'

This was a long speech for Morris. His forthcoming Christmas roast and plum pudding must mean a lot to him.

'Those birds,' I said, 'will be kept somewhere alive for another three weeks. Even if they are country-reared, they will now be fed as town birds.'

'That's why you want to go out into the country and buy one off the farm,' Morris informed me. 'Not everything sold in the market around Christmas is what it claims to be.'

'Morris,' I said, 'we are here to find Billy Scroggs, not our Christmas dinner. And here, if I'm not mistaken, comes Constable Barrett to help us.'

I had sent a request earlier to Deptford for the services of Barrett. Finding Scroggs was unlikely to be easy. The more of us were covering the area, the better. A local man like Barrett should prove useful. Also, when we did find our quarry, he might prove very difficult to capture. We were dealing with a killer, a man with nothing to lose.

'Good morning, sir!' said Barrett brightly, coming up to us. 'Sorry to keep you waiting, sir. A barrow has overturned just around the corner and the road is blocked.'

'Did it have turkeys on it?' asked Morris with interest.

'As a matter of fact, it did,' confirmed Barrett, surprise on his face. 'Two of the crates broke open and the birds escaped. They went running off in all directions. A few people will have caught a free dinner.'

'Well,' I said, 'I don't want us to lose *our* bird, Billy Scroggs!' I hoped that the incident with the turkeys was not a portent. 'We also need to find a collector of rags and old clothes named Jeb Fisher, popularly known as Raggy Jeb.'

'The rag-picker?' Barrett nodded. 'I've seen him about the area. Not this morning, I'm afraid, but often enough. He's quite well known, is Raggy Jeb.'

'Do you know where he lives?' I asked eagerly.

'Sorry, sir, no idea. I could ask around the public houses.'

I remembered Britannia washing the floor at the Clipper public house, and shook my head. 'I don't think we should ask in such places, at least not at first. Scroggs's sister washes floors in at least one tavern, perhaps more than one. If someone lets her know we are searching, she will run off and warn her brother. It is a pity because such places are usually good sources of information. We must ask along the river. If we are really lucky, we may find a former shipmate of his. Remember, he has a tattoo on his arm reading "Ma".'

'Yes, sir!' said Barrett briskly. 'Where shall I report to you, sir?'

'Here, before the railway station, is as good a place as any. In an hour?'

We watched Barrett stride purposefully away. Morris said, 'We could use him at the Yard.'

'I doubt Phipps would want to let him go, but I agree with you.' My gaze had been wandering around the area as I spoke and I had spotted something familiar. A bent figure, wearing a tarred hat, was working methodically along the frontage of the railway station, picking up bits and putting them in a cotton bag. 'Wait here a moment, Morris,' I said. 'I want to have a word with that old fellow over there.'

The old scavenger took no notice of my approach; and not until I stood right before him and blocked his progress did he look up. Then he straightened partly but somehow still remained crouched, so that his hunched stance resembled a question mark. He greeted me with, 'Morning, Cap'n!' as he touched a forefinger to the battered brim of the tarred hat.

I smiled at him. 'I have never had the honour to captain a ship,' I said. 'I am a police inspector and my name is Ross.'

'Officers is officers,' he said placidly. He face was as wrinkled as a walnut and a lifetime of exposure to the elements had tanned his skin like fine Russia leather. His eyes were a faded blue in the irises and the surrounding part of the eyeball yellowed like old ivory. His gaze was somewhat milky and I wondered if he had cataracts. But he seemed able to see well enough to spot the scraps of cigar ends. I realised he was very old indeed.

'You are a naval man, I think,' I said. 'You have served aboard ships of the line, not a merchantman.'

'Aye, Cap'n!' It seemed I was to remain a captain as far as he was concerned. 'Charlie Mott is my name. I began as cabin boy aboard the old *Billy Ruffian*.' His face crinkled in a proud smile.

'Billy Ruffian?' I asked, puzzled.

He chuckled. 'HMS *Bellerophon*, she was rightly called. But the sailors called her "*Billy Ruffian*". She was a fine ship. The French almost sank her, you know. But the old ship was too quick for them.' He moved closer to me, peering up into my face. 'I saw the French emperor!' he confided. 'Old Boney, I saw him with my own eyes. He came aboard the *Billy Ruffian* and surrendered, after the great battle at Waterloo. We were blockading a French port at the time. A big grey coat, he wore, and his hat set across his head, like you always see it drawn.' He made a motion to indicate how Napoleon had worn his hat. 'They always say now he was a small man, but I saw him with my own eyes and he wasn't so small. He was ordinary height. O'course, I was very small myself, being a nipper, cabin boy, like I told you. But even so, I could see he was about the same height as our officers.'

Confidentially, he added, 'I overheard one of our officers talking to another, when Boney came aboard. He said, "Upon my word, Bonaparte will regret this, for we shan't let him go again!"' He shook his head and added mournfully, 'To think the Royal Navy is to quit its dockyard here at Deptford. It's a sad thing.'

It was also a sad thing, I could not help thinking, that a man who had served his country since a boy, aboard a ship of war, must end his days picking ends of cigars from the gutters.

'You are always in this area, I think, Charlie,' I said to him.

'Aye, Cap'n.'

'Then you will know some of the local – characters.'

'I'm one meself,' he said complacently.

I had not meant to insult him; but luckily it seemed he had taken no offence. Rather, I fancy, he thought I had paid him a compliment.

'A collector of old clothes and rags,' I said. 'A man called Jeb Fisher, sometimes called Raggy Jeb.'

A degree of sharpness I wouldn't have expected entered the faded blue gaze. 'Raggy Jeb?'

'You know him!' I said firmly, not giving him the chance to deny it.

'I wouldn't say that, Cap'n. I know of him, mebbe.'

'Have you seen him today?'

'No!' He shook his head in a kind of relief. 'Not today, Cap'n.'

'Recently at all? Because I need to find him. I have a couple of questions for him, just one, really.'

'He's been about,' admitted Charlie.

'Do you know where I could find him?'

In reply Charlie gestured at the scene around us. 'He'll

very likely turn up anywhere, Cap'n. He sails these seas, as you might say.'

Nautical expressions obviously meant more to Charlie Mott than landlubbers' talk. 'Do you happen to know his home port?' I asked. 'Where does he drop anchor at night?'

'Old chandlery,' said Charlie, 'down by the river. Big old wooden building, not used no more. The old Safe Return Inn used to lie alongside it, but that burned down nearly ten years ago and no one bothered to build it up again. It was a rough place, mostly seamen off foreign ships drinking there and fighting most nights. Naval men didn't drink there. Some said at the time the Safe Return was torched deliberate, after the landlord barred some fellows that had caused trouble once too often. At any rate, the fire spread to the chandlery next door; and part was damaged. After that, the chandlery moved its business elsewhere.'

'A quiet spot down there now, then?' I remarked in a conversational tone.

'Mortal quiet,' said Charlie. 'No one goes there much now. It's got a name for odd sights and sounds, not of this world. Some have said they've heard laughter and men singing when they've passed by the burned-out hull of the Safe Return. Seafarers, they're a superstitious lot. If Raggy Jeb wants to make his berth there, no one is going to want to take it off him.'

An ideal place for someone wanting to lie low and not be disturbed, like Billy Scroggs, I thought. I thanked Charlie Mott and told him it had been a pleasure talking to him. Then I rewarded him suitably.

He wished me, 'Fair weather!' as he pocketed the shillings. Then he resumed his patient search for old tobacco.

'Let's see if we can find Barrett,' I said when I returned to the waiting Morris. 'We may have a lead and I have a fancy we'll need Barrett's support.'

As we set off in search of the constable, I told Morris what I had learned. He agreed it was just the sort of place someone on the run from justice, like Billy Scroggs, might seek out as a hiding place. We were in luck, for we spotted Barrett a little way ahead of us, asking questions of a shopkeeper. We signalled to him to return to us and he came back.

'I've had no luck yet, sir,' he said to me.

'I may have some,' I told him and recounted my conversation with Charlie Mott.

'Ah, old Charlie,' said Barrett knowingly. 'Did he tell how he saw Napoleon, when he was a cabin boy aboard the *Bellerophon*?'

'As a matter of fact, he did. I suspect it is the truth. More to the point, we should go at once to this place, the former chandlery. You'll know the spot?'

'I know the site of what's left of the Safe Return Inn, sir. It's a while since that burned down. There are some other buildings down there, most in temporary use. I think I know the one Charlie Mott calls the old chandlery.'

We made our way down to the river. The tide was out, leaving an expanse of glistening yellowish-brown Thames mud above which the gulls swooped and dived in sweeps of white wings, seeking anything edible. Also searching the mud we saw a group of young boys, digging energetically for whatever they might find. They squelched through the morass in their bare feet, risking all manner of injury from hidden objects, and who knew what kind of disease. The more they disturbed the mud, so the stench of it became stronger as every foulness it contained released its gases. No wonder Billy had carried the smell about with him and I had noticed it at his mother's home. I would have put my handkerchief over my nose, but I did not want to show over-sensitivity before Morris and Barrett, who strode sturdily on. The wooden ribs of a boat, beached and rotted, stuck up like an animal carcass. After we had passed that, we met fewer people of any sort and eventually found ourselves walking through a wasteland of deserted – or apparently deserted – buildings, some of them very old indeed.

'The Safe Return Inn,' I asked Barrett, 'what kind of a place was it? Very old?'

'They say it had been there since King Henry's day,' said Barrett. 'I don't know if that was so. It was a rickety place, as I recall from when I was a boy. The top half of it leaned out so far you'd have thought it would fall down into the street at any moment. It had a name as a place smuggled goods changed hands, so the police knew it well. Then one night it went up in flames and that was the end of it. We kids all ran down there to watch it burn.'

'Arson?' I asked.

'So the rumour went. But it was such an old place, all

wood, and still lit by candles and oil lamps, that it wasn't a surprise. Nothing was ever proved. But there was no loss of life, nor even injury, and that was odd for such a blaze. Those who saw it burn said so many rats ran from the building, they were like one of the plagues in old Egypt. I can vouch for that myself. They were everywhere in the streets running round our feet.'

A quarter of an hour later, we found ourselves walking down a narrow lane lined with decrepit buildings. There was little sign of physical life, yet we were surrounded by noises, many of them strange. The wind blew through cracks and crannies, whistling eerily. The wooden beams and planks forming much of the structure of the buildings groaned like a ship under full sail. It was like being accompanied by ghosts. Even Morris looked uneasily about him.

At last we came to an open patch where the Safe Return Inn had once stood. Charlie Mott, with his seaman's way of looking at the world, had referred to the shell of the building as the 'hull', as of a ship. With the blackened beams sticking up into the sky like the ribs of a ship, such as we'd seen earlier in the mud, and the charred remains of planks of wood amid the rubble, the scene did suggest a wooden man-o'-war that had met its fate in some desperate sea battle.

'Here, sir,' said Barrett unnecessarily.

'So that,' said Morris, pointing ahead, 'will be the old chandlery.'

Beyond the ruins of the inn stood another wooden building, two storeys high, constructed of tarred planks above a low brick foundation. The planks nearer to us showed dark scorch marks; but considering its flammable structure and proximity to the site of the Safe Return, it was a miracle it had not been reduced to cinders in the flames that had consumed the old inn. It was not surprising the chandlery as a business had subsequently moved out and away.

'Someone is at home, sir,' said Morris in a low voice.

A thin spiral of smoke came from an iron pipe sticking out of the side of one wall. It probably connected with a stove of some sort inside.

'I'll go in,' I said. 'Morris, you stay outside at this end of the building and Barrett, you stand guard at the other end. If anyone comes out and tries to make off, stop him.'

'What if someone comes along this lane intending to go in?' asked Morris. 'He'll see us waiting here, Mr Ross, and change his mind fast.'

'True. You can both stay out of sight, I think. There are doorways enough and these places around look empty.'

I pushed at the door into the chandlery. To my relief, it gave beneath my hand and swung inward with a creak. If we had had to break in, that would have ruined any chance of catching our man, if he were there.

I stepped into a narrow passage leading into a large open area. To my left, a wooden stair ran up to a floor above. To my right, the 'room' had been fitted out as a dwelling place. There was a table, some rough chairs that looked knocked together by someone with rudimentary joinery skills and a bedstead I guessed made by the same carpenter who had fashioned the chairs. Stacks of old clothes and rags along the back wall awaited sorting. At the very far end a primitive iron stove smoked villainously, filling the air with an acrid stench and making my eyes water. The iron pipe supposed to take the smoke outside was working imperfectly, either badly fitted or just too narrow. In the corner a slatternly young woman stooped over a washtub, wielding a bar of soap in an attempt to do some laundry. Two children crouched nearby watching her. One of them was little Sukey, so I knew I had found the right place. The other child was a boy of about ten years of age and he looked familiar, too. To my right, hanging on a hook, was a sailor's heavy pea coat of dark woollen cloth.

At my entry, the woman looked up from her labours at the washtub, staring at me through a curtain of loose, dishevelled hair. Then she dropped her bar of soap into the water and opened her mouth.

'Don't scream!' I ordered sharply. 'I am a police officer.'

She remained staring wildly at me with her mouth open. Sukey simply looked at me. The boy, however, began to edge along the wall.

'You stay there, young fellow!' I told him. 'You have been following me about all over the area for these past few days, a very efficient little spy. So you might as well remain now to see the end of the adventure.'

The boy froze but Sukey spoke up. 'I've seen *him* before,' she said, pointing at me. 'He spoke to Granddad.'

'You hold your tongue!' snapped her mother, coming out of her trance. She straightened up. 'What do you want? I'm a busy woman. I got work to do.'

'You have a husband?' I asked.

Despite herself, her glance drifted to the pea coat before she turned a defiant stare on me. 'What's it to you?'

'Just answer me. These children have a father?'

'O'course they got a pa!'

'So, then, what's his name?'

She had had time to gather her wits. 'Fisher,' she said brusquely. 'But he ain't here. I ain't seen him in a long time. He's left us.'

'I dare say your name is Fisher,' I told her. 'But the father of these children is Billy Scroggs. Where is he?'

Even as I spoke my ear caught a creak of wood behind me. The boy's eyes turned in that direction. I spun round and saw him at last.

Scroggs was a big, solid brute of a man, certainly the most substantial 'ghost' I would ever come across. His bulk did not come from height. He was of no more than average in that. But he was broad and heavy in the shoulders with long arms. His head was thrust forward and sunk into his shoulders so that he appeared to have very little neck at all. His skin was weather-beaten and tanned, his hair dark and curly, flecked with grey. He wore a heavy sweater of oiled wool. It covered his arms so that I could not see the tattoo, but I did not need to. He stood at the top of the wooden stair and now began slowly to descend it, keeping his mean little eyes fixed on me. I knew I had to stand my ground; and that it would be difficult. Morris and Barrett were outside. But they watched for someone approaching the chandlery or possibly rushing out. They might not immediately realise there was a confrontation inside. I kept my voice as authoritative as possible.

'I believe you are William Scroggs,' I said to him. 'Who also gives the name of William Jones. You sold a pair of earrings recently, to a pawnbroker by the name of Sharp. I had good reason to believe those earrings were stolen in the course of a violent crime. I arrest you on suspicion of murder—'

But that was as far as I got. Something hit me on the back of the head. It was not a heavy blow, but the suddenness of it caused me to step forward and automatically duck, off-balance. Something flew past and skidded along the floor and I saw it was the bar of soap. The woman had flung it at me with unerring accuracy. With a roar, Scroggs leaped down the last few stairs and launched himself at me.

The weight of him and the force of the collision slammed me down on to the floor, the breath knocked out of my body. As I struggled to regain control, Scroggs's fist crashed into my face. At the same time, the woman threw herself into the mêlée, screeching. Somehow I managed to free one arm and flung it up towards my assailant's face. My forearm, by a stroke of luck, caught Scroggs across the bridge of his nose and a stream of blood sprayed down on me. He gave a great roar and his thick fingers fastened on my throat. I was sucked into a black world shot across with blinding streams of light.

Just when it seemed I would sink into total oblivion the pressure on my neck was gone. So was the weight on my chest. The blackness cleared. Distantly, through the throbbing in my ears, I heard a police whistle. (I later learned it was Barrett calling for any help that might be nearby.) Then Barrett himself pounded through the door and joined Morris who had thrown both arms around Scroggs and hauled him away from me. By the time I sat up, they had him securely manacled.

The woman was still screeching at me. I pointed at her and managed to gasp, 'Take her too! Where are the children?'

'They came running out the door, sir!' Morris told me. 'But I already reckoned something was going on. We heard the woman yelling. The kids ran off down the street, gone to warn their grandfather, most like.'

'We'll pick him up later, sir!' Barrett assured me. 'He's well known, is Jeb Fisher, and we won't have any trouble finding him quickly.'

I was on my feet by now and able to take action. I ran to the stove, hooked open the little door in it and peered in. As I had guessed, the reason it was smoking so badly was because they had been burning wads of paper, or trying to. No doubt alarmed when he heard from his sister that the earrings were in police hands, Scroggs had decided to burn the bundle of IOUs taken from Clifford's house. Any attempt to use them, once the hunt for him was on would be useless. The charred remains, blackened but still legible in parts, would hang him, anyway.

Chapter Eighteen

THANKS TO Billy Scroggs's fist, one side of my face was swollen out like a balloon and had turned a colourful purple and yellow. I saw a gleam of satisfaction in Britannia's eyes as she surveyed me.

She was being held in the women's area of Newgate Prison. I sat at the table in the little room where she had been brought for questioning, and met her sardonic gaze. A brawny wardress stood at the wall behind her, hands folded, face impassive. Such light as entered through the narrow barred window was cold and grey, like the gown the wardress wore. Britannia, too, wore a drab prison garment. This lack of colour made me feel we formed a group in some black and white scene printed in a book.

'It was a wicked thing you and your brother did, Britannia,' I said. My voice was hoarse from having Scroggs's hands clamped round my throat.

Britannia's look of derision increased. 'Old Clifford should have stayed upstairs. Then she wouldn't have got hurt.'

'Are you going to tell me it was your employer's own fault your brother killed her?'

'She should've stayed upstairs!' Britannia repeated obstinately.

I sighed and wished my throat were not so sore. I had never had a single conversation with Britannia Scroggs that had been easy and this was to be no different, even without a painful throat. She subjected the world to her own distorted view, as if she looked at it through a prism, and could not be persuaded to see it differently. Leading the life she had led, this was perhaps not surprising. But one thing did surprise me.

'You told me,' I croaked, leaning towards her. 'You said that Mrs Clifford had been good to you. That was after Sergeant Morris took you to identify her body.'

'I know I said that,' returned Britannia impatiently. 'What did you expect me to say?'

'For goodness' sake, Britannia! She employed you. She gave you a room of your own. You lived there, all found, and had enough money to pay your mother's rent for her wretched room! Why would you risk that? Why on earth would you collude in her murder?'

'We didn't mean to kill her!' snapped Britannia. 'She should've stayed upstairs. How many times have I got to tell you? Then she'd have been all right. She came downstairs, she saw Billy and she saw me standing at the desk. Billy had just got the lock open.'

'Was he already in the house when Wellings called to see Mrs Clifford? Was he upstairs in your room?'

'No,' said Britannia. 'He was outside in the yard, waiting until old Clifford went to bed. I let him in. I didn't know she was going to come downstairs, did I?'

'So you and your brother planned robbery. Even if things had gone differently, as I suppose you hoped they would, it was a treacherous act on your part. Let me tell you what you and Billy intended. Your brother would make off with whatever spoils he found, and you would go back upstairs until the next morning. Then you could have come down and pretend to be surprised there had been a burglary. Billy would have damaged the lock on the back door before he left so that it would look like a break-in. Mrs Clifford might have been suspicious. But she might have believed you had nothing to do with it; and you could have stayed there.'

'No, I couldn't have stayed there!' shouted Britannia at me with such force that the wardress, alarmed, stepped forward.

I signalled to the woman to stay back. 'Britannia,' I said, 'why could you not have stayed there? Did you think Mrs Clifford would not have believed in your innocence?'

In reply, Britannia thrust her hands out towards me. 'Look at them!' she ordered.

I found myself looking at her distorted knuckles and finger-joints.

'They're getting worse!' said Britannia sullenly. 'The pain of them sometimes makes me weep. Only I couldn't show it, not until I'd gone to bed; because if old Clifford had seen me crying, she'd have wanted to know why. Then she'd have turned me away straight off! If I couldn't work, she'd not have kept me for a day. A couple of times I broke dishes, because my hands were so stiff in the

319

morning. She stopped the cost out of my wages. When I drew the picture of those earrings for you, it was all I could do not to scream out, it was so painful for me to do it. But I had to hide from you how bad it was, just as I had to hide it from old Clifford. You had to think there was nothing wrong with me, just like she did. You hadn't to guess how desperate I was – me and Ma were. Billy, too. He's got two little'uns and a wife. He couldn't give Ma any money. We were in such a fix. And she had money. She had money in the house! There, just for the taking!'

There was a pause. Britannia's words, ringing around the tiny room, faded away. I wondered just how much money Mrs Clifford had kept in the house. 'How much?' I asked Britannia. 'How much money did Billy find?'

Britannia's glowering looks worsened. 'Not enough,' she said. 'You can believe me or not, but there wasn't much cash there. She'd gone out earlier that day and she must've taken the money to the bank. Another night and we'd have done really well. But it was just our bad luck we didn't find much that night. That's what made Billy so angry, started him swearing and making threats of all sorts. The risk we were taking and for so little! It's why he took the papers, signed by all the debtors. He thought the people named on them might like to buy them back for, say, a quarter of what was owed. After all, it would have been getting them cheap, and they could destroy them, so that no one would ever know they'd borrowed from a moneylender. Respectable families don't like to think any of their relatives had got into debt. It makes all of them look bad, you know?'

I did know. The news that Edgar Wellings had been a client of Clifford had horrified his family, prompting the scenes described to me by my wife.

'So, Billy lost his temper and battered Mrs Clifford to death. Then you – or Billy – one of you, took off her wedding ring and fob watch and pulled out her earrings.'

'We had to have something,' muttered Britannia, 'and she didn't need them no more. Billy was that angry still, I was afraid he'd turn on me. I told him we could sell the earrings and ring, and the little watch, just to calm him down. She was always looking at the little watch. Everything had to be done on time with her, like clockwork. She wasn't easy to work for, you can believe that!'

'You lied about the colour of Mrs Clifford's earrings, claiming the stones were rubies instead of sapphires,' I said after a pause. 'Did you really think that would be enough to confuse us?'

'Why not?' snapped Britannia sulkily. 'I made a good job of those drawings, didn't I? I got an "eye". They said so, at Sunday School.'

'Too good a job, Britannia. We knew we had the right earrings and you must be lying about the stones.'

Britannia bit her lower lip and I noticed the chipped front tooth again. 'It ain't fair,' she said.

Life wasn't fair, she meant to say, or it had never been fair to her. It wasn't an excuse for what she and her brother had done, but she would not be brought to agree. It was her own vanity regarding her skill at drawing that had led us to the truth; but that she was in any way responsible for the fact that both she and Billy were awaiting trial was another thing she and I would never agree on. In Britannia's view, she herself, not Mrs Clifford, was the victim.

'Tell me about moving the body.' It was best to stick to the practical questions.

That gained me an exasperated look. 'I had nothing to do with the *moving* of it. They did that. It had to be moved because otherwise I'd have seen it in the morning. I couldn't have pretended I hadn't seen it, could I? I had to pretend I didn't know what had happened to her, wait a bit before I went to the police station. That was so Billy had a chance to get away, find a ship and leave the country for a few months. But he couldn't find one that was taking on crew.'

'When you say "they" had to move it, you mean your brother and Jeb Fisher. Was he in on the robbery?'

She shook her head. 'No, Raggy didn't know nothing. Billy had the idea to move her. I thought about it and agreed it was a good plan, so Billy went out to find his wife's father, because he had a cart.'

'They are legally married, your brother and Fisher's daughter?'

Britannia raised puzzled eyes to my face. 'As good as,' she said.

'And pretending not to find the bloodstains on the carpet until later in the morning of the day, that was also to give Billy time?'

'I tried to clean it off,' said Britannia, scowling. 'But I

couldn't. So I had to think of something else. I covered it over.'

There was a horrible practical logic to all of this. I still persevered.

'Billy, too, must have had blood on his clothing, surely?'

Britannia nodded. 'On his shirt. He took it to Ma to wash it. She didn't know that the blood was old Clifford's! He said he'd been helping out at the slaughterhouse, fetching and carrying the carcasses. He didn't want to take the shirt back to his place to be washed because his nippers would see and remember bloodstains on their pa's shirt. They might go mentioning to some other kids, and word get round.'

I tried to question her about Harry Parker, but learned nothing.

'You keep asking me!' snapped Britannia. 'I didn't kill her. I didn't move her and I didn't leave her in that yard. All I did was let Billy into the house.'

'Nothing excuses crime, Britannia. Nothing excuses what happened to Mrs Clifford. Nothing excuses your colluding in robbing her or your attempts to mislead the police. You cannot claim you did no wrong.' I was so angry with her now I was almost shouting myself.

'That's it!' snarled Britannia. 'Everything *I* did was wrong. Mrs Clifford, she had rights, according to you. She was as mean as they come and I never had a kind word from her. Me, I've got no rights. I can starve. Ma can starve.'

Britannia threw out her hand. 'The fuss you're making

about her! You'd think it was someone special who'd died. It was only old Clifford! No one cried over her, the mean old witch! She didn't have no family, no friends. The people who borrowed money from her hated her. Well, Mr Inspector Ross, what about me – and Ma – and what about my brother's little'uns? Ma will finish in the workhouse. My brother's wife and kids very likely end up there, too. What about them? You've got nothing to say about them, have you? Well, I've got no more to say to you.'

Britannia swivelled on her chair to face the wardress. 'I want to go back now. I've finished talking to him. I'm not saying another word. Not if you make me sit here all day, I'm not.' She turned back to me. 'So you can go home. You've probably got a nice cosy home to go to. Well, out there . . .' Britannia flung out a hand to indicate the world beyond Newgate's walls, 'out there half the people don't know where their next meal is coming from! Some of them has no homes to go to. Some of them commit what you'd call crimes because there's nothing else they can do!'

She pressed her lips together. 'I'm finished,' she said.

So was I. I took my leave of her, but the memory of her scowling defiant face remained with me for a long time.

There was no getting anything out of Billy Scroggs. He had retreated into a private hell of simmering rage and spite. When he did speak, it was to hurl abuse at us. Then, when he learned how talkative his sister had been, he'd found more foul language to use about her. He made no inquiry about his wife and children, or even his wretched father-in-law whom he'd made a reluctant accomplice.

Raggy Jeb himself had begged us to believe he had not known of the planned robbery. He had been dismayed when Billy came to tell him what had happened. He had not wanted to move the body. He swore to this with such passion that we believed him. But Billy was the father of his grandchildren. What could he have done but try to help? They'd had to abandon the original plan to take the body to the river, because there were so many people about that evening. Raggy Jeb Fisher, scared out of his wits, had been too much of a tremble even to push the cart! So they'd dumped the victim in Skinner's Yard and parted company. Raggy Jeb had gone to the Clipper public house, where he'd left Billy's little girl, Sukey, in the care of the barmaid, and found her asleep in a corner. Raggy had a pint or two of ale, to restore his presence of mind, and while he was drinking someone came running in and said a body had been found in Skinner's Yard.

Raggy had nearly fainted with the shock of it. They'd expected it would be some hours, daylight perhaps, before the murdered woman was discovered. Raggy started off home with the child on the cart. Where Billy had gone, he had no idea. Scroggs had not come home until dawn, and then so drunk they'd had to carry him into the old chandlery and leave him on the floor to sleep it off.

To question either Billy or Raggy Jeb about Parker had been useless.

*

I was on my way back to Scotland Yard from Newgate when, once again, I felt that tingle between the shoulder blades, the sense of being stalked. It increased until it became a certainty. Whoever followed me, he was hurrying his step. He was trying to catch up with me. It was a strong step, not a stealthy one. I decided he did not intend to attack me. Rather, he wanted to speak to me. To oblige him, I stopped and turned to face him. Then I received a shock.

About ten feet away, breathing heavily, stood Harry Parker. For a moment I really believed it was Harry himself, even though I had viewed his dead body on a mortuary slab. My pursuer was a small man with those same pinched features and little dark eyes. His gaze flickered nervously as he debated whether to stand his ground or turn and flee. Then the answer to the riddle struck me.

'You are Harry Parker's brother, the one who lives in Limehouse,' I said.

To be recognised both startled and frightened him. I thought he would run away, so I added quickly, 'Don't be alarmed! You bear a remarkable resemblance to your brother. Were you twins?'

He ventured a little closer, studying me all the while with those rat's eyes. 'No,' he said hoarsely, 'not twins. Two years between us. He was my younger brother. I'm Barney – Barney Parker, stableman by line of work.'

Now he was nearer I could see he was an older man. His hair was touched with grey, the lines around his mouth deeper. He was a little heavier in build than the late Harry.

'You're Inspector Ross, right?' he asked.

'I am.'

'You got Billy Scroggs in the clink?'

'He's locked up in prison, yes.'

'Not going to let him go, are you?' asked Barney anxiously.

My nose caught the acrid tang of horses. He was a stableman, as he claimed.

'He's a bad'un, is Billy Scroggs,' croaked Barney. 'I couldn't come to you before. I wanted to, mind!'

'When you learned of your brother's death? That's when you wanted to contact the police?'

'Yus!' He blinked several times and nodded, resembling an automaton that had been set in motion. 'But not *any* p'lice officer! It had to be you, Harry said so. But I couldn't come to you while Billy Scroggs was out there on the loose. I couldn't finger him to you. He'd have heard about it. I'd have joined poor Harry in the river!'

'You believe Scroggs killed your brother?'

'He done for poor Harry, right enough. Harry was afraid of him. He left Deptford and came to me because he was scared. But then he went back. He shouldn't have gone back. Billy found him. Harry was afraid that Billy would. He told me, if anything happened to him, I was to go and find you. That's what I'm doing now. Billy's locked away, so now I can tell you what Harry told me, the night he came over to Limehouse.'

'You're doing the right thing, Barney,' I told him. 'Do

you want to come with me to Scotland Yard? We are not far from there. Or would you prefer to talk elsewhere privately?'

I hoped he would come to the Yard. I needed a witness. But I didn't want to frighten him off.

After a moment's deliberation, he said, 'I'll come to the Yard with you. I don't like standing about talking to you on the street like this. Anyone could pass by and see us. Same in a pub. You don't know who's looking, do you? It might get back to Billy. I know you've got him in a cell. But he's got friends, ain't he? Out here . . .' Barney waved a hand to indicate our general surroundings. 'That's why I couldn't come to you in Deptford. Best thing is, I'll follow you. When we get near the Yard, you turn and grab me. You march me into the building like you've arrested me. No one could blame me for going with you then!'

I understood his logic. Informers are not liked. So I set off again, knowing he was dogging my footsteps a short way behind. Near the Yard, I turned, took his elbow and said sternly, 'Come along with me. No nonsense, now!'

And so we entered the Yard, linked like a courting couple. As it turned out, the first person we saw was young Dr Wellings, apparently on his way out.

'What are you doing here again?' I asked sourly. I had had more than enough of the young wastrel.

'The superintendent called me in,' Wellings said, eyeing me nervously. 'He told me you have arrested the person responsible for the death of Mrs Clifford and I am no longer a suspect.'

'You are extremely fortunate, Dr Wellings, and I trust we shall not see you at the Yard again!'

'Who's the young gent?' inquired Barney, when Wellings had scuttled away.

'Just someone who came to make a statement, as you are about to do,' I told him.

When we were seated in my office; and Biddle had appeared with his notebook, Barney at last relaxed. He looked round him with interest and studied Biddle in particular.

'That one's going to write it all down, is he? Everything what I say? Because I don't talk fancy.'

'We only want you to use your own words. Then you will have a chance to read it and sign it.' Doubt struck me. 'Can you write?'

Barney looked shy. 'I has to make my mark.'

'That's all right. We'll read it out to you. You will make your mark and I will sign my name beneath, with a statement that it is your mark, made in my presence.'

Biddle held up his pencil at the ready. Barney gazed at him admiringly. 'It's a wonderful thing to have an education.'

Biddle blushed scarlet.

'Well, the night it all happened,' Barney began, 'was just like any other. It goes to show you never know what's going to hit you. Harry, my brother, was walking along, minding his own business, as you might say, when he saw the rag-picker ahead of him with his cart. That's a fellow called Raggy Jeb; they know him everywhere. Been around for years! But the funny thing was, what took

Harry's attention, that Raggy Jeb wasn't pushing the cart. It was all piled up with rags and old clothes, like it might be at the end of the day. But pushing it was Billy Scroggs, and that did make Harry wonder. He never knew that Billy had anything to do with collecting old clothes! He would sign on as deckhand on any ship that would take him, though he's got himself a bad name on account of his violent ways. The way Billy was pushing the cart, too, like it was really heavy. Billy is a big strong fellow. Why would he be making heavy weather of pushing a cart of rags? So, all in all, Harry got curious and he followed. He took care they didn't see him, because Billy Scroggs wouldn't like anyone wanting to know his business.

'They got near to Skinner's Yard and they stopped. Raggy Jeb had put his hand on Billy's arm. Raggy looked really scared. He was looking all about him and the people. It was busy, streets crowded with all sorts of folk. Some seamen went by, arguing. Harry tucked himself in behind them and got a bit closer. He heard Raggy Jeb say, "It's too far to the river, I tell you. There's too many people about!" Then he pointed into the yard and said, "Leave her here!" It seemed like Billy wasn't keen on the idea, and the two of them argued a bit. Harry couldn't hear it all. But, in the end, they turned into Skinner's Yard.

'Harry waited until they came out. They wasn't in there for long. But when they did come out, it was Raggy Jeb pushing the cart, like he usually did. So Harry reckoned they'd shed part of the load, the heavy part. Raggy went off in one direction, with the cart. But Billy turned right round and walked back the way they'd come – and he walked right up past Harry and saw him! So Harry, he just mumbled, 'Evening, Billy!' and went on, like there was nothing unusual. He was afraid Billy might come after him. But Billy didn't; and when Harry had enough courage to look behind him, there was no sign of Scroggs.'

Barney paused and said sadly, 'If Harry had had any sense, he'd have got as far away from there as possible, as fast as he could. But he was curious, see? When he was certain Billy Scroggs really had gone, he went back. He slipped into Skinner's Yard and looked to see what they'd left there. He stumbled over something, looked to what it was and— he near died of fright, Mr Ross! It was a woman's dead body! That's what he told me and that's the truth, you can believe. Why, even when he was telling me about it, he was all of a-shake. He turned and ran out of the yard – and straight into a constable on the beat! Talk about bad luck! Of course, the bluebottle grabbed Harry and wanted to know what was wrong? It would have been no use Harry telling him nothing was wrong, not in the state Harry was. So he took him in and showed him the body.'

Barney paused. 'And that was it. He knew, poor Harry, that when it got out that the body was found and the police had been led to it by a local man, naming Harry, well, Billy would hear of it. He'd remember he'd seen Harry that evening, near where he and Raggy Jeb had left the body. Harry could have told you, the police, that he'd seen Raggy Jeb and Billy, pushing that cart and all the rest of it. But Billy would know that, too! He'd be looking for Harry.

'I told Harry he could stay with me in Limehouse. But Harry had no money and he couldn't get work that side of the river. So he went back, back to Deptford. He shouldn't have done that, Mr Ross.'

'He should have confided in the police, Barney. That's what your brother should have done. If he'd told me the whole tale, I could have protected him.'

'Easy to say that,' retorted Barney. 'Not so easy to do, not for people like us.'

We read him his statement. Superintendent Dunn came in to witness Barney make his mark. When Parker had left, Biddle opened the window despite the icy chill of the air flowing in. It was needed to dispel the strong aroma of horses and manure that Barney had left behind him.

Dunn said, 'You will be able to tell Mrs Ross that the matter is now cleared up, and young Wellings has nothing more to fear.'

'She will be relieved, sir.'

'Mm,' said Dunn. 'She and Miss Wellings went out to Egham and fetched that young fool back to London, after he decided to run off, didn't she?'

'Yes, sir.' There was no point in denying it now.

'Pity we can't enlist her in the force,' said Dunn with a rare smile. 'Although, if we did, I dare say there would be no need for the rest of us!' He paused. 'Not for the detection part of it, anyway. I suppose we males will be needed for the violent side of things!' He indicated my swollen cheek. 'A medical man has seen that, I suppose?'

'Yes, sir, he doesn't think it broken but I was lucky.'

'Good,' said Dunn, and went back to his own office. One doesn't expect thanks from one's senior officers and it is just as well.

Chapter Nineteen

'THANK MR Dunn for his kind words,' said Lizzie, when I reported the day's events that evening. 'Of course, women make excellent detectives, why shouldn't they?' She frowned and studied my bruised face. 'Is your throat still very sore?'

'Getting better,' I told her.

'Well, I do think Mr Dunn should have shown you more consideration. He could have given you a day or two at home to recover from that horrible man's attack.'

'As far as Dunn is concerned, if an officer can walk into the Yard on his own two feet, he is fit for duty. Anyway,' I added, 'I am fit for duty. The bruises will fade and I will be able to swallow properly.' I was on a diet of soup and stews and felt myself no better than an invalid.

'You see?' said Lizzie. 'Men always have to be so – strong and show no weakness, and such nonsense.' She turned her face to the fire and watched the crackling flames for a few moments.

'My dear,' I rasped, 'there is something ticking away in your always active brain and it has nothing to do with my injuries.'

'Oh,' said Lizzie, 'it's just that, well, that maid, Britannia . . .'

'Ah, Miss Scroggs, once encountered, never forgotten.' I'd never forget her, certainly, nor that murdering ruffian of a brother of hers.

'They won't hang her, will they?' Lizzie stopped watching the fire and stared anxiously at me.

'I have no idea,' I replied, taken aback. 'I am not judge or jury. She and her brother – and Jeb Fisher – have yet to stand trial. I dare say Billy Scroggs will go to the gallows. As for Britannia? Well, she did conspire to rob her employer and she did let her brother into the house. But personally I don't believe that murder was any part of her plans. I am not so sure about Scroggs himself. We have discovered he has a reputation among the seafaring community and had been unable to sign on as deckhand on any ship for some weeks. Britannia feared it was only going to be a little time before Mrs Clifford realised she could not do her work, because of her increasingly crippled hands. They decided to steal the cashbox, sure it would be full of money.

'But things went wrong from the outset and the robbery ended in bloody murder.

'Britannia had to stay in the house. There was nowhere she could run to! But there was a slim chance Billy might yet find a place as crew and escape. So they concocted a plan and, I must say, it was a clever one. I wonder which of them thought it up? Billy is not a thinker. Britannia, on the other hand, has a hard head and a quick brain. The money and the IOU's went to her mother's hovel where, as Morris suspected too late, they were hidden beneath a foul-smelling stew. The cashbox went into the river with the murder weapon. Father Thames has received many objects into his watery bosom throughout history! The IOU's were moved from Ma Scroggs's home when the police showed a disconcerting habit of turning up at the door. We were just in time at the old chandlery to prevent Raggy Jeb's daughter burning the lot completely.'

'There is little to be said in her defence,' said Lizzie with a sigh.

I sought to cheer her, since Britannia's fate seemed to worry my wife. 'She has turned Queen's Evidence. Now she realises her brother is going to hang, she's laying everything she can at his door. Possibly she will get away with a lengthy prison sentence. I only hope she has the sense, when the trial takes place, to show remorse. It won't come naturally to her. In her conversations with me the only regret she's expressed was that there was less money in the house than she and her brother had expected. That wouldn't go down well with a jury. But if she can manage to look as if she's repented; and if the jury takes account of the fact that she was under the influence of her brother; and her desperation at the thought of losing her place as maid because of the advancing rheumatism in her hands . . . She might escape the death penalty.

'If you have pity for anyone; save it for Raggy Jeb Fisher. He knew nothing of the robbery until Scroggs came to fetch him to move the body. Unfortunately, his ignorance may not save him from the gallows. Fisher recognised me as a police officer that same evening. He couldn't resist asking about the murder.

'The other thing that went wrong for the villains was that Harry Parker saw them and was curious. He followed them, discovered the body and, in his flight, cannoned into Constable Barrett. They had not thought the body would be discovered so quickly.

'Mind you, they had a bit of luck, too. Edgar Wellings, accompanied by you and his sister, obligingly turned up at the door the following day while the police were at the house. Fate must have appeared to be smiling on the Scroggs siblings. Britannia was able to point him out to us as a likely suspect. You know, Lizzie, young Wellings has been very lucky to escape standing in the dock on a charge of murder himself! I think Superintendent Dunn has impressed that on him.'

'The child, Sukey,' said Lizzie sadly, 'she and her brother and mother will all end up in the workhouse, I suppose. Old Mrs Scroggs, too.'

'It probably can't be avoided, at least, as far as the old woman is concerned. The children's mother may find some way of keeping herself and her children from going on the parish.' I paused. 'It is the way of the world, Lizzie, that the innocent suffer from the wrongdoing of the guilty.'

Lizzie sighed. Then, making an effort to brighten the mood, said, 'Frank and Patience are to be married in the spring.'

I groaned. 'I never want to see eyes on that young fellow again!'

'It cannot be avoided. You will need a new coat for the wedding.'

I groaned again.

'Edgar Wellings is not to stay in London.'

'Well,' I told her, 'that, at least, is good news!'

'Bart's told him they didn't want him back. But his family has insisted he return home, anyway. They wouldn't hear of his remaining so far away from them. They want to know what he is doing. He has been found a place as a junior doctor in a local hospital, in their town. I think Frank may have had some influence there. Frank was anxious to remove Edgar from London, too.'

'Lizzie,' I said, 'if the Wellings family imagine that Edgar will not get into trouble in his hometown, they will be sadly disillusioned. Can you imagine that young dandy being satisfied with toiling on the wards of a provincial hospital? Or, when he is not working, be content with the limited entertainment available? To say nothing of living in a town where everyone will know who he is! He will be recognised and his comings and goings reported back to his parents. The family will also be watching him like a hawk. He will not last there above a year; and then he will be off and getting into trouble somewhere else, mark my words! But, so long as it is not here in London, I don't have to worry about it.'

'You are right, of course,' said my wife. 'But I do worry a little, all the same, because whatever Edgar may do in the future, it will affect Frank and Patience.'

I leaned forward and took her hands. 'Lizzie, my dearest, if there is one person in the world you don't have to worry about, it is Frank Carterton. Edgar may be the sort who will always get into scrapes and have to be helped out. Frank, I am convinced, is a born survivor.'

Lizzie looked at me, her gaze sombre. 'And you, Ben? That man could so easily have killed you. Or he might have injured you so severely you could no longer work as a police officer.'

'You would send me back down the pit, would you?' I asked. It was a poor joke but I wanted to lighten her mood.

'Don't be foolish!' she said sharply.

'Then there is only one thing for it,' I gasped out. I had been talking too much and my throat now felt as if Billy Scroggs still had his hands clamped round it. 'I shall have to work even harder and get promoted. If I can ever make superintendent,' I whispered, 'I shall be able to sit at a desk like Dunn and criticise fellows like me who must take care of the donkey work.' I remembered to add, 'Ably assisted by you, my dear, of course!'

Then my voice gave out completely. But my wife looked satisfied.

**Discover Ann Granger's previous thrilling Victorian mystery
featuring Inspector Ben Ross and his wife Lizzie . . .**

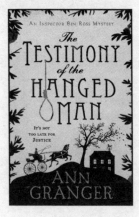

A hanged man would say anything to save his life. But what if his testimony is true?

When Inspector Ben Ross is called to Newgate Prison by a man condemned to die by the hangman's noose, he isn't expecting to give any credence to the man's testimony. But the account of a murder he witnessed over seventeen years ago is so utterly believable that Ben can't help wondering if what he's heard is true.

It's too late to save the man's life, but it's not too late to investigate a murder that has gone undetected for all these years.

And don't miss the other novels in the series:

A Rare Interest in Corpses
A Mortal Curiosity
A Better Quality of Murder
A Particular Eye for Villainy

headline

www.headline.co.uk
www.anngranger.net

THRILLINGLY GOOD BOOKS
FROM CRIMINALLY
GOOD WRITERS

CRIME FILES BRINGS YOU THE LATEST RELEASES FROM TOP CRIME AND THRILLER AUTHORS.

GN UP ONLINE FOR OUR MONTHLY NEWSLETTER AND BE THE FIRST TO KNOW ABOUT OUR COMPETITIONS, NEW BOOKS AND MORE.